THE PIZZA-PYRE

CHARLEIGH BRENNAN

BALANCE OF SEVEN
Dallas

For information, contact:
Balance of Seven, www.balanceofseven.com
Publisher: dyfreeman@balanceofseven.com
Managing Editor: tntinker@balanceofseven.com

Cover Illustration by Emily Zelasko
www.emilyzelaskoart.com

Cover Design by Cait Marie, Cait Marie Designs
www.caitmarieh.com

Developmental Editing by Amanda Mills Woodlee

Developmental Editing, Copyediting, and Formatting by TNT Editing
www.theodorentinker.com/TNTEditing

Proofreading by Amanda Mills Woodlee

Publisher's Cataloging-in-Publication Data

Names: Brennan, Charleigh. | Templeman, Charlene, 1977- .
Title: The pizza-pyre / Charleigh Brennan.
Description: Dallas, TX : Balance of Seven, 2021. | Series: The pizza-pyre ; book 1.
Identifiers: LCCN 2021945513 | ISBN 9781947012158 (pbk.) | ISBN 9781947012165 (ebook)
Subjects: LCSH: Life change events – Fiction. | Pizza – Fiction. | Vampires – Fiction. | Video games – Fiction. | Young men – Fiction. | BISAC: FICTION / Occult & Supernatural. | FICTION / Fantasy / Humorous. | FICTION / Fantasy / Paranormal.
Classification: LCC PS3602 R46 P5 2021 (print) | PS3602 R46 (ebook) | DDC 813 B74--dc23
LC record available at https://lccn.loc.gov/2021945513

25 24 23 22 21   1 2 3 4 5

For my mom,
who has always been my most
enthusiastic supporter,
and for my dad,
who will always motivate me to be
a better and stronger person.

CONTENTS

PROLOGUE

Pizza . . .

Rich, red tomato sauce, aromatic pesto, tangy barbecue, creamy white sauce. Regular crust, thin crust, stuffed crust, deep dish. Cheese—all kinds of cheese, the gooier, the better. Pepperoni, olives, bell peppers, sun-dried tomatoes, chicken, sausage, anchovies, garlic, Canadian bacon, and yes, even pineapple. Hey, if they can eat bananas on pizza in Sweden, a little pineapple isn't going to be the end of the world. I've had stranger things on pizza before, like oysters. It's all good. All of it.

Oh, how I loved pizza.

After graduating high school, I realized I was on my own to finance college. My dad had to invest his money in his small-town hardware store to keep in business, and I didn't want him to feel obligated to pay my way. So I decided to take some time off from school to work. I could save up money for tuition and fees instead of being in perpetual debt until who knew when.

Where did I decide to apply for a job? That's right. Gino's Pizza. I became their ace delivery boy—ahem, ace delivery professional. I'd get free pizza in between deliveries and one pie every night I worked to take home for my room-mates and me. It cut down my budget for groceries and kept us neck-deep in the food of the gods.

If pizza were a goddess, I'd worship at her feet. And I did. I knelt in prayer to give thanks every time the heady aroma of pizza enveloped me like the finest of expensive colognes. I revered every bite of melting cheese and sauce that met my tongue. I'd close my eyes in pure rapture as the combination of flavors made my taste buds sing hymns in Lady Pizza's honor.

That is, until that day. The day pizza was utterly taken from me. That harrowing day when what was once my go-to meal became nothing but sand in my mouth.

DAY 0

THURSDAY

Hey, Josh! How's my best delivery boy doing today?"

I flashed a broad smile at Gino, my boss and pizza-making maestro. He was short and balding, but despite his obvious gut, anyone could see he wasn't just fat. His past as a high school linebacker showed in his powerful arms and legs. That layer of fat hid his massive core, which hid an even more massive heart. Everyone who worked for Gino knew they were family, whether they were related by blood or not.

I took his hand and gave him a bro hug. "I'm ready for my first customer, Gino!"

"I like that attitude, kid. I'll throw some extra cheese on the pizza tonight for you and your friends."

"Thanks, man!" Gino offered extra cheese every night, but he was such a decent guy, I couldn't let his warm-hearted offer go without thanks every time.

"Your old car holding up okay?" He looked out the window at the collection of duct tape and rust spots with a little silver paint that I called a car. It had seen better days, but I'd bought it off my dad when I was sixteen after saving for a couple of years doing odd jobs around the neighbor-hood. I could have a car of my own, and he could buy the new one he had been hoping to get for some time. It was a win-win situation for us both.

"Yeah, it's managing fine. Some cars just know how to last, and this baby is reliable . . . for the most part."

Gino patted me on the back. "Good, good." He looked over my shoulder at the door and grinned. "Harriet! Ready to make some pies?"

I held my breath as I turned and caught sight of Harriet. She strode through the front door with a cheerful hop in her step. One of her long chocolate braids fell across her shoul-der, partially obscuring the image on her black tee shirt of the opening screen of a classic sixteen-bit video game. She reached up to push her cat-eye glasses up her slender nose, drawing my gaze to her serious gray eyes.

If pizza were a goddess, Harriet would be her hand-maiden. I'd had a crush on Harriet since I was a freshman in high school. She was two years my senior, and once she found out I was painstakingly saving my lunch money to pay for my future car instead of using it to eat, she started bringing extra food for me. She'd find me in the cafeteria with my friends Desmond and Brian; I'd be reading comic books while they ate. She'd perch on the chair next to me and, in her quiet voice, tell me she had been experimenting with her cooking the night before. She would insist I'd be doing her a favor if I gave her my opinion or helped her finish the leftovers. We'd all sit together, sharing Harriet's food while we talked about comic books, movies, and video games. We four nerdy misfits somehow became a pack. A nerdy pack of weirdos.

I smiled at her, hoping I wasn't blushing like a schoolgirl in the dim glow of the light overhead. I couldn't keep my heart from fluttering, even after years of knowing her. While she tended to come across as shy and reserved, I knew better. She had the heart of a warrior and the wisdom of a sage. She was smart as a whip and knew how to let you know you were acting like an idiot without hurting your feelings. It was like she possessed some kind of magic.

I couldn't tell whether she noticed how into her I was, but Des and Brian knew. They teased me relentlessly about my infatuation with "Princess Harriet," as they jokingly called her. I just couldn't bring myself to tell her how much I loved her.

"I'm ready, Gino," Harriet responded gently. "Let me just grab my apron, and I'll get to work."

She gave me a quick smile and wave, then ducked behind the counter to wash up and set up her station.

Gino and Harriet were impressively efficient at making pies. They had the ingredients separated carefully in a perfect, mouthwatering assembly line, and watching them work was like watching a finely choreographed dance. Gino's wife, Graziella, would answer the phone, print up the order, and put it on the order rack. Gino or Harriet would grab the order receipt and get to work. Sometimes they'd work as a team; sometimes one would take lead on a pizza they specialized in. They were so quick, yet somehow, every pizza they put in a box looked mouthwatering and smelled amazing.

The phone rang, shocking me out of my thoughts. "Want me to grab that, Gino?"

"Sure, kid!" Gino replied as he joined Harriet in the kitchen to finish prepping for the busy night ahead. "I doubt anyone's calling for pizza yet."

I picked up the receiver after the third ring. "Gino's Pizza, home of the world-famous Gino's Special! How can I help you?"

While I listened for the voice at the other end, Harriet mouthed, "It's 'may I.'"

A young-sounding voice spoke nervously from the receiver. "Hi. Um, uh . . . is there an Amanda there?"

I heard a few tittering giggles at the other end and couldn't help but smirk. It was obviously a prank call from a familiar group of middle school kids. Since they were young, I decided to humor them. "Amanda who?"

More giggling came from the other end, and the one I was talking to exclaimed, "Shut up, guys!" Once the giggles were a little more under control, he continued. "Hugginkiss." I heard one huge snort of laughter and several loud instances of "Shhh!" coming from the background.

"How about I make you a deal? We're actually closed right now, so if I call for this Miss Hugginkiss, there's not really anyone to hear it. It won't be that funny. What I can do is, if you order a pizza, I'll shout that I need her, and you'll get some free cheesy breadsticks with your order. How's that?"

The line went silent for a moment, and then I heard muffled whispers. A few times, I heard a "How much do you have?" and some counting. Finally, the voice came back on the line.

"What can we get for ten dollars?"

"I can get you a large with extra cheese or one topping." The voices began whispering again.

"Okay, one large pepperoni and those breadsticks, and you have a deal!" came the eager voice from the other side.

"Sounds good. Now hang on. I'm going to stand on a stool and shout it. Keep your phone on. When I'm done, I'll get your address and bring you the pizza. Okay?"

More giggles. "Okay!"

I climbed up on one of the stools. Probably not the best

idea since the tops of the stools spun, but if I was going to embarrass myself for a few prankster kids, I figured I'd just go all out.

Harriet stuck her head out of the preparation area to look at me. "What are you doing, Josh?"

"Just entertaining our first customers of the evening." I stood up straight, my head almost hitting the ceiling. "Ahem. Where's Amanda Hugginkiss? I need Amanda Hugginkiss!"

A chorus of laughter came from the phone. "He said he needs a man to hug and kiss!" one kid shouted.

I carefully climbed down off the stool and picked the phone back up. "Okay, guys. Now let me get your info, and I'll have that pizza over to you pronto."

I put the address into the system, along with the order, in between giggles from the kids at the other end and gave the order to Harriet.

She took the order receipt and handed it to Gino. "Josh, you are much too nice to those kids."

"It's not that big a deal. They call once a week. I might as well humor them and get them to buy something too." I smiled and ducked around the counter to get my red Gino's Pizza cap and jacket for delivery. "Besides, I know those kids. They live in my neighborhood, and one of their parents went around warning people they might do this. They watched an old movie that showed kids making prank calls and decided it might be fun, even though we have caller ID and can figure out who they are easily. I'm not going to ruin that for them."

She rolled her eyes but smiled. "Well, let's hope it's just a phase."

"Let's hope what's a phase?" Graziella walked in the front door and turned on the lights for the Open sign in the window.

While Gino easily looked the part of a pizzeria owner, Graziella looked the opposite. She always had her hair perfectly styled in an updo that must have required at least one hairnet and a couple bottles of hair spray to keep every bleached-blonde hair in place. Today, she was wearing a familiar red blazer with a matching skirt. She wore it every time she thought she was on the verge of making a sale on a home. She was the number one realtor in the county, and she was good, whether or not she wore her lucky suit. Nobody could sell a house like she could . . . or a pizza.

"Just a prank call Josh managed to turn into a sale," Gino replied after putting the pizza in the brick oven. He came out from behind the counter and gave his wife a chaste kiss on the cheek so he wouldn't mess her suit up with his floury, doughy hands. "Hello, my sweet dove."

Graziella smiled and patted him playfully on the shoulder. "Get back to work, *amore mio*, and let me congratulate Josh on his business savvy."

Gino laughed and walked back around the counter and into the kitchen area to continue prepping while he waited for the pizza to cook.

Graziella leaned on the counter, her chin perched on her slender fingers, and gave me an appraising look. "Now, Josh, how did you manage that?"

I explained what had happened, and she grinned. "You know, you may have a future in sales. If you ever decide you want to go into selling houses, just let me know. I'll teach you."

"Yes, ma'am."

It wasn't really my plan to go into business. Not that I really had much of a plan for the future beyond saving up for college. I figured I'd take a few classes and find something that felt right. Since I would be paying for school myself, I didn't have to feel pressured about navel-gazing while I tried to figure out what to do.

Gino boxed the pizza and breadsticks after a few minutes, and I grabbed them for my first delivery run. The warm afternoon quickly faded into a cool evening as I made delivery after delivery. It was a Thursday night, so we were easily managing the slower influx of phone orders and dine-in customers. Not too busy, but it was that point in the week when people were starting to feel a bit worn down from work and wanted a break from having to make dinner. Our only real competition for fast food was a national chain down the road, and they didn't deliver, so it was just me and Renato, Gino and Graziella's son, ducking in and out of the restaurant to deliver as quickly as we could.

I knew the town like the back of my hand. I knew all the clever shortcuts and secret ways to get to each house, so I rarely had to speed. Frankly, with the money I was trying to save, it wasn't worth it to get a ticket from Officer Monroe and his cronies. I had a special arrangement with the local police. I gave them extra breadsticks when the department ordered pizza and pasta, and if I went a touch over the speed limit every once in a while, they'd let it pass. I'd gotten so good at making quick deliveries without speeding that the agreement wasn't necessary anymore, but it didn't hurt to keep the cops happy.

After several hours of deliveries, I came back to the restaurant, ready to wind down for the night. The last customers were leaving, and one of the waitstaff was bussing and wiping down tables. Renato sat at the counter, eating a slice of Greek goddess pizza, and I sat next to him just as Gino served me a slice of the same.

"I know it's not your absolute favorite, but eat your veggies, kid. They're good for you." Gino's comment earned a laugh from Harriet, who was tidying up.

"I dunno. If I have to, I have to," I joked back. He knew I'd eat whatever he put in front of me, and after sitting in my car for hours with the lingering smell of deliciousness seeping into the upholstery, I was famished.

Renato looked hungrier than I was. When I was about halfway through the masterpiece of pesto, spinach, feta, and artichoke hearts Gino had given me, Renato pushed his plate to the edge of the counter. "Another slice, Dad?"

Before Renato could finish asking, Gino picked up the plate and dished out another mouthwatering slice, this time a meat lover's special. "Of course, son. Hard work deserves a good meal." He messed up Renato's hair affectionately as Renato began to chow down in the way only a growing teenage boy could manage.

As I finished my last bite, the restaurant phone rang again. "I'll grab it," I announced since I was closest. Everyone continued what they were doing as I ducked around the counter and picked up the receiver. "Gino's Pizza! How may I help you?" I asked, remembering Harriet's correction from earlier.

"Yes, I'd like to order a pizza," answered a mellifluous voice. The tone was a bit mesmerizing, and I found myself struggling to put two words together in response.

I finally took a deep breath. "Okay, what can I get you?"

I listened to the order and wrote it down, relieved I didn't have to speak too much. As I became used to the voice on the other end, Gino's training for how to take orders kicked in. Once the call was over, I put the ticket on the rack. I then sat back down on my stool and ruminated over the call. Something didn't feel quite right.

"Hey, Graziella, do you know this address?" I grabbed the ticket from the rack to show her. She looked it over and put it back on the rack so Gino could start on the order next.

"Yes, I sold that one about a year ago. It's the big mansion on the hill that's been empty for a decade. They were doing renovations on it, but they must be done if there are people calling from there."

"Wait," Renato spoke up. "You mean that place with the outdoor pool that all the kids used to sneak into on Friday nights to go skinny-dipping?"

"You knew about that, hmm?" Graziella looked at him with one raised eyebrow. Whenever Graziella raised her left eyebrow, you knew there could be trouble. When it was her right, though, there was definitely trouble. I was relieved it was her left, for Renato's sake.

Renato put down his slice and sat up with his best posture. "I've heard stories. You know . . . from the other guys."

Graziella swooped forward with seemingly preternatural speed and grabbed Renato's ear. "Is that the truth?"

"Ow! Ow, yes, it's the truth! I know better than to mess with your houses!" Renato tried to worm his way out of her grip, without success.

Graziella grabbed his chin with her other hand and turned it so she could look him straight in the eye. "Is—this—true?"

Renato nodded, and I could swear I saw a bead of nervous sweat slide down his acne-riddled cheek. I couldn't help but feel bad for him. I'd have been terrified to have Graziella as a mother. At the same time, I knew her fierceness could be transferred to anyone who tried to hurt her only son in the blink of an eye.

She let go, and Renato let out a sigh of relief. "Good

boy." Graziella patted him on the head. "You going to take this last delivery?"

I spoke before Renato could. "I'll take it. Renato's been working hard, and it's getting late."

Gino spoke up from the kitchen. "I'll make your pizza and theirs, and you can take the delivery straight to them on your way home. They paid by credit card, so you just need to bring me the signed receipt tomorrow."

I gave him a salute. "Aye, aye, captain."

Gino laughed as he assembled the two pizzas. Harriet worked on cleaning, Graziella began to close the register for the night, and Renato and I finished eating our slices while arguing over whether the high school should start a curling team. Renato thought it was too weird a sport for the school to have a team, while I thought it was just too weird a sport for the school not to have one.

We bantered back and forth until Gino shouted, "Order up."

I gulped down the rest of my soda and grabbed the pizzas. I slid them securely into the insulated delivery bag as I said my goodbyes.

"Do you need a ride too, Harriet? I can drop you off on the way, if you want."

Renato, well aware of my crush, began making overly exaggerated kissy-faces at me. It was hard enough to keep a normal expression on my face when talking to Harriet about potentially being alone with her. Renato's antics weren't helping.

"Oh, no, Josh, that's okay. I have the car today, so I'll be fine. Besides, one more stop would mean your pizza would be that much colder once you got home." She patted me on the shoulder. "See you tomorrow, though!"

"Yeah, you too!" I cringed as my voice rose half an octave just because she touched my shoulder.

Renato snickered, and I tossed him a mock glare. Gino did me a favor and smacked the kid lightly on the back of the head. Even though Gino knew I had a crush on Harriet, he, at least, was kind about it.

Walking out to my car, I quickly got on the road. I was really curious about the old mansion. Back in high school, I had been one of those kids Renato mentioned who liked to sneak into the place when I could. While most of the other students just used the pool, my friends and I liked to sneak into the mansion and do mock ghost-hunting investigations. We never found or learned anything, other than the fact that just about anything that happens in the near dark is going to seem like it was caused by something supernatural.

My favorite spot in the mansion had been the old study. The shelves had been empty, but a large antique desk and matching chair had remained. I had liked to sit there and pretend I was opening a box of cigars. I'd clip the imaginary end of one, light it with an imaginary lighter, and then prop my feet up on the edge of the desk.

I wondered if the desk was still there as I drove up the winding road to the mansion. I had to park a short distance from the front door, as the brick driveway out front was filled with a variety of expensive cars. I couldn't help but gaze at some of them longingly, especially a gentian-blue Porsche 911 Carrera that I knew would pay for college a couple times over.

I didn't want to waste too much time, though, drooling over cars I could never afford when there was a garlicky, meaty pizza for me to get home. I redirected my attention and jogged to the front door. Ringing the doorbell, I looked around at the elaborate, swirling ironwork over the windows on either side of the front door. I hoped I'd get a good tip from a place this fancy, but the amount of pizza they'd ordered seemed absurdly minimal for a party big enough to have that many cars parked out front.

Laughter mixed with classical music playing in the background, which only made me more curious. I liked a good pizza myself, but it wasn't exactly caviar and champagne.

As I waited, I glanced at my watch impatiently. I was just reaching to ring the doorbell again when the front door finally opened. A man in a crisp black suit with a grim appearance and enviable posture stood before me and glared at me as though I were an insect.

My jaw immediately dropped. A butler? Did people even have butlers in real life anymore? There was no doubt he was one. Everything about him implied order, precision, and propriety.

"Um, hi there. You ordered a pizza?" I said once I got my jaw working again. I opened the insulated pizza bag and pulled out the box.

"Yes."

There was something eerily nondescript about the butler. His white-gloved hand touched mine as he took the box, and the hairs along my arms stood up. Something just didn't feel quite right, but it wasn't my place to judge. I'd seen weirder things on delivery runs, like the delivery I made to Mr. Costello's house a couple of weeks ago. It had been strange seeing my high school principal dressed up in bondage gear in the background while a dominatrix answered the door and took the pizza.

I shook off my discomfort. "I just need you to sign this receipt, and I'll get going."

"Of course, sir."

I offered him the cheap pen from my pocket, but he

went over to a side table, pulled out a fancy ballpoint pen, and signed the receipt with a flourish. Then he handed it back to me. I was impressed. His signature looked like it belonged on the Declaration of Independence, not a greasy slip of paper.

Just as I was about to leave, a man and a woman walked through the hallway and spotted us in the foyer. "Oh, Mr. Wellington, is that the pizza boy I ordered?"

It was the same mesmerizing voice that had called with the order. I wasn't surprised to find it belonged to a tall man with dramatically flowing black hair and a perfectly tailored suit.

Now, I wasn't generally a jealous person. I didn't need all the finer things in life. I just wanted to go to college, get a decent job that paid well enough I could splurge on comic cons every once in a while, and get on with my life.

I couldn't help but be envious of this guy, though. He was handsome and wealthy, and he had a stunning woman on his arm. I tried to imagine myself in that suit with Harriet on my arm, wearing a beautiful dress the color of the Porsche outside. I failed miserably. It was just too unrealistic that anything like that would ever happen to me.

"I'll just be going, then. Have a good night!" I began to walk out the door.

"Wait," came that amazing voice.

I immediately stopped. It didn't seem right not to wait, even though I had a pie with linguica, mushrooms, and artichokes cooling on the front seat of my car. The way I stopped, however, as if I'd walked into a glass wall, was incredibly odd. My heart began to beat a little faster. Something wasn't right.

"Turn around, pizza boy," the slick, silvery voice murmured.

I promptly turned around. Though my heart was still set on that pizza, I couldn't help but follow his instructions. It was like I was a puppet and the owner of that voice controlled the strings.

The long-haired rich dude approached me. "What's your name?"

Despite the condescending amusement in his tone and my growing instinct to just get out of there, I replied tightly, "Josh. It's Josh."

"Did you hear that?" exclaimed the woman who'd accompanied him. "What a perfectly, delightfully ordinary name!" She fluttered dark lashes over her emerald eyes as her perfect red lipstick framed the words as though she were the star of a cosmetics commercial.

"Hmm . . . yes." Long-Haired Dude smiled. "Come with us, Josh."

Again, I did as he said, though I still didn't understand why. For some reason, my initial panic had started to slip away, only to be replaced by a foggy calm. I followed Long-Haired Dude and Red Lipstick from the foyer, down the hallway, and into a large room filled with people lounging on overstuffed white sofas, dancing to the music being played on a white grand piano in one corner, or making out in the more secluded corners.

I blinked, trying to clear the hazy, almost drugged feeling that was starting to form in my mind, and noticed more details. There were spots here and there on the white furniture where it looked like wine had been spilled. I almost laughed. It seemed klutzy for such elegant people to spill wine so carelessly like that.

I blinked again. Some of the couples were making out pretty violently. Was this some kind of weird orgy?

Long-Haired Dude clapped his hands together to get

everyone's attention. "Tonight's entertainment has finally arrived."

I felt somewhat drunk at this point. When people turned to face Long-Haired Dude, I barely registered that some of the people they were making out with collapsed to the floor. I nearly collapsed myself and probably would have if Red Lipstick hadn't grabbed my arm in an iron grip.

I almost thanked her, but my mouth felt vaguely dry and a little swollen, as though I had just had a cavity drilled at the dentist. I kept my mouth shut. I didn't want to drool in front of a woman as hot as Red Lipstick.

Another woman in the room clapped her hands. "Oh, delightful! We haven't done this in ages! I want to place the first bet."

I listened distractedly to the conversation. Something about a bet . . . people were sharing time amounts: days, weeks, months. The highest was a year. I was confused, but I didn't really think too hard about it. I couldn't. My brain just didn't seem to be working quite right.

As everyone quieted down, Long-Haired Dude approached me. He swept his arm wide to encompass the room. "Choose one."

"One what?" I croaked out.

"One of the people in the room, of course, young Josh."

Several people snickered, and I heard someone make a snide remark, but I didn't quite catch what they said. All I heard was the word *vampire* and my name. The room filled with snorts of laughter, and I vaguely smiled. I felt like I was missing a joke at my own expense, but I wasn't quite sure.

"Oh, do choose me, Josh," came Red Lipstick's voice from my side.

I nodded. It was easier to just go along with whatever

she wanted than to think too hard about the other people in the room.

"Excellent!" said Long-Haired Dude.

I turned and gave him another vague smile. Not only did I feel like I had been to the dentist, but I had that weird feeling a person can get after having their wisdom teeth pulled, as though anesthesia were still working its way through their system. I thought about the word mentioned earlier: *vampire*. If someone had told me these people were vampires while I was in this state, I probably would have believed them.

I chuckled. Red Lipstick squished my cheeks as though I were a chubby baby. "Oh, look! He's so adorable and cooperative! Now, Joshy, tilt your head to the side like a good boy."

"Okay." I grinned and tilted my head.

Everything after that was a blank.

DAY 1

FRIDAY

I woke to the sound of chirping birds and the emergency brake poking uncomfortably into my ribs. Groaning, I sat up and rubbed my forehead with the back of my hand. My eyes felt strangely sandy, and I yawned and stretched as well as I could in the front seat of my car.

As the fuzziness left my mind, I realized I had slept in the car all night for some reason. I jerked to attention and accidentally honked the horn as I looked around. I was at the bottom of the hill leading up to the mansion. Had I stopped and slept in the car because I was tired? I groaned. I remembered being really out of it the night before, and my mind scrambled to pull together bits and pieces of what had happened at the mansion. I cringed to think I might have made a fool of myself in front of potential repeat customers. While Gino's pizza was so good it spoke for itself, I didn't want to make Gino look bad at all.

I fumbled around to find my keys since they weren't in the ignition, and I eventually found them stuck in the pocket of my jacket. I held them up and squinted at them in confusion. Why hadn't I left them in the ignition?

I finally sighed and gave up on that line of thought. Who knew why an exhausted person did anything?

Deciding not to think too hard about it, I put the key in the ignition and started the car. Something niggled at the back of my mind, some warning that it was best to get the hell away from that mansion and get myself home. It was a weird instinct, as I couldn't really remember anything beyond getting the receipt signed by the butler. That was strange, but it still fell within the realm of a relatively normal delivery. I wanted to deny the inner urge to run, but it won out. I quickly turned at the corner and made the five-minute drive home in four minutes.

I parked on the street in front of the tidy little suburban house I called home. After the night I had had, it was a relief to know I could return to a pleasant, normal, modern house. From the sidewalk, I walked down a cobblestone path, which cut through a neatly trimmed lawn just starting to get crunchy from the autumn leaves that had begun to fall, and up to a clean white house with a black-painted door and large, airy windows.

If not for my best friend Desmond, I'd either be living in one of the shitty apartments down on the corner of Lincoln and Grand where the druggies hung out or still at home with my dad. Des was a successful pro gamer, so he'd been able to rent a three-bedroom house in a decent neighborhood and had invited Brian and me to live with him.

I fumbled tiredly with my keys in one hand while balancing the pizza in the other. When Des initially said Brian and I could live there rent-free, I had argued that I should pay some rent. I finally wore him down, and Des negotiated me down to one hundred dollars per month and unlimited free pizza. It still seemed much too little, especially since the unlimited free pizza was just part of my job.

I awkwardly managed to get the door unlocked and open, only to be greeted by an eye-watering combination of severe body odor and cheap aftershave.

I rolled my eyes. "Brian? Did you forget to take a shower again?"

I placed the pizza box on the kitchen counter and walked into the living room to behold Brian in all his glory, wearing boxers while playing video games. I watched in fascination as he put down his controller and took a huge gulp from a liter of soda while scratching his belly.

I had to admit, there were days when I wouldn't have minded hanging out on the couch, vegging out on games, and not having to get dressed. But every day? How was Brian not bored after months of this?

He'd moved in after his dad threatened to kick him out if he didn't join the military or go to school and then made good on his threat. Des and I thought his dad was being unfair, but after a few weeks, we'd started to understand why his dad was so strict. Without someone telling him what to do, Brian didn't bother to do anything. Our friend was now a professional-level couch potato. Even his skin had taken on a ghostly pallor because he barely left the house anymore.

"I'll take one tomorrow." He shoved what looked like a peanut butter sandwich in his mouth and continued playing an unfamiliar war-shooter game Des had probably just gotten.

I picked up a controller and sat in one of the leather armchairs. It was as far as I could get from him and his cloying miasma. The stench was so thick, I could have grabbed a handful and worked it into a miniature model of Brian. I was starting to wonder if the smell was on the verge of becoming sentient.

"Did you finally get some with Princess Harriet?" Brian quipped, his eyes glued to the screen.

I glared at him, holding back my instinct to punch him in the face. Punching him would have involved getting closer to the stench, which was enough to keep me in check. Instead, I changed the subject.

"You know, if you bathed more often and took some pride in your appearance, you'd be able to get a girl for yourself."

I looked Brian over. His stomach bulged, and his un-shaved stubble made him look more slovenly than trendy. It was a sudden, shocking transformation from the track star he once was.

"Damn it!" Brian threw the controller to the floor in frustration.

"Hey, don't wreck the controller because you can't play for shit," Des said as he walked down the stairs to join us. He immediately began to gag, covering his mouth and nose. "Okay, Brian, you need to take a shower now."

"Why the hell do I care about getting a girl? Chicks suck. They only go for chads like Des."

Des walked in front of the couch and put his hands on Brian's shoulders. "Dude, don't go full incel on us, okay? We need the Brian we know and love back. Hell, I'm a pro gamer, and even I know when to put down the controller to get some exercise and take a shower. Now go. Clean yourself up. You reek."

Grumbling under his breath, Brian stood and walked upstairs to the bathroom. Des and I waited for the telltale sound of the shower being turned on before we traded matching looks of worry. We didn't have to put into words how concerned we were that Brian wasn't trying to make things better for himself. Neither of us was adult enough to know how to handle the mess he'd become.

I looked away first, picking up the blanket Brian had been sitting on. My gag reflex kicked in as Brian's smell wafted from it, and I almost started hyperventilating.

"I'll take that."

Des grabbed the blanket from me and held it at arm's length as he walked to the laundry room, where he immediately put it in the washer with soap and bleach. With Des being an organized neat freak and me growing up doing all the chores in a single-parent family, neither of us was okay with Brian's level of mess. I didn't mind a few things strewn about here and there, but the Brian piles were an exponentially higher level of gross than even most guys our age would be okay with.

"When did we become his parents?" I batted my eyes, pretending to be a 1950s housewife, as Des returned to the room with some cleaning supplies.

"When he's like this, he's *your* son," Des joked in a husky dad voice as he wiped down the coffee table. He then picked up the controller as though it were a baby bird with a broken wing. "Sorry, baby. The bad man won't hurt you again." He carefully cleaned it with an alcohol wipe.

I couldn't hold back and began to laugh a little hysterically. The combination of the previous night's weirdness, Brian's grossness, and Des's obsessive care of his gaming equipment finally got to me.

Des gently placed the controller in its designated storage container beneath the television. "You okay there, man?"

"I don't know. I feel kind of weird." I opened a window

to help air out the room and sat down. "Last night was . . . odd."

Des sat down on the edge of the couch. "Okay, talk to Papa Des. What happened? Did you see Mr. Costello in bondage gear again? Did you get pictures this time?"

I groaned and started to gag a bit. "Don't ever mention that again. You promised you wouldn't."

"Never again, my friend," Des stated solemnly, giving me a mock salute. "You look kind of pale, though, even for a white guy. You sure you're all right?"

"Well, last night, my final delivery was to that mansion up on the hill. Did you know there are people living there now? I delivered the pizza to the butler, but somehow, the rest of the night turned into this weird blur, and I woke up in my car at the bottom of the hill this morning. I can't remember anything. It was . . . strange." My right hand shook a little, and I clenched it into a fist to stop the tremor.

"You think they roofied the pizza boy? Did you check to see if they took one of your kidneys or something?"

"Shit!" I jumped out of the chair and pulled up my shirt to see if there was any sign of a nefarious operation. After a short investigation, I was clearly free of open wounds and stitches. I realized how ridiculous it was for me to freak out like that since I would have obviously been in pain if someone had stolen a kidney. I jerked my shirt back down and slumped into the armchair, my jeans creaking against the leather. "Fuck, man, don't say shit like that!"

Des laughed for a moment, then gave me a piercing look. "Really, man, you don't look great. Maybe you need to eat something?"

"Yeah, you could be right. Plus, now that we've aired the place out a bit, I think I can handle eating something."

"See, at least you still have your sense of humor. That's

a good sign." Des strode into the kitchen, turned on the oven, and opened the pizza box. "Oh, man, it's a little squished."

"Crap. I think I used it as a pillow last night. Sorry." I walked over to the counter to check the damage. There was just a small spot where the cheese had stuck to the inside of the top of the pizza box. "It doesn't look too bad, though. Thank goodness Gino invested in those little table things that prevent the tops of the pizza boxes from caving in."

"Yeah, Clarissa loves using those to make tables for her ponies. I think she has enough for a whole restaurant now." Des smiled proudly as he talked about his little sister and slid the pizza into the oven. "It's no big deal. We'll just make Brian eat the messed-up part to make up for subjecting us to his foul, unearthly stench."

We both snickered. As we waited for the pizza to reheat, I sat on a barstool at the kitchen counter with my head in my hands and yawned a few times, while Des started taking out plates. I couldn't shake the lingering fog from my mind. I hated being unable to remember what had happened last night. Since we'd eliminated organ harvesting from the possibilities and I didn't feel hurt in any way, they couldn't have done something that horrible. Could they? Maybe I was just more tired than I thought.

Unconsciously, I scratched at an itch on my neck. When I felt something wet, I jerked my hand back and examined my fingertips, finding a small amount of fresh blood beneath my nails.

"Hey, Des? Is there something on my neck?" I tilted my head to the side so he could see where I had been scratching.

He took a quick look. "Yeah. Looks like a couple of wicked mosquito bites. Maybe there were a bunch of mosquitoes up at that mansion because of the pool."

I shrugged. "Yeah, probably."

"Or maybe you were bitten by vampires." Brian appeared on the stairs in his now-familiar uniform of a video game tee shirt and baggy sweats. "Chicks dig vampires. Watch. You'll turn into a vampire, amping up your coolness factor to Des levels, and you guys will both get all the ass you want. I'll just have to wait around for your sloppy seconds."

I snorted, taking in an unwelcome menthol, oaky scent, and glared at him. "Can you cut it out with the cheap cologne? Only old guys wear that."

Brian glared back.

Des stepped in before Brian could retort. "Bri, look man, all we're saying is, you need to start taking care of yourself. If there's one thing I've learned from only having sisters, it's that girls care more that you smell clean than that you wear cologne. Plus, you used to be in great shape from all that running you did for the track team. Girls had crushes on you."

"No, they didn't." Brian's self-loathing seeped from his pores and spread throughout the room as much as his body odor / cheap cologne combination. "You're a hot Black dude with money, and chicks are all over money. Josh isn't as much of a chad as you are, but he's tall and good-looking enough to bag Harriet anytime he wants. I'm just—"

Des slammed a plate on the counter, where it shattered into a few jagged pieces. Brian and I jumped and stared at Des. He was usually pretty mellow, even when he was being thoroughly trounced while gaming. But it seemed the past few months of Brian's inability to take the driver's seat in his own life was wearing on Des as much as it had on me.

"That's enough! Do you think we would be friends with you if we thought you were a loser? Do you know how many girls asked me about you, only to come crying back to me later because you had told them they weren't hot enough for you?" Des pulled the pizza out of the oven and put it on the counter. "This is your last pizza, Brian. You're going on a diet, and you're going to exercise with me until you lose some of the weight you've gained."

"And you're taking a shower every day," I stated as I helped Des pick up the pieces of the broken plate. "And no more fucking cologne."

Brian looked as though he had been slapped in the face. I had a feeling his parents had never properly put their foot down with him until they kicked him out. He stared at the pizza for a moment. "Are you guys gonna kick me out too?" His voice was small and weak.

Des grabbed a new plate, put a piece of pizza on it, and then served one to Brian. "No, we're not kicking you out. We just want you to act like a man. Maybe even get a counselor if you need one. This has to stop. When you hate on yourself, you blame everyone else, and women can pick up on that anger a mile away. That's why they don't want to be with you."

He took a bite of pizza and paused thoughtfully. "You know why I'm good with women? Because of my sisters. Jocelyn wouldn't let me get away with anything. She made sure I knew good and well what women have to struggle with. Clarissa taught me how to be patient and nice to her when she'd ask me to play with her. You can't expect someone to cater to you like your mom did. Most women don't want to feel like they have to mother their boyfriends. You have to meet people where they're at and compromise. It's not looks. It's not money. It's making women feel like you care about them and know that you care about yourself too."

I grabbed a piece of pizza while Des lectured Brian. The gooey, stringy cheese made my mouth water, and the smell of the sausage just about broke me. I opened my mouth to inhale as much of that pizza as I could in one bite. I knew just how good it would taste.

My teeth tore through cheese and crust, and I was about to close my eyes in heavenly bliss when I realized something was horribly, excruciatingly wrong. I could smell the pizza. It smelled amazing. I could feel the texture of the pizza in my mouth, and it felt completely normal for pizza. It was the right temperature. Everything was right except . . .

It tasted like nothing.

I chewed and swallowed, then tried another bite, this time smaller. Nothing. It smelled right, looked right, felt right, but tasted as flat as water.

I jumped off my stool in horror. "Guys! Stop arguing and put down the pizza!"

They both turned and stared at me as though I had two heads.

"Um, you okay, man?" Des asked, looking extremely concerned.

Brian looked at me, down at the pizza, and back at me again. "Well, if this is my last pizza, I'm eating it." He took a bite and closed his eyes. "Oh, god, I can't believe you're going to make me give this up! This is the best."

I looked down at my slice of pizza. "You can taste that, Brian? And it tastes fine?"

"Hell yeah. Gino makes the best fucking pizza. You know that." Brian took another bite. "Oh. Pure heaven."

Des put his slice down and gave me a penetrating look. "What's wrong, Josh?"

I gulped and looked at him with wide eyes. "I can't taste

it. It . . . has no flavor. Do you . . . do you think they really drugged me at that mansion and this lack of taste is some sort of aftereffect?"

"I dunno." Des picked up his slice again and took a bite. "It tastes fine. I think it's just you. Do you want me to call Jocelyn? I think she's on shift at the hospital now. Maybe they can do a blood test or something."

I gazed at the precious slice of heaven on my plate in sorrow. "Call—her—now."

I didn't know what was going on, but there was no way anyone was taking my precious pizza away from me.

Des sped into the hospital parking lot, screeched the car into an empty spot, and stopped just before the car would have ended up on the curb.

"Quick, Brian! Go grab a wheelchair for Josh!" Des was out the door and running into the hospital while Brian and I were still trying to get out of the car, shaky from Des's insane driving.

"You really need a wheelchair?" Brian asked as we watched Des do his impression of an Olympic sprinter.

I shook my head. "It's my tongue, not my legs. I can walk just fine."

"Yeah, I figured."

We quickly walked to the hospital entrance and entered through the automatic doors. We were immediately met by the sight of Des nearly tackling his sister Jocelyn, who had just walked into the lobby. Her hair was up in a tidy French twist, and she looked every inch the reliable, steady medical professional she was.

"Okay, Des, calm down. Just tell me what the problem is." Jocelyn's manner was sedate but supportive, even as she pushed Des back a bit so she had some space.

"Okay, so we were eating pizza, and Josh couldn't taste it. We think he might have been roofied or something," Des explained in a rush. "Can you check him out to see what's wrong?"

Jocelyn's eyes widened. "Wait, did you say Josh can't taste pizza? Josh—the guy who can eat pizza twenty-four/seven and never grow tired of it? That Josh?"

I stepped into the conversation. "Yeah, I had a weird experience last night, and I've been feeling strange all morning. When I ate a slice of pizza, I couldn't taste it at all, even though I could smell it and my mouth wasn't numb or anything."

Des gave Brian a stern look and whispered sharply, "I told you to get him a wheelchair, man!"

Brian rolled his eyes. "He doesn't need one. He can walk just fine!"

I ignored them. "Do you think there's some kind of test that could find out what's wrong?"

"Dr. Sinclair is on vacation right now, or I'd have you see him since he's your GP. This sounds odd, though. Why don't I take you back to an exam room? We can talk about what happened and run some labs to see what's going on." Jocelyn's bedside manner was welcoming and reassuring. She turned to Des and Brian. "Gentlemen, I'll need you to stay in the lobby."

"Okay, Sis! Make sure Josh gets his taste buds back!" Des gave her a thumbs-up, then grabbed Brian and sat him down in a nondescript chair typical of hospital waiting rooms. He grabbed a random magazine, shoved it at Brian, and took one for himself.

"This way." Jocelyn guided me down a sterile hall to an empty exam room.

Once she'd sat me down in a chair next to a small desk, she asked me to explain what had happened. I went through the whole story: making the delivery, forgetting what happened afterward, waking up in my car, feeling a little off all morning, and a detailed account of what I experienced while eating the pizza. While she listened, she checked my eyes, ears, and throat, as well as my blood pressure and heart rate. Then she spotted the two marks on my neck.

"What's this?" She put on latex gloves and adjusted my head so she could see better.

"I don't know. I just scratched at them this morning. They weren't there yesterday, and Des thought they were mosquito bites or something." I furrowed my brow. "You don't think they have something to do with this, do you?"

She looked at the two spots carefully, gently prodding the skin around the scabs. "I'm not sure. They could be insect bites or injection sites, but they're a little odd. Almost like an animal bite that's had a few days to heal? If this was from last night, though, I'd guess insect or injection, which could mean you were drugged like Des suggested. Weird place to inject someone, though. If they were trying to drug you without you knowing, I'd think they'd choose a less obvious spot or put it in your drink or food."

She stood straight and nodded, removing the gloves. "Okay, I want a urine sample, and I'll have the phlebotomist take a blood sample. Also, I need to ask this: do you think you need a rape kit done?"

The question surprised me. "I don't know. I don't feel like anything like that happened to me. I don't feel injured or anything, other than the mosquito-bite things on my neck." I looked at her, suddenly feeling lost. "Do—do you think I should?"

She sat down across from me. "It's a good idea, just to be sure. Have you bathed or changed your clothes at all since last night?"

I shook my head. The idea that someone might have done something like that was disturbing and took this whole situation to a level I wasn't sure I'd be able to handle.

"Have you gone to the bathroom at all?"

"No, not yet."

"Okay. I'm going to have a nurse come in to perform the exam." She stood and walked toward the door, then turned and gave me a small smile. "Josh, I'm glad Des brought you right away. Hopefully, we can get you some answers soon. It should take twenty-four hours, at minimum, to start getting a return on the test results. Do you have to work tonight?"

"No, I'm off tonight," I replied. "I have to drop something off there, though."

She smiled. "Good. I want you to take it easy. I'll let Dr. Sinclair know that I saw you today when he gets back in a couple of weeks. I'll ask if one of the guys can get you a change of clothes, too, since we'll have to take your clothes for the rape kit."

I nodded, more scared than I had felt when I woke up in the car. Shortly after, the nurse came in and gave me a somewhat awkward exam and a cup for a urine sample. Once that was taken care of, I was rushed off to get my blood taken. The emotional weight of the situation must have really worn me out by then because I became really dizzy after my blood was drawn.

"Whoa, don't get up too fast," the phlebotomist said as

I collapsed back in the chair. "You're looking a bit pale. Have you eaten enough today?"

I thought about that beautiful slice of pizza forlornly. "Just a bite of something."

"I'll get you some juice. That should perk you up."

I smiled flatly and nodded. I was starting to feel numb inside; it was all just too overwhelming. My hands were still clammy from the rush of getting to the hospital, and while the fear still lingered, it was distant, as if I were watching everything from the outside. I could only hope these tests would give me some answers soon and that losing my sense of taste was temporary.

While I brooded over my misery, the phlebotomist left and came back with a juice box and a banana. "Here you go. Your friends in the lobby are worried about you. I told them you'll be ready to go soon."

I nodded, drank the tasteless juice, and then ate the tasteless banana. At the very least, I could smell them, so I could imagine how they tasted. I realized bananas were pretty weird to eat when you couldn't taste them. I could have been chewing a mushy, squashed slug, for all I knew.

I finally stood up slowly, making sure my feet were firmly planted on the floor. I was determined not to get dizzy again and fall down. Once fully upright, I took a deep breath and gave the phlebotomist a nod of thanks. The nurse who had helped me earlier gave me the clothes Des must have brought for me and led me to a room where I could change out of the hospital gown I'd been wearing. I felt halfway back to normal by the time I walked out to the lobby.

Brian bolted out of his chair. "You okay?"

Seeing the genuine concern on his face, I kind of felt bad for being so hard on him earlier. "Yeah, I think so. I won't have any results for at least another day, though, so Jocelyn told me to take it easy today." I noticed my hands didn't feel quite so clammy anymore. Maybe that was a sign I'd be okay for now. "Can we drop off the receipt from last night's delivery and my work stuff on the way home?"

"We got you covered," Des said. "All you have to do today is chill out, play a few games or watch some movies or something, and . . . well, eat, I guess?"

I thought about eating. I could still eat. Nobody had told me otherwise. I nodded. "Yeah. I can still at least smell my food while I eat it."

"Sounds like a plan. Let's get you home. You'll be back to normal in no time." Des patted my shoulder supportively, and the three of us left the hospital.

Of course, I was never going to be normal again.

DAY 2
SATURDAY

I woke up on the living room couch to the sun shining directly in my face. I grunted in annoyance and turned over to hide from the bright light. My desire to get more sleep fought a valiant battle against the garish light, only to surrender in utter defeat.

Groaning, I reluctantly opened my eyes. The grain of the couch's black leather filled my vision in detailed relief. That was odd. I had never bothered to look closely at the leather, but now I could clearly see pores and wrinkles I hadn't noticed before. I scratched my head and sat up, wondering if my vision being so sharp was another symptom of whatever odd illness I had.

I yawned and stretched, glancing around the room. Brian lay on the other section of the L-shaped couch, snoring, and Des was nowhere to be seen, which figured. Being all about order, Des had strong feelings about sleeping in a proper bed instead of just about anywhere else. Brian and I both had blankets on, so Des must have made sure we were comfortable before heading off to his room.

I chuckled and then yawned again, shutting my eyes. When I opened them, I noticed something. Something different. The details I had picked up from the leather of the couch hadn't been a fluke. Everything I could see seemed extra sharp. It was enough to make my head start pounding.

Hoping a pair of sunglasses might help, I quickly got up and made a beeline for the hall closet. I checked through the pockets of a couple of my jackets, shuffling around awkwardly as I squinted to let in as little light as possible. I managed to find a pair and quickly shoved them on my face, almost taking an eye out in the process. Opening my eyes slowly, I found, to my relief, that the sunglasses were enough to stave off the impending headache.

"Hey, Josh!"

I jumped and turned as Des greeted me with the kind of enthusiasm only a true morning person could possibly possess. He stood a couple of feet behind me, clearly dressed to go running, tee shirt and shorts worn over compression pants.

"You want to come with?"

I shook my head. "I think I'll sit this one out. I'm still having some weird symptoms. Whatever I got drugged with must have been pretty intense."

Des looked like he was about to ask a question but stopped and smiled instead. "Okay, man. Take it easy, then." Des jerked his head toward Brian, who was just barely waking up. "You gonna help me get him ready to run?"

I gave him a conspiratorial smirk, and Des returned it with a twinkle in his eye. We immediately went into stealth mode. Des angled from the side where the corners met on the sectional sofa, while I sneaked up from the other end. Luckily, Brian was extremely slow to wake up. Once we were properly in position, we both shouted, "Surprise attack!"

Brian freaked out as we tackled him, kicking his legs and flailing his arms.

"Oof, man, you really did gain some weight!" Des complained as he finally hooked his arms under Brian's armpits.

"But the feet still work!" I shouted, still trying to get hold of Brian's legs as they waved around with wild abandon.

"What the hell are you guys doing?" Brian shrieked in horror.

"It's time for you to get started, remember?" Des shouted as Brian tried to loosen the grip on his shoulders. "We're getting you back in shape so you can feel better about yourself. Step one to defeating your inner demons!"

By that point, I had both of Brian's feet under control, holding his ankles in a death grip. "Yeah, Brian! You can do this, man! You used to do it all the time when we were in high school!"

Des and I stood there with Brian struggling vainly to escape. Suddenly, I was hit with the realization that our plan hadn't included what we would do after lifting Brian up. When I looked to Des for answers, he seemed to have had the same thought.

"Um . . ."

"Yeah, uh, let's . . ."

Brian stopped struggling and folded his arms across his chest in irritation. "Put me down! I'll get my damned shoes on and go running!"

I let go of Brian's feet, gently placing them on the ground. Des helped him stand. Brian glared at us, then quickly jumped over the couch, darting away like a cockroach exposed to light, and locked himself in the bathroom.

"Crap!" Des exclaimed. "He's going to hole himself up in there unless we make him come out!"

We closed in on the bathroom and began pounding on the door.

Brian pounded the door back. "Can't a guy pee in peace? For fuck's sake, guys!"

"Fine, as long as you come out right when you're done!" Des shouted.

I stepped away from the door. "I'll go grab some socks and shoes for him. He can run in his tee shirt and sweats just fine."

Des gave me a thumbs-up, and I ran up the stairs to Brian's room. When I opened the door, a putrid, unwashed smell oozed out, and I pulled the neck of my shirt up over my nose to block the stench. I slogged through the reeking mass of dirty laundry and random trash to get to Brian's dresser. One single pair of socks resided in his sock drawer. I grabbed it and rifled around the mess on the floor until I found decent shoes for running. I began to leave, but then I turned back and opened the window to air out the room. The next step of Mission Make Brian a Man was definitely getting him to do his own laundry.

As I left the room, I pulled my tee shirt back down and heaved a sigh of relief. I could have sworn the smell was even worse than usual. I slid down the banister to the bottom of the stairs, hoping it would get me away from the smell just a little faster.

I handed the shoes and socks over to Des. "It's all up to you now, man! If you need to abort the mission, send me a text, and I'll pick you guys up."

Des saluted. "Aye, aye, captain." He looked down at the shoes and socks in his hands. "You sure these are clean?"

Before I could reply, Brian opened the bathroom door. "Give me those." He grabbed the socks from Des, sat down on the floor, and put them on. "Idiots. Both of you. Idiots."

Des and I chuckled, but I think we were both relieved he was cooperating. We wanted our old friend back, and if this was what it took to get an improved, more grown-up Brian, it would be worth it.

Des and Brian headed toward the door. As he hopped with both feet to pump up his energy, Des gave Brian an enthusiastic pep talk, saying things like "You're gonna do this, man!" and "You'll be ready for the Olympics before you know it!" Brian merely yawned as he followed Des out the door and closed it behind them.

As I went to the kitchen, I heard Des shout, "House of champions!" I watched through the window as he and Brian took off down the street.

I was kind of relieved to have a little time alone. It would give me a chance to get in my own head and try to figure out what was going on. Pulling a carton of orange juice from the refrigerator, I poured a small amount in a cup. I took a tentative sip to see if my sense of taste had changed any overnight. Nothing. I went over to the sink and filled the glass with water instead. I wasn't really feeling hungry, just thirsty.

I sat back down on the couch and lifted the sunglasses to rest against my forehead, squinting away from the harsh glare of light coming in through the east-facing windows. I'd never had migraines before. Was that part of what was going on? I held up my right hand and examined it with my strangely sharp vision. I observed pores, tiny hairs, and wrinkles I had never noticed before. It was kind of cool, but kind of creepy at the same time. Was that normal for someone with migraines? While I hoped the taste problem was temporary, the vision thing could be useful.

I settled the sunglasses back on my nose and decided not to think too much about it. Whatever happened would happen, as long as my health was okay enough for me to keep working and saving for school.

I grabbed a basket, some cleaning supplies, and latex gloves from the laundry room. There was no way Brian would get his room clean by himself when it was this bad; the smell alone might get us evicted if the landlord ever had to come in for some reason. With a sense of dread, I climbed the stairs to grab Brian's dirty laundry. Hopefully, I could force him to get it done once he came back.

I opened the door once more and put on a mask left-over from when we did some painting after we first moved in. I figured it would help suppress the noxious fumes better than my shirt would. After putting on the gloves and kicking a few things aside to create an empty spot for the laundry basket, I began to pick up anything that remotely looked like laundry.

The state of the room was depressing. This was Brian, my friend since elementary school. His mom had been a doting housewife, doing everything for him and his dad. That was nice and all, but Brian had never learned to take care of himself. As awful as my recent experiences had been, seeing my friend fall apart over the past handful of months was heartbreaking.

I picked up some socks that were so stiff with dirt and grime, they could have walked away on their own. I paused for a moment, wondering if it was more than just dirt, and immediately dismissed the thought from my mind, tossing the socks in the basket. I could throw away the latex gloves I was wearing when I was done, at least.

As I kept up a slow and steady pace, I wandered through memories of growing up with Brian. My heart felt heavy as I thought of who he'd become in the past few months. Could we get the Brian I remembered back in some way? He might be lazy and grumpy all the time now, but he had always been fun to hang out with. The guy deserved some good in his life, or so I hoped. He just needed to learn to make goals and take pride in taking responsibility for himself. And if Des and I could teach him some of the things we knew about girls, maybe he could actually get a girlfriend.

Once I'd gotten the laundry off the floor, I grabbed a trash bag and began to pick crumpled junk food wrappers and torn-up magazines up off the floor. As I rifled through the trash, an image on one of the magazines caught my eye. Picking it up, I found it was a photo of the same Porsche 911 I had seen outside the mansion.

I blinked for a moment. Suddenly, the memories started flooding back. The butler, Long-Haired Dude, the weird auction, and Red Lipstick all popped back into my head. I began to feel dizzy and sat down on the edge of Brian's bed, my heart pounding.

At first, scattered thoughts ran through my head without sequence, almost like a deck of cards being shuffled. I somehow managed to slow the thoughts as I fought through a sudden feeling of nausea. Taking several deep breaths, I gathered the scattered bits and pieces in my mind, looking for some memory of being drugged. After picking through the memories carefully, I realized the last thing I remembered was Red Lipstick telling me to tilt my head. There was nothing after that.

I clenched my now-clammy hands into fists, relaxed them, and repeated the process multiple times as I tried to control my frustration. I just couldn't remember eating or drinking anything, and I definitely did not remember getting injections in my neck. Maybe that had happened after Red Lipstick told me to tilt my head?

Even greater than my anger was my fear. Would

whatever had been done to me last forever? Would I be stuck with some health problem I'd have to manage for the rest of my life? Would I be well enough to handle working and going to school? I propped my elbows on my knees, dropped my head into my hands, and groaned. I needed all this like I needed a hole in the head.

"No, not going down that road," I muttered. I needed to stay positive. Anything could be overcome. I didn't need to follow Brian's current example and just give up on myself. It wasn't an option. My options were to stay calm and wait to hear back about the test results, try to eat even though I wasn't able to enjoy it, and if I was in the clear, go back to work tonight. If I couldn't go back to work, I'd rest and follow whatever instructions I was given.

I stood and finished picking up the trash. I had to keep moving forward. There would be no point to anything otherwise.

As I walked down the stairs with two bags of trash, Brian and Des came back in the front door. Des looked fresh and ready to meet the day; Brian looked like death warmed over.

"Uh, how'd it go, guys?" I put the trash bags on the ground by the front door and went into the kitchen to grab them each a bottle of the weird Japanese electrolyte drink Des swore by. I tossed one to Des, who grabbed it with a smile. I almost tossed the other to Brian, but he was hunched over with his hands on his knees, trying to get his breathing under control. I twisted off the cap and handed it to him.

He looked up and took the drink. "Why did I use to love doing that? It was never that hard before."

"You're just out of practice. You'll be back to outrunning Des soon. You just have to keep up the work." Maybe it wasn't one of Des's enthusiastic pep talks, but it was all I had to offer.

Unexpectedly, a huge grin shone on his face. "Yeah, you're right! I used to beat Des all the time! I can do it again!"

"Good! Now, let's get you doing your laundry. If you can outrun Des again, you can definitely do your own laundry." I pointed to the overflowing baskets in the laundry room.

Brian gulped down some of the drink and glared at me. "You had to ruin it, didn't you?"

Des took another sip from his bottle. "Didn't your mom ever tell you that laundry and dishes are the chores that never end?"

"I'm going to help you, Brian. It's easy once you know the basics. Taking it home to your mom is probably way more work than just doing it yourself. Once it's dry, you don't even have to fold everything. Put everything you can on hangers and anything that's left can be stuffed into drawers."

I gave him a friendly push into the laundry room and instructed him on what to do. Making sure he didn't overdo the soap, I helped him get a load of whites into the washer. Then I sent him upstairs to take a shower once Des came down the stairs, fresh from his own. Even though Brian moaned and complained, he followed my instructions. I was probably spending too much time focused on Brian, but it was easier than facing my own problems.

Grabbing a banana and one of Des's energy drinks, I sat on the couch. I took a bite of the banana and, again, couldn't taste it. I gulped it down anyway and took a sip of the drink. Weirdly, I could kind of taste it. It wasn't as strong as I was used to it being. It was supposed to have a grapefruit flavor. I could almost taste a hint of that, but what I got more of was a somewhat saline taste.

I was so excited that something akin to flavor was hitting my tongue that I was tempted to quickly gulp the rest of the drink down. Then I realized if I did that, I wouldn't be able to enjoy what taste there was. I slowed down and savored that bottle of chemicals suspended in liquid like I was one of those wine-tasting experts.

Grabbing a controller, Des sat down next to me and gave me a quick glance. "Josh, you look weirdly blissed out. Are you on something?"

I looked at him with what must have seemed like a really odd smile. "Des, I can kind of taste it!" I held up the bottle.

"What, really?" He had been facing the TV, watching for the start screen of his game. He put down the controller and looked at me intently. "Your sense of taste is already coming back?"

"Well, I couldn't taste the banana, but I can kind of taste this stuff. It's something, at least."

"Progress, man! You'll be chowing down on pizza again in no time! Let's celebrate with a game!" Des got up to grab another controller and handed it to me.

We played some of Des's favorite game, *Midnight Murder Mansion*, with Brian joining us after his shower. It was easy to just zone out for the next few hours and let my friends distract me from my worries. We laughed and yelled at the game, I helped Brian do his laundry, and everything felt utterly normal, like any other weekend of hanging out.

I almost didn't notice when my phone vibrated in my pocket. Pulling it out, I saw it was a call from the hospital, and my buzz was effectively killed.

I put down my controller. "I gotta get this, guys."

They just nodded and kept playing without me. I stepped into the kitchen and answered. "Hey, what's up?"

"Hi, Josh, it's Jocelyn," came the voice from the other end of the line. I couldn't decide whether I was relieved it was her. It was probably better to just rip off the bandage than to draw out the process.

"Hey, Jocelyn. How did my results turn out?"

"We haven't gotten everything back yet, but our new lab tech, Dr. Chen, pulled some strings to get things moving a little faster with the blood work. The guy's weird, but he definitely has connections. Anyway, so far, we haven't found a trace of anything concerning, other than that you seem a bit anemic. Does anemia run in your family at all?" Jocelyn sounded pretty calm, so I took it as a sign that it wasn't too big a deal.

"Not that I know of. What else could cause it? Why would that impact my ability to taste anything?" I sat on one of the kitchen barstools and leaned on the counter, trying to focus on Jocelyn's words instead of the sounds of the game in the background.

"It could be caused by blood loss or low iron. There are some more concerning health issues that could cause it, but you're generally pretty healthy, so I can't imagine it being something that can't be solved with a minor change to your diet or by taking supplements." Jocelyn paused. "None of it explains your sudden lack of taste, though. I think we should keep an eye on that."

"I did kind of taste something today, so maybe it's just some weird fluke?"

"Oh, really? That's good news. Maybe the best thing to do is monitor what's happening with your taste. My only concern is if those bumps aren't mosquito bites. Maybe someone took blood from you, which would explain the anemia. Usually, they'd take it from your arm, though, not your neck."

I thought about the memories that had returned to me while cleaning Brian's room. The moment Red Lipstick asked me to tilt my head suddenly seemed much more significant. Did she draw blood from me? Why would she draw blood from me?

Jocelyn continued. "Also, just so you know, your rape kit came back. Strangely quickly too. Usually these things sit around for a while because of backlog, but you must have someone interested in your situation."

"Should I be worried about that?" My voice wavered a bit.

"I don't know, Josh. It's weird. Dr. Chen must have some pretty important connections, I guess? He did say there would be a delay on the rest of the results, but I'm not going to look a gift horse in the mouth, especially because he's been so reliable. If something's going on, though, or if someone is taking an interest in you, maybe it's related to whatever happened. Unfortunately, that would be more of a police matter than a medical matter, so I'm not sure what to tell you.

"However, in regard to the rape kit, nothing suspicious or worrisome came up, so hopefully that means nothing happened to you. If you remember something, though, you can always come talk to me. You know, not just as a doctor, but as a friend." Her voice was comforting. If anything was wrong, she'd be my substitute older sister like she'd always been when I was younger.

I took a deep breath. The news was good at the very least, despite the weird quickness of the tests. "Thanks, Jocelyn. I mean it. What do you think I should do for now?"

"We'll want to wait until we get more results from the tests, but in the meantime, even though you haven't fully gotten your sense of taste back, be sure to eat some healthy food. If it was just some blood that was taken from you, then you'll probably be fine with rest and good nutrition. I'll have one of the nurses call you later about coming in for further tests, if needed."

I nodded, even though I knew she couldn't see me. "Okay. I'll do that."

"Bye, kid! And remember, call me if there's anything else you need."

"Will do, captain!" I replied jokingly. She laughed before hanging up.

I had to admit, I was relieved. At least we were a step closer to narrowing down what was going on with me. There were still a lot of questions, though. I pushed the sunglasses I was still wearing up the bridge of my nose and realized I'd forgotten to tell Jocelyn about the sharp vision and light sensitivity. Maybe it was simply a side effect of the anemia. I grabbed another of Des's sports drinks, figuring it might be good to load up on electrolytes, and walked back into the living room.

"But why do they call it Sweat?" Brian was asking. "It makes it sound like the drink is made with sweat."

"I don't know, but what I do know is, I like it way better than most of the other sports drinks out there," Des responded, deftly navigating the video game controller with agile fingers.

"You want back in, man?" Brian asked as I sat back down with them.

I took off the sunglasses for a moment to see how my eyes handled the rapid action on the TV screen and instantly regretted it. Everything was just too bright and sharp. "Nah. I think I'm going to just watch for a bit."

"Hey, is everything okay?" Des asked.

"Yeah. Jocelyn said I have anemia but I wasn't drugged and nothing else seems wrong. She doesn't know why I'm having issues with taste, though." I took another sip of the sports drink. "I might have to go in for more testing sometime soon, though."

"That sucks. Maybe you'll meet a hot nurse." Brian smirked.

I grabbed my controller back from Brian. He protested weakly but didn't attempt to take it back. The three of us played all through the afternoon until I realized I had to get to work.

By the time I got there, the sun was starting to go down, and I was relieved to finally take off my sunglasses. Though some of the streetlights were a bit brighter than my eyes were comfortable with, it wasn't as headache inducing as the sunlight. Thank goodness for that since my job relied on me being able to drive.

Harriet spotted me first after I'd entered through the back door. "Hi, Josh! How was yesterday? Des said you had a cold or something?"

I plopped down on a stool and watched her prep. "I had to go to the doctor."

Harriet dropped a serving spoon on the floor in surprise. She scrambled to pick it up and brought it back to the sink. As she washed it, she scrutinized me over her shoulder. "Are you okay? You do look a bit pale. Maybe you should call in sick today?"

"I can't do that to Gino. Renato can't do it all by himself, and Gino needs to be in the kitchen. It's not even really a cold." The look she gave me made me feel a little guilty. "I'll be sure to get plenty of rest when I get home."

Harriet nodded, still looking concerned, and returned to what she had been doing. Gino joined her in the kitchen and gave me his trademark smile. "You ready for tonight, kid?"

"I will be." And I meant it. I just wanted to forget everything and do my normal job in my normal town without all this weirdness hanging over my head.

Harriet furrowed her brow. "Gino, Josh went to the hospital yesterday. Maybe we should make him go home or just have him take it easy."

Gino looked me over carefully. "Josh, if you're not okay, you can go home. We'll figure something out."

"I'm okay. I'm just a little anemic, and I can't taste anything for some weird reason. But I'll be fine. Maybe just give me some of the easier deliveries or something."

I thought carefully for a moment about all the memories that had rushed back into my head while cleaning Brian's room. "Also, I don't think we should deliver pizzas to the mansion on the hill. Something . . . weird happened night before last. If they call again, don't let Renato go."

Gino's usually warm expression became ice cold. I knew that look. He was in papa-bear mode. "What did they do, Josh?"

I was a bit rattled by how quickly he changed from his usual cheery self to this more ferocious state. I knew Gino was protective of the people he cared about, but his anger seemed to fill the area around him with an aura of intensity. I was suddenly grateful that Gino made pizzas instead of working in another, far more violent profession.

I explained everything that had happened with the delivery and the doctor's appointment, minus a few of the more confusing details. Harriet and Gino both listened carefully, without interruption, until I was done spilling my guts.

They looked at each other as though they were communicating telepathically, then turned to face me at the same time. Gino spoke first.

"If you insist on working tonight, giving you the easier deliveries is fine with me. It's time for Renato to take a little more responsibility anyway. We won't make any more deliveries to the mansion. If they want something, they can come here, and if they give us any trouble, they'll be getting a piece of my mind instead of a piece of pizza. If any of them ever give you trouble again, even when you're off the clock, let me know."

I nodded solemnly. "I was thinking it was best to stay away from them myself."

Harriet came around the counter and hugged me. "Be careful, Josh. I don't want to see you hurt."

I hugged her back, hoping she wouldn't pull away too soon. On one hand, I didn't want her to see me blushing from the sudden hug. On the other, getting a hug from the girl I had a crush on was pretty exciting. I glanced over at Gino and saw that the ice had melted from his gaze. He even gave me a little smirk.

Harriet pulled away. "Let's get to work, then. People will start calling any minute." She quickly returned to prepping without giving me another glance.

I stood for a moment in the warm kitchen, strangely cold as her body heat dissipated from my arms. Did she know how I felt about her? Was she just giving me a little space to compose myself? I'd been trying to keep my feelings secret for a while now, and I had thought I was doing a good job, but who knew?

As if my weird health issue and all the events around it weren't preoccupying enough, now I had to wonder if I should say something to Harriet. I glanced at her as she finished kitchen prep and chatted with Gino. Maybe, hopefully, she was just giving me time to figure things out before I decided to say anything.

I put on my Gino's hat and jacket and sat quietly. I'd started clenching my jaw and grinding my teeth, so I grabbed a warm breadstick to chew on. I may not have been able to taste it, but at least chewing on something helped reduce my anxiety.

The rest of the evening went by in a blur. There were too many orders for me to stop and brood over all the strange thoughts running through my head. Once everything was done, I grabbed a chopped salad from Gino instead of a pizza, explaining that Des and I were trying to get Brian back in shape.

I was exhausted by the time I arrived home, so I offered the guys a quick hello and handed over the salad. Then, in an almost zombie-like trance, I made a beeline up the stairs to my room and fell into a dreamless sleep as soon as my head hit the pillow.

DAY 3
SUNDAY

osh! Hey, Josh! Want to run with us?"

I woke to the sound of fists pounding on my door. I lifted my head and realized the number of fists required to make that much noise meant it wasn't just Des on the other side. The clock read 8:26 in sharp, red digital numerals. The brightness of the digits did nothing to help reduce my headache.

"Come on, Josh. Don't leave me to this slave driver," Brian complained through the door. "I need at least one person who isn't as in shape as Des. That way, I won't feel like such a failure."

Thanks for the vote of confidence.

I groaned and got out of bed gingerly. If both of them were at the door, there was no way they would leave me alone unless I made an appearance. I probably deserved it for hijacking Brian yesterday. Also, that Brian was outside my room, ready to run, was promising, so I would take my lumps.

"I'm up, I'm up. Give me a moment!" I sat on the edge

of my bed for a moment and massaged my scalp. My shoes were still on my feet from last night, so I toed them off, one after the other. Then I kicked them aside and pulled off my socks. My head protested every movement. "Fuck it," I said, choosing to ignore the pain, and stood upright.

Another series of persistent knocks came from the door. "Yeah, I'm coming. Just a moment!"

I quickly peeled off my jeans and put on some sweats and a new pair of socks. My armpits smelled okay, so I left on my tee shirt from the night before. In anticipation of another round of knocks, I opened the door to find an enthusiastic Des and a slightly less enthusiastic Brian. While the guy looked bored and annoyed, I thought I could spot a bit of a twinkle in his eye.

"Finally! We were starting to wonder if you had died in there or something," Brian quipped.

I took a deep breath and realized my headache was gone. "Huh, that's weird."

"Well, you could have died since you've been all weird the past couple of days," Brian said.

Des backhanded him against the chest to silence him. "What's weird, Josh?"

"My head was pounding just a moment ago. Now it's completely fine. I was going to tell you guys I might just walk while you run, but maybe I can handle joining you now that the headache's gone." I shrugged. "Might as well, I guess."

"Yes!" Brian punched the air with his fist. Des and I both looked at him, and he immediately backtracked. "Uh, yeah, I mean, it's cool if you join us and all, I guess."

Normally, I would have poked fun at him for trying to hide his enthusiasm, but I didn't want to see him take a step backward again. "My running shoes are downstairs."

"Hey, man, you sure you're okay?" Des asked. "Did Jocelyn say anything about you exercising in your condition?"

"Wait, now you ask, after waking me up to drag me out for a run?" I began to walk down the hall toward the stairs. "Let's go. If I start to feel bad, I'll stop."

I took a few steps down the stairs. As soon as I'd descended out of the shadows and into the light coming in from the floor-to-ceiling windows of the living room, searing pain shot through my eyes. I shut them immediately and blindly scrambled for the railing at the side of the stairs to steady myself.

"You okay, Josh?" Des asked.

I shook my head, squinting my eyes open. I managed to see okay while squinting, but the headache was beginning to come back. "Uh . . . I just wasn't ready for it to be this bright." I tried to hide that if my eyes could speak, they'd be screaming bloody murder.

Brian made his way past me. "It's just as bright as it usually is this time of day."

I ignored him and turned around to face Des. "Could you grab me some sunglasses? Maybe this weird health thing is affecting my vision."

"Yeah, man. No problem." Des looked concerned as he stepped around me. I sat down on the step behind me, and once my face was in shadow again, my eyes felt fine. I looked down into the living room and noticed again how detailed my vision had become. Everything white looked a touch brighter. Shadows didn't hide as much as they should. I noticed a few specks of something on the floor near the kitchen. I was a little surprised; the wood was stained a dark brown that should have hidden such signs of dirt. I definitely wouldn't have noticed it from this far away before.

I groaned but tried to focus on gradually getting my eyes

used to the bright rays of sunlight, hoping my eyes just needed to adjust.

"Here you go."

Des walked up a few steps and casually held out the sunglasses. It didn't fully register that the sunglasses were right in front of me. Instead, I noticed the pores and wrinkles on his wrist, as well as a couple of veins. I must have sat there a little dazed because he repeated himself.

"Here you go. You sure you're all right?"

I shook my head to clear my thoughts and looked him in the eye. "I'm fine. Thanks." I took the sunglasses, and once they were on, I sighed in relief. With my vision that sharp, wearing the sunglasses almost made it like my vision before . . . well, whatever was happening to me.

I stood and began to walk down the stairs, but Des didn't move out of my way. Was it his turn to act weird now?

I waved my hand in front of his face. "Des, you there?"

He blinked for a moment. "Sorry about that. It's just your eyes. They looked . . . different."

A small ball of anxiety started to form in my stomach. "Different how?"

"I could have sworn when the light shone on them, they looked kinda like cat eyes. Like your pupils were slits instead of circles." He laughed. "But that's ridiculous . . . unless you're turning into a werecat or something."

He turned and walked down the stairs like nothing had happened. I was a little scared, though I wasn't sure I wanted to admit it. I decided to file the cat-eye issue in my mental procrastination file.

I was following behind him, trying to clear my thoughts of any fear or worry, when I got hit in the face by one of my running shoes. I looked over to see Brian grinning mischievously.

"What the hell, Bri?" I grabbed the shoe and began to throw it back at him when Des stepped in the way.

"Be chill, dude. Calm."

I rolled my eyes and sat down to put my shoe on instead.

"Sorry, Josh. I couldn't help it. You were so out of it, you were kind of an easy target." At least Brian had the decency to look a little sheepish.

Des handed me my other shoe, and I shoved it on irritably. This day was already going downhill, and I hadn't even been awake half an hour.

Hopping from foot to foot, Des looked eager to get going. "Come on, guys! Let's get moving!"

I sighed and followed him and Brian out the door. They both owed me. I'm not sure what, but considering I felt like the unwiped ass of a geriatric cat, I was going to ask for something big.

We'd been running down the street for a while when Brian stopped and grabbed Des's arm. "Oh, crap! Hide Josh!"

Des looked in the direction Brian was looking and quickly ducked me down behind a convenient car. I opened my mouth to speak when I heard a voice . . . *the* voice.

"Gentlemen! How are you this morning?" Mr. Costello's booming resonance oozed with authority as he greeted Des and Brian.

"Hi, Mr. Costello!" my friends responded in unison.

"Out for a run, I see. Good. I like seeing that kind of discipline in my former students."

I only barely kept myself from laughing out loud, remembering the time I had delivered a pizza to a dominatrix at Mr. Costello's house. Des kicked me softly in the side to remind me to keep my mouth shut, so I bit my lip and decided to bide my time until the conversation was over.

"Yeah, I'm trying to get back into shape, Mr. Costello." For some reason, Brian had always responded well to Mr. Costello. Maybe it was how structured and systematic Mr. Costello was as a principal, much like his overcontrolling dad. I guess it left Brian with fewer decisions to make.

"Good on you, Mr. Dunning. I always liked seeing your performance at track meets," Mr. Costello said in his commanding voice. "How about you, Mr. Adebowale? Is your family doing well?"

Des tensed. He had always been bothered by Mr. Costello's keen attention to his family. Des was pretty sure Costello was always trying to suck up to his family because of their wealth; it never felt like his interest was genuine.

"My family is fine, Mr. Costello." He said it politely. Only someone like Brian or me could have picked up on the slightly sharp tone that indicated he wasn't pleased to be speaking with him.

Mr. Costello didn't notice at all. "Good, good. I hope your parents will join us for our upcoming fundraiser. They've been so helpful in the past."

I could almost hear Des grinding his teeth. "You'll have to ask them that, sir. I don't know what their plans are."

"Ah, yes, of course," Mr. Costello replied quickly. "You're probably enjoying your newfound adulthood. I hope you follow in your father's footsteps and become a lawyer. Or maybe do like your mother and sister and go into medicine? You were always a smart young man." There was an awkward pause before he added, "What about that friend of yours? Josh, was it? How's he doing?"

My ears perked up at the mention of my name. Kind of

odd that he was pretending he couldn't quite remember it. I had absolutely no doubt he remembered me from the dominatrix-pizza incident quite well.

"He's fine, Mr. Costello! He's working hard to save money for school," Brian replied.

"I see." Mr. Costello paused for a moment as if in deep thought. "You know, I've never really told you boys this before, but I've always had a bad feeling about that boy. He never seemed very . . . honest. Considering his upbringing, with his mother running off and how scattered his father can be, I have to wonder how that affected his character."

I froze in shock. Mr. Costello had always been nice to me to my face. My grades had always been in the upper 10 percent of my class, and I had never gotten in trouble. I may not have stood out the way Des did with his positive, gregarious personality, or Brian with his athletic skills, but I was hardly a bad kid.

Then it hit me. He was scared. I knew something about him that, if it got out, could end his career. Instead of talking with me about it like an adult, he had decided to smear my good name. My blood started to boil.

"Really, Mr. Costello?" Des began. "Josh has always been a good guy. He may not stick out much, but he's always been a loyal friend. When I invited him to be my roommate for free, he insisted on paying rent anyway. There aren't a lot of people as responsible as he is."

Brian shrugged. "Yeah, he's always been a pretty cool guy, sir."

"You never know when a person will turn on you, though," Mr. Costello insisted. "It's always the quiet kids who keep to themselves who end up shooting up schools or becoming serial killers."

My blood turned to ice in my veins. But before my

anger could get the better of me, I realized what I could do as the perfect revenge.

Before Brian or Des could respond, I stood up from my spot behind the car. "Oh, hey, Mr. Costello! I'm sorry I didn't pop up and say hello right away. Shoelaces . . . you know."

Mr. Costello's face turned beet red. "Oh, right, Mr. Buckmilter. Yes. Shoelaces can come loose when you're running. Of course."

I felt a perverse sense of glee watching this once-intimidating man fall apart at my mere presence. I couldn't help but continue, playing like I hadn't heard a word he'd said about me, even though we were all well aware I had heard every single syllable of his attempt to smear my name.

"I've been doing pretty well too. I've been working hard, and I've been saving loads of money. I may end up being able to start college sooner than I expected! Everyone else seems to think I'm being a bit of a masochist . . ." I paused for effect, hoping Mr. Costello would pick up on my use of the word. "But hard work pays off in the end. Don't you think so, Mr. Costello?"

With my keen eyesight, I observed little droplets of sweat beginning to form on his still very bright-red forehead. He reached into his pocket, pulled out a handkerchief, and began to wipe his forehead. "Yes, yes. Sometimes working hard is its own reward."

"Oh, definitely," I continued in an enthusiastic tone. "Delivering pizzas is a great first job too. You get to see all kinds of people in their natural element. Makes me want to study something like anthropology or sociology. I think I recall seeing a cool anthro class available at the community college . . . something about deviations in human sexuality?

Maybe I should start off taking that class. I'm sure I have enough money saved up that I could just take that one."

"Wise idea, young man." Mr. Costello anxiously stuffed his handkerchief back into his pocket with a shaking hand. He suddenly turned around and looked at his house. "Oh, dear, was that my wife? I should go see what she wants. Boodguy, boys! I mean, goodbye, boys!"

We watched him run for the house and then glanced at each other.

"Did you hear his wife at all?" Des asked.

"Nope. Not me," I replied.

"Nada," Brian said.

"What do you bet he's looking out his window at us right now?" I asked.

"Likely, I'd say," Brian responded.

"Let's keep running until he can't see us, then we can laugh," I suggested.

We ran down the street and around the corner. Once we were sure we were out of sight, the three of us nearly collapsed in laughter. Strangely, it was the best I'd felt in a long time. It reminded me of being back in high school together, our old, normal selves, with nothing to worry about except homework. The future had seemed so bright only a few months ago. Now, what had looked like a bright, shiny brand-new copper penny was starting to look a little worn and tarnished.

I looked up from where I was leaning against the side of a house and holding my sides, which were starting to ache, and spotted a toddler sitting on a lawn across the street. The little boy must have been drawn by our laughter because he was looking at us and giggling. I smiled, and the kid suddenly jumped up and started running toward the sidewalk. I stopped laughing immediately and scanned the area. A woman sat on the porch of the house he was in front of, her eyes glued to her phone. If she was the one responsible for the kid, she clearly wasn't paying attention.

I was about to say something to get her attention when I heard a sound that made my blood run cold. Turning my head, I saw a car speeding down the street. With my newly sharpened vision, I could see the driver was looking down at his phone instead of at the toddler, who was now stepping off the curb.

Everything felt immediately slow and fast at the same time. Without thinking, I ran out into the street, grabbed the kid, and cradled him to my chest as I threw myself onto the lawn he had previously been sitting on. As I tried to make my heart stop beating so hard, I watched the car speed by at about ten miles per hour above the speed limit. The driver was completely unaware of what had almost happened. I glanced over at the woman on the porch, who was still fiddling with her phone. Then I looked across the street at Brian and Des. They stared back at me with bewildered expressions.

When I turned back to the kid in my arms, he was staring at me with big eyes. I sat up and put him down next to me. Fortunately, he was free of any injuries. The woman still hadn't noticed anything, so I got up to speak with her.

"Hey, excuse me, is this your kid?"

She looked up from her phone at me, then at the little boy, who stood beside me, chewing on his finger. He looked like he didn't know whether he should cry.

"Yeah, that's my son." She appeared baffled that I had asked her.

I crossed my arms and gave her a stern look. "You need to pay better attention. Your kid walked out into the street and would have gotten hit by a car if I hadn't grabbed him."

She blinked a couple of times. "W-what? There was a car?"

I nodded. Brian and Des joined me.

"Yeah, lady," Brian said, backing me up. "The car almost hit your kid. You might want to make sure he's okay."

The kid grabbed my leg. I looked down at the little guy. He was just so small. I didn't understand how someone could be so careless with someone so tiny and fragile. Then he wrapped his arms around my leg and held on so tightly, I started to wonder if I'd lose circulation. Tiny but strong.

I patted him on the head. "Stay out of the street, kid, okay?"

He nodded. "Zoom!"

The kid's mom looked haggard as she stood and shoved the phone in her pocket. She quickly stepped forward and pried her son's arms from my leg. "Thanks," she mumbled. "Let's go, Tommy." She took the little boy in her arms and walked back into the house, closing the door behind them.

"Uh, you're welcome?" I responded to the door, a little surprised by her lack of enthusiasm. "Is it me, or was that a little odd?"

"Dude, what the hell?" Brian suddenly jumped in front of me. "How was that even human?"

"Seriously, Josh, what the hell did you just do?" Des looked concerned for the second time today. "How did you move that fast?"

"What do you mean? I just ran to save the kid. You know, like a person does when someone's in danger?"

I was really disturbed by their expressions. They weren't looking at me like I had saved a kid's life. They looked at me like something was wrong with me. While, yeah, something was wrong with me, it wasn't this.

Des looked straight at me while Brian babbled to himself about comic book characters. "Josh, you were really fast."

"Sure, I mean, adrenaline, right? Nobody in their right mind wants to see a little kid get hit by a car, right?" I scratched my head. I couldn't make sense of why they were acting so strange.

Suddenly, Brian grabbed me by the shoulders. "Josh, you were like some kind of superhero! You moved so fast, you were a blur. I'm not even joking! I've never even been that fast at my peak when running on the track team!" He grabbed his hair in his fists and sank to his knees. "No! Both you guys can't be faster than me!"

"Huh?" It was my turn to give Brian an odd look.

Des rolled his eyes at Brian's dramatics and turned back to me. "He's not lying. Josh, you looked like something out of a comic book movie. How is that even possible?"

I looked down at my feet and wiggled my toes in my shoes. Were they exaggerating? I mean, it was a little strange that I was able to get all the way to the lawn with the kid well before the car hit either of us. Everything had happened so fast, I hadn't really thought about it.

First, loss of taste. Next, light sensitivity and extremely sharp vision. Then possibly cat eyes. Now super speed? What the hell was going on? I clenched my hands into fists to prevent them from trembling. I was completely confused, and I had more questions than answers.

"Let's head home, guys. Let's just . . ." I sighed. "Let's just go home."

"Okay." Des grabbed Brian and gave him a stern look. "Come on, man."

Brian nodded and pulled himself together. "Sure."

We jogged the rest of the route since it would be faster to finish the run than to go back the way we had come. An oppressive silence hovered over us. Even though I was freaked out about what was happening to me, I kind of felt bad for Brian. I didn't want him to be discouraged. The last thing he needed was to fall backward after two days of progress.

We had just rounded the last corner by our house when Brian stopped. He put out an arm to prevent me from moving forward. "Do it again."

"Huh?" I asked. Des and I both turned to look at him.

Brian gazed at me without flinching. "Run. Really run. Run from this corner to the front door. Don't think about what you should do; just do it."

I turned to the house. It was maybe an eighth of a mile from where we stood, at the most. It would be a quick jog to get to the door anyway. I opened my mouth to protest when Des chimed in.

"Maybe . . . maybe you should, just to see. If it was an adrenaline fluke, then we'd at least have an answer. If not, maybe it will help us figure out what's going on with you, right?"

I glanced back and forth between Des and Brian. They both stared back at me with expectant, sober expressions.

"Fine, I'll do it." I didn't really feel up to it. Everything was going sideways so fast, I was starting to wonder if I'd sprout blue fur next and start running around town collecting rings.

My friends stepped back, and I took a deep breath.

"Remember, don't think about what you should be able to do; just do it. Just go," Brian said.

I nodded. I hopped a couple of times and let out a breath. Then I ran.

Barely a second later, I slammed into the front door

with a grunt. I fell on my ass on the front porch as my friends jogged over to me.

"Ow." I rubbed my forehead, which must have had a huge pink welt on it.

Des helped me to my feet while Brian looked back and forth between me and the front door, brow furrowed in confusion. "Josh, I don't think you just have some kind of weird cold or something. And if they gave you drugs, they should have worn off by now."

"Yeah, I'm kinda not thinking about that right now. How's my forehead?" I started to rub my sore tailbone as well.

"Not a mark or a scratch," Des said. "That's odd. Usually, your white ass turns bright pink in an instant when you get hit by something."

"Wait, dude. Listen. So Josh has super speed, and maybe he has a healing factor as well!" Brian looked like a kid on Christmas morning. "Anything else, Josh?"

"There's the vision thing," I tossed off casually as I tried to turn, unsuccessfully, to see my own ass. I wasn't sure why I thought I could manage that, but hey, if I could run with super speed, maybe I had contortionist powers as well? Who knew?

Des unlocked the front door and opened it. "Maybe we should talk about this inside."

"Right." I followed him into the house.

Brian followed us, suddenly more energetic than I'd seen him since the day he moved in. While I was glad to see it, I was a little irritated that it came at the expense of my being a complete freak right now.

I pulled off my shoes and threw them in the hall closet, then sat down on the living room couch, while Brian threw out ideas about what could have happened to me to make me go superhero. Des went into the kitchen and grabbed some drinks for us, then sat down next to me. Brian sat down on the other side of the couch so he could stare at me expectantly.

"What vision thing?" Brian asked. If the guy had had a tail, it would have been wagging in excitement.

"Josh, I'm still not sure if I saw what I saw earlier," Des warned. I think he was also a little disturbed by Brian's excitement.

"Okay, then let's check that." I closed my eyes and took the sunglasses off. As I opened my eyes, piercing light lanced through them, followed by sharp pain. I squinted and then did my best to carefully open them wide enough that the guys could take a good look.

"You seeing what I'm seeing?" Brian asked Des.

Des nodded sagely. "Yeah. That's what I saw before."

I sighed and put the sunglasses back on. "Cat eyes?" They both nodded.

"Maybe we should start writing these down, Josh," Des suggested. "The more we can keep track of, the closer we can probably get to figuring out what's going on." He got up and grabbed a pad of paper from the kitchen, then sat on the coffee table instead of the couch. "We have"—he began to write—"no sense of taste, vision stuff, cat pupils, enhanced speed . . . anything else?"

I glanced at Brian, who watched me eagerly. "Well, slight sense of taste for certain things. Maybe it's something to do with electrolytes?"

Brian looked disappointed. "Nothing else?"

"Does there have to be anything else?" I asked, irritated. "It's not like this has exactly been fun for me."

Realization dawned on Brian's face, as if he finally understood. "I'm sorry, man. I didn't mean to—I mean—I—"

Though I'd been trying to keep my cool, something in my tone must have been a little threatening because Brian jumped out of his seat and headed toward the stairs. "I'll go take a shower before you guys hog all the hot water."

Des and I glanced at each other in surprise, then watched Brian head upstairs. I heard a door open and close and then sounds of the shower turning on.

"Did Brian just go take a shower without prompting?" I asked once I was able to form words.

Des raised an eyebrow and gave me a look that consisted of one part doubt, one part surprise. "It seems like he did. That was unexpected."

I smiled. "Yeah. But good."

Even though I was becoming increasingly confused about what was going on with me, at least I could feel good about Brian making progress. After making the list of my symptoms, the rest of the day felt relatively mundane. I was grateful to get to work a few hours later and go through my normal routine. I was done with weird.

DAY 4
MONDAY

I ran on automatic for the rest of Sunday, following the discovery of my bizarre super speed. Or rather, I avoided running at all costs and *worked* on automatic. We didn't have quite as many orders last night as we usually did on Sundays, so it was easy enough to just show up, get the work done, and leave.

My behavior over the past few days must have let on that I wasn't quite myself, though, because come Monday at lunchtime, Harriet and Jocelyn showed up at the house with worried looks on their faces.

"Josh." Harriet gave me a huge hug when I opened the door. "Des and Brian invited us. We're all worried about you."

Jocelyn patted me on the back as Harriet hugged me tighter and tighter, which made me wonder if I looked worse than I felt. "Let's talk, kid."

With my head shoved against Harriet's neck at an odd angle, all I could get out was, "Mmfff morf."

Harriet pulled back, suddenly bashful. "Oh, was I hugging you too tight? I'm sorry. When Des called and said you were going through some stuff, my heart just dropped. I could tell something was up at work, but you didn't say anything."

I felt like a total idiot. Harriet had always been there for me. Why hadn't I told her anything? Was it that I hadn't wanted her to worry? Seeing the sad look in her big silvery-gray eyes, I realized keeping her in the dark was probably worse than telling her the truth.

"I'm sorry. I just didn't know what to tell you."

She smiled weakly. "Well, you can tell me now, and maybe I can help make work easier for you if you need me to, okay?"

Feeling guilty, I looked at her shirt in a cheap attempt to both avoid her eyes and change the subject. Today, she was wearing a shirt with a really cool design of an anime character I liked. For some reason, Harriet seemed to find the best fandom tee shirts, and this one was no different.

"Cool shirt?" I offered, hoping that giving her a compliment might make her feel a little better.

"Yeah, it is a cool shirt, but that doesn't mean I've fully forgiven you yet for keeping things from me."

I chuckled. Maybe she understood me a little too well. "Yeah, I know, I know. Let's go sit down and talk."

Jocelyn led the way to the living room and sat down on the couch next to Des, while Brian lounged in the armchair, finishing up a video game. I sat at the other end of the L-shaped couch, with Harriet sitting right next to me.

Sometimes, I felt so close to her and yet so far away at the same time. I was so afraid if I said or did the wrong thing, I'd lose not only my chance to make our relationship . . . more, for lack of a better word, but also my friendship with her. Maybe I was being completely and utterly stupid about all this and there was a perfect way to let her know I wanted to be the one who protected her heart from the world. I was even more scared of telling her I loved her than I was of whatever the hell was happening to me.

Des stood and walked over to Brian. "Time to put the controller down, dude."

Brian looked around and only then seemed to realize Harriet and Jocelyn were there. "Oh, yeah, sorry."

He quickly found his save point and turned off the console.

Des remained standing. "Okay, it's time to start Operation WTF."

I chuckled. Des gave me a pained look that said he meant business. "Sorry, man. I just laughed because it made sense."

Harriet immediately spoke up. "After talking with Jocelyn on the way here, I get the feeling I know less about the situation than everyone else. Can you explain what exactly is going on so we're all on the same page?"

Brian opened his mouth to speak, but Des put a hand on his shoulder and nodded at me. I took a deep breath and explained everything, from the mysterious pizza order last Thursday to my newfound super speed. Jocelyn and Harriet listened intently. Jocelyn helped out when the discussion turned to the medical tests, but other than that, it only took a few minutes to explain everything. Amazing. It felt like the last few days had been a lifetime, and crunching it all down to a simplified explanation made it seem clinical and detached.

We all sat quietly for a moment to digest the information.

Brian finally broke the silence. "He's a vampire."

"Brian, there's no proof Josh is a vampire." Jocelyn had

always found Brian irritating and had no qualms about telling him off for saying stupid or inappropriate things. "Not only do vampires not exist, but he doesn't even do things vampires are supposed to do. It's not like he spontaneously combusts when he goes out in the sun, for example."

"Yeah, I guess not," Brian replied. "But something's up. He's at least a mutant or something. Maybe those people shot him up with radioactive goo?"

"I'm not a mutant either, Brian."

Brian crossed his arms and rolled his eyes. "Well, you're not exactly normal."

I could see I had taken the wind out of his sails, but I couldn't bring myself to care. This wasn't about Brian. This was about me, and I had every reason to be worried.

"Look, I can still walk around in the daylight without combusting. I can go to work at a pizza restaurant, where there's garlic everywhere. It just doesn't make sense." I sighed. "This is serious. Even if it turns out to be some kind of mutation, that doesn't mean I'll survive this."

Brian uncrossed his arms and huffed out a sigh of frustration. "Fine! Fine, I'll just shut up now."

Harriet reached out to touch his arm. "It's okay, Brian. You're trying. That's what's important."

Brian took a deep breath and blew it out. "So, what then? There aren't any real explanations for what's happening with Josh."

"Well, having super speed could just be an adrenaline response," Jocelyn said. "That kind of thing does happen. However, considering all the test results, Josh should be more fatigued than he seems to be, especially after expending that much energy when showing signs of anemia. Maybe we can do some more tests? Not just blood samples but some physical tests and scans as well?"

"And how about your dad?" Harriet asked. "Have you told him yet?"

The room went quiet as Harriet's question hit like a ton of bricks. I hadn't told him. I hadn't even called him in a few days. My heart suddenly felt unbearably heavy. Since I was a baby, it had just been him and me. I owed him some explanation, even just for forgetting to check in on him.

Dad had never quite recovered from Mom's disappearance, according to family friends. He had once been a confident man with a bright future. But Mom's sudden disappearance had broken something inside him. He'd nearly lost the hardware store he inherited from his grandfather because he'd lost so much of his drive.

Nobody knew why she left. They had been happy together. They had been looking forward to raising me and giving me a couple more siblings. Then, with no explanation, Mom was gone. She was the town mystery, and that mystery was a burden Dad couldn't quite carry.

"I-I should call him," I said, guilt coloring my tone. I ran fingers through my hair in frustration. "I can't believe I forgot to tell him."

Harriet scooted closer and rubbed my back. "Don't feel bad, Josh. These are strange circumstances. You can call him today, maybe?"

"Yeah, but I should have called him a couple of days ago." I propped my elbows on my knees and cradled my head in my hands. "He's probably worried right now."

"You have a good excuse for being a little forgetful. I know I'd be a mess if weird, unexplained things were happening to me," Harriet reassured me.

"Josh, Dr. Chen has been looking over your blood samples. He likes odd medical puzzles. If you're okay with it, I'll let him know your other symptoms," Jocelyn offered. "I have to say, though, some of the symptoms you guys listed sound a bit unbelievable. Light sensitivity is one thing, but catlike pupils?"

I made eye contact with her, then got up and walked over to the wall of windows. The light wasn't coming in the way it did in the morning because the noontime sun was directly overhead. I did feel a bit of eyestrain from the sunlight still coming through the window, however, and hoped it would be enough to show Jocelyn that the cat eyes were real. She got up and joined me, examining my eyes carefully. Then she pulled out a pen flashlight and shone it carefully on my eyes, which were starting to water.

"Okay, cat eyes." She clicked off her flashlight and stepped back. "I'm perplexed, Josh. I've never heard of anything like this. I spent a lot of time after Desmond called me trying to figure out what all these symptoms could add up to. There's nothing. Either you have a few different co-occurring health problems or you have something entirely new. The cat eyes, though, that should be impossible."

I sighed in frustration as I sat back down on the couch. "What do I do, then?"

"There has to at least be something, Josh," Des said. "This is too weird, and we don't know if this is all that will happen or if things will . . ." He paused and glanced at me, his concern clear on his face. "If things will get worse."

"We monitor him," Jocelyn assured. "Josh comes in for regular testing to see how he's doing. Despite all the changes, Josh seems to be in relatively decent health. If things get worse, we may have to get some specialists involved, maybe hospitalization . . ."

"I can't afford all that," I whispered. Everything I was

saving for, to try to make some kind of better future for myself, was starting to fade away. It all seemed like a pipe dream now. Maybe this was what it meant to grow up.

"If we get you connected to a research or university hospital, which would be the most likely situation, there's a good chance you might not have to pay much, if at all," Jocelyn explained.

I stood up and looked at my friends. They were trying to help, but this conversation was only making me feel worse. "I think I'm done talking about this. I need to go see my dad and explain everything."

"I'll go with you, if you want, Josh," Harriet offered gently, taking hold of my hand. "If there's anything I can do to support you, even if it's just a quiet ride to your dad's house, then I'm happy to do it."

I nodded. "Thanks. Thanks, really. I probably don't seem to appreciate this enough right now, but knowing you guys care helps a lot."

Des nodded. "We'll never give up on you. We're a team. Always have been, always will be."

"And this is when it's okay to give each other bro hugs, guys," Jocelyn said, watching our awkward attempt to hide that we wanted to do just that.

"Oh, guys." Harriet sighed and stood up. She pulled a grumbling Brian out of his chair, gestured to Des to join us, and grabbed my hand again. "I'll join the hug so you don't have to feel so emasculated. Come on, you dorks!"

She pulled us into a hug, and we, plus Jocelyn, gave in to Harriet's request. I would never admit it, but I really did need it.

Jocelyn left after that since she needed to get back to work. I needed to wait until my dad was done at work before calling him, so Harriet hung out with us for a while. We all helped Des with his latest review for a new multiplayer horror game. I was relieved to just focus on playing the game with the three of them. It was a great excuse to avoid talking anymore about my health.

Once we'd wrapped up, Des retreated to his computer for edits with a quick "Great work, guys." Harriet pulled me into the kitchen.

"Let's call your dad now. See if we can drop in before work starts tonight." There was no question in her voice. It was clear she wanted me to tell him as soon as possible.

"Yeah, that makes sense." I pulled out my phone and quickly made the call.

Harriet turned, grabbed a glass from the cabinet, and filled it with water from the tap. I could tell she was listening, and the fact she was trying to hide that she was almost made me laugh in the middle of my brief phone call. She was always easy to read when she was worried about someone. Her tendency was to get as involved as she possibly could.

"Okay, bye, Dad," I said after keeping the conversation as simple as possible. I shoved my phone back into my pocket and leaned against the counter as Harriet took a sip of water.

"So?" she asked expectantly.

"So, he said he's home and we can stop by anytime." My voice was steady, somehow managing to hide the dread I felt. I wasn't scared of my dad. That wasn't the case at all. I just wasn't sure how he'd react. If I was sick enough that the worst could happen, he could be left alone. I didn't even want to imagine how much that would hurt him.

Harriet dumped out the rest of her water, placed her cup in the sink, and started walking toward the hallway. "Let's go now."

I gulped. "*Now*, now?"

"Yeah, now. Things like this are like peeling off a bandage. Just rip the thing off so you can get past the pain." Her voice drifted back from the hallway. "I'm going to grab my stuff. You'll have to drive me home at the end of the night, by the way, since I got a ride here with Jocelyn."

I stood blinking for a moment.

Harriet peeked back into the kitchen. "What are you waiting for?"

"R-right," I mumbled. Then I cleared my throat. "Right, I'm coming." I grabbed my keys and a spare pair of sunglasses, while Harriet went back to the living room.

"We're heading off now, guys. See you again soon!"

I walked to the entrance to see her giving Des and Brian each a hug back in the living room. I felt a pang of jealousy, even though I knew Harriet always hugged everyone. I just wished that when she hugged me, it meant something different from when she hugged them.

"Have fun!" Des shouted to me.

"Yeah, make sure you have *lots* of fun," Brian teased as Harriet joined me at the front door.

I grabbed a foam ball from the hall closet and threw it at him. With a satisfying *plonk*, it hit Brian right in the middle of his smug forehead.

"Hey!"

I just smirked and followed Harriet out the front door.

Explaining everything to my dad wasn't easy. Every time I got to something that was hard to say, Harriet stepped in and took over the conversation, assuring that she and everyone else would be there to support me while the doctors figured everything out. Dad seemed to take it well, but he tended to cover his worry with a poker face.

"I'm sorry I didn't tell you right away, Dad," I said once we'd finished explaining.

Dad sighed, looking a little tired. "This all started three days ago, right?" The faint wrinkles around his eyes and on his forehead deepened. He looked disappointed. "You know you can tell me anything, son. If you need to stop working and move back in, it's okay."

"I'll tell you everything I know as soon as I know it from now on," I said.

"You'll make sure he does that, Harriet?"

Harriet gave him a smile and a quick salute. "On my honor, Mr. Buckmilter."

"Good. I'm glad Josh has such loyal friends."

Dad looked a little lost after that, so I reached over and squeezed his shoulder. "It'll be okay, Dad. We've been through hard times before. We'll figure this out."

He nodded. I could tell he was holding back because Harriet was there.

I remembered seeing photos of him from before Mom had left. There were so few since he had thrown out any photos of him and Mom that he had had. He used to be full of confidence, his brown hair thick and neatly cut, his clothes flattering his wide shoulders.

That was a man I hadn't had a chance to know, though. The man I knew had unkempt hair that was starting to gray at the temples and tended to hunch his shoulders. He no longer filled out his clothes as nicely; his time for hitting the gym had been cut down over time by working and raising me by himself. I sometimes wished I'd had a chance to know the person he was before. I couldn't blame him, though. I knew how tough things had been on him.

Dad lifted his hand to mine and squeezed back. He may not have been quite the man he was before, but the strength was there in his grip, and it made me feel a little better. He had never fully given up. There was still a spark of strength in his heart.

"We'll figure this out together," he stated firmly, then let my hand go.

I stood up from the worn-out couch. "Harriet and I should get to work now, Dad. I'll call you tomorrow?"

"I'll be expecting it. Oh, and Josh," Dad began as he walked Harriet and me to the front door. "You won't make the same mistake when you finally ask Harriet to marry you?"

If it were possible for my face to burn hotter than the sun, it would have. Harriet just laughed. "Mr. Buckmilter, you'd absolutely be the first to know."

I was relieved Harriet could answer him back so smoothly because there was no way I could have said anything without looking like an idiot. The way she answered him, however, left me with a little glimmer of hope. She didn't say it wasn't a possibility. With all the weirdness going on, it was a relief to know there might be a little something I could hope for.

After saying our goodbyes, Harriet and I hopped in the car and headed to Gino's. The solar-radiation levels of heat emanating from my face gradually reduced to cheery bonfire levels as I drove. It might have helped that I had the air conditioner going full blast.

"I'm glad you told your dad," Harriet said. "I could tell he wants to help."

"Yeah. Sometimes he doesn't know the best way to help, but he's good at letting me know he wants to support me no matter what." I kept my eyes focused on the road, thankful I had a good excuse to avoid looking Harriet in the eye while feeling so embarrassed.

"You'll tell all of us how things are going, won't you?" Harriet sounded a little worried. I glanced over quickly to see the serious expression on her face.

"Yeah, of course." I turned back to watch the road carefully.

"I just wanted to be sure." I could feel Harriet's gaze turn away from me. "You know, I bet Gino would be impressed by how carefully you keep your eyes on the road when you drive."

Of course she could tell I was deliberately avoiding eye contact. Instead of blushing more, I burst out laughing. She immediately chimed in, and our laughter seemed to chase away the tension that had built up throughout the day.

"Let's get to work," I said, parking behind Gino's.

"Let's."

Luckily, that was the beginning of an incredibly mundane night of pizza orders and deliveries. Mondays were never very busy at Gino's anyway, so I was grateful for a relatively lazy night.

Right before closing, I took the trash out. I went out the back door and walked around my car to the dumpster, which stood at the far end of the lot near some bushes and trees. As I got closer, I heard rustling from the nearby foliage.

"Is someone there?" I put the trash bags down on the ground and approached the dumpster slowly. "Whoever's back there, come out," I said in a deep voice I hoped sounded almost as stern and scary as one of the local cops.

Closing in, I hoped it was just a raccoon or two trying to get a bite to eat. I cautiously peeked around the side of the dumpster. While my newly sensitive eyes were better at seeing in the dark than they used to be, I still had a hard time seeing what was going on in the pitch-dark shadows.

"AHHHHHHHHHH!" shrieked two voices . . . and my own.

I fumbled with a flashlight I kept in my pocket and turned it on to find myself face to face with a teenage couple. I could tell by the hickey reddening the guy's neck and the way the girl was rearranging her clothes that they had been making out.

Once we had all calmed down, I spoke. "Um, dude, I hate to ask this, but what kind of guy makes out with his girlfriend behind a dumpster? Couldn't you take her someplace less smelly and gross?"

The girl slapped her boyfriend's shoulder. "He has a point, you know."

"Yeah, but you know we can't go to your house or mine," the boy replied. "We had to find someplace to meet up."

"So . . . that meant behind a dumpster?" I asked again. "Not even your car or a friend's car or something? Or the park? Anywhere more comfortable and less smelly?"

"The cops patrol the park at night, and my friends and I aren't old enough to drive." I could tell the guy was starting to get annoyed at me for making him lose points with his girlfriend.

"Look, sometimes raccoons hang out around the dumpster. I'd hate for one of you to get bitten or something. Just find somewhere a little safer and . . . healthier to make out, okay?" I backed up and gestured for them to get out from behind the dumpster.

The girl looked a little ill. "Yeah, let's just go. We can find somewhere else, right, Gabe?"

"Yeah, let's go." Gabe put an arm around her shoulders and walked her out of the parking lot.

I chuckled as the young couple walked away. Turning off the flashlight, I put it back in my pocket and grabbed the trash bags. As I lifted the lid of the dumpster to throw them in, I heard the bushes rustle once more.

I sighed. "Oh, come on. Is Gino's dumpster the new trendy date spot? At least come inside and eat some pizza."

I walked around the back of the dumpster again, a little annoyed. As I turned the corner, a pair of reflective eyes flashed through the darkness, and a menacing growl came from the same direction. I backed up slowly. The eyes looked too big for a raccoon's, and the growl sounded like it came from a much larger animal. Even with my sharper vision, I couldn't fully make out the dark form, only that it was fairly large. A dog? A wolf, maybe?

I kept eye contact while I tried to figure out what it could be. It growled again as I inched back and suddenly darted forward. I tripped over my feet as I tried to turn around and ended up landing on my backside.

Everything happened so quickly, I couldn't make sense of what I saw. Suddenly, a woman in Victorian-style clothes, complete with a tiny top hat and an intricately jeweled walking stick, stood in front of me, facing the creature who had jumped out at me. I couldn't fully see it, but in the dim light, I thought I saw a human arm. It was hard to tell around the skirt of the woman's dress, which was long and full and filled most of my vision.

"Now, now, it's time to quiet down. The boy meant no harm, I'm sure." The woman's gentle voice was almost as mesmerizing as the voice of Long-Haired Dude.

A wave of fear washed over me. Was she one of them? I couldn't deal with more from those people, whoever they were. I scooted back a bit, hoping to get away as stealthily as possible.

"Stop," the woman said calmly.

I gulped, recognizing the feeling that followed. I wasn't in control anymore; she was. Just like the night I made the delivery to the mansion on the hill.

Get up, get up, GET UP! my mind screamed, but I still couldn't move.

The woman stepped toward the creature as I tried and failed to resist her commands. "Come to me." She clearly wasn't talking to me, so I didn't move an inch. As I watched her close in on the creature, I saw that it was definitely humanoid. She reached down and clipped something to its neck, then stood and led the creature toward me.

As they came closer, I thought back to the night I had delivered pizza to Mr. Costello's house while the dominatrix was there. The creature definitely looked like a man. He wore leather pants and some sort of harness, and a leather hood covered his head, exposing only his eyes. He nuzzled happily against the woman's skirts.

Now that the woman was facing me, I could see that an eyepatch covered one of her eyes. Several long scars like claw marks extended beyond the edges of the eyepatch. Despite that, she was clearly quite beautiful.

"My apologies, young man," the woman said as they approached me. "He shouldn't have gotten out. Usually, I'm much more careful about these things."

I couldn't quite put words together to respond. The situation was just too absurd, and my adrenaline was still pumping hard. It didn't matter how polite she was. It was clear she was one of them, and I didn't want to risk being taken back to the mansion.

"Umm . . ."

The woman nodded. "I relinquish control of your body back to you, and again, I apologize. This will not happen again."

"Uh-huh." I stood up, still jittery and on guard.

She held out a business card. "My name is Ms. Heliotrope. If you need your clothes dry-cleaned, I'll have it done for you."

I stayed as far away from her as I could as I reached out to take the card. It was sleek and black with *Ms. Heliotrope* and a phone number printed on it in fancy cursive script.

"I'm Josh, Josh Buckmilter." I reluctantly offered my hand for her to shake. I wasn't quite sure why I offered a handshake; it seemed like the most normal reaction I could give under the circumstances.

Ms. Heliotrope's one exposed eye widened slightly before she took my hand and politely shook it. "A pleasure, Mr. Buckmilter."

"I don't think I'll need a dry cleaner," I added. "They're just jeans. I can throw them in the wash."

Ms. Heliotrope gave a small nod. "Understood. If I may say so, Mr. Buckmilter, I get the feeling we may see each other again soon. Until then."

"Yeah, sure." I watched as the strange woman and even stranger man walked out to the street and rounded the corner.

I shoved the card into my pocket and returned to finally uneventfully throw the trash in the dumpster. It wasn't until I got to the door that I fully registered the whole incident. Her voice had stopped me, and then she had said that she relinquished control of my body back to me. What the hell was that? Even though I'd gotten another chance to see how it all worked, I still had no idea what was going on.

I dropped Harriet off at her place, then headed home.

Thoughts swirled as I walked into the house, up the stairs, and fell into my bed. I couldn't tell anymore if the exhaustion was from my physical condition or from all the weird things that kept happening.

84

DAY 5

TUESDAY

I sat on the couch and flipped the jet-black business card between my fingers. The silvery lettering glinted in the sunlight as I played with it. By the time I woke up, I'd nearly convinced myself that the happenings behind the dumpster were just some wild imagining of an exhausted mind. I had almost fully settled on it being some weird stress dream when I realized it was my day to do laundry. I had brought my clothes downstairs and started throwing things into the wash, emptying pockets as I did.

Of course, there it was. The card was slightly bent from having been in my pocket, but no less mysterious. So there I sat, reexamining the card for any information other than the name *Ms. Heliotrope* and a phone number with a nonlocal area code.

"What's that?" Des asked as he sat down on the couch with his laptop. He started up a game from a developer friend of his.

I shrugged and handed the card to him. "Just a sign that my life keeps getting weirder and weirder, I guess?"

Des examined the card. "Ms. Heliotrope? What's a heliotrope?"

I shrugged again. "No clue." I took the card back. That Des could see the card too just further confirmed that it was real and last night had happened. "Do you know if there were any conventions in the area this past weekend? Like a steampunk convention or some kind of BDSM expo or something?" Des usually knew when all the cons were scheduled because he often got invites to speak on panels and connect with other gamers.

"Nope, nothing." Des started tapping on the keyboard. "Did something happen last night?"

"Yeah. *Something* being the operative term." I explained the weird interaction with Ms. Heliotrope and her strange companion in the parking lot of Gino's.

Des shook his head in amazement. "You know, maybe this is a good thing. Maybe having a weird mystery on your hands that isn't your health can help take your mind off the medical stuff for a while."

I might have been inclined to agree if I wasn't dealing with a few too many strangers showing up in my tiny hometown with questionable motivations. Besides, it was hard to take my mind off all the weird changes I was experiencing when my cereal still tasted like cardboard. Hell, even though the bacon I had with it smelled amazing, it was just an empty crunch in my mouth. My sense of smell was stronger than usual. I was still extremely light sensitive. Sometimes I moved a little faster than I meant to, making me clumsy. None of it seemed to be going away. Thinking about the changes was unavoidable when they were constantly reminding me they were there. Ms. Heliotrope was a distraction, but not enough to make a difference when I seemed to be undergoing some bizarre second puberty.

As I shoved Ms. Heliotrope's business card in my pocket, it hit me: I needed normal. I needed to spend a day doing the most ordinary things I could imagine. Jumping over the back of the couch, I sat down to watch Des try out the new game while I racked my brain for ideas.

Mow the lawn? Nope, Des did it yesterday. Plus, I'd have to be out in the sun, which would strain my eyes. Wash the car? Nope. Took it through the car wash a few days ago. Plus, same issue with the eyestrain. Okay, what about indoors? Laundry is already started, and I won't need to do anything with it for a while. Shopping—

That was it! Shopping! We could probably use some groceries, and it was the most mundane thing I could imagine. Maybe I could even find some food I could taste.

"Hey, Des," I said as he paused the game to type up some notes.

"Yeah, Josh?" His eyes never left the screen.

"Do you need any food from the store? I think I'll go out and get groceries today."

"Um, yeah, sure. I think I left the list in the usual place on the refrigerator."

"Oh, right." Of course Des had a list. As laid-back as he seemed in his gameplay videos, he was the most fastidiously organized person I'd ever met.

"Just keep the receipt. I'll pay you back for whatever you pick up for me." He continued playing. "Maybe you should ask Brian, though. You know he always forgets to write what he wants on the list."

"I always forget what on the list?"

Brian's voice came from directly behind me. I jumped and jolted Des, who nearly dropped his laptop. With a deft twist of his wrist, he managed to catch it right before it would have hit the floor.

I sighed in relief, then turned around. "What the hell, Brian? Des's computer could have been destroyed."

He was dressed for running. Wiping a few beads of sweat off his forehead, he stared at me quizzically.

"Maybe don't sneak up on me right now?" I asked, irritated. While it was good he found some motivation to run by himself today, his interpersonal skills were still pretty bad.

"Chill, Josh," he snapped back. "The world doesn't revolve around you, even if you are turning into some kind of mutant weirdo."

His cavalier attitude about what I was going through felt like a stab in the heart, but then I remembered how his claims of me turning into a fictional creature or superhero had been dismissed yesterday. He'd probably be nursing his wounded pride for a few days, at least. That didn't change anything, though. I was confused and scared, with no answers yet. I was about to tell him off for being a shitty friend when Des spoke up.

"I'd be jumpy too if I stumbled upon Mr. Costello and his steampunk dominatrix role-playing in Gino's parking lot last night."

Brian and I looked at Des for a moment and then started laughing. I might have felt bad for Mr. Costello if he hadn't tried to slander me in front of my friends. As it was, the thought of that weird beastly man in bondage gear being Mr. Costello was pretty hilarious.

I didn't laugh for long, though. That guy definitely hadn't been Mr. Costello, and nothing about the stern politeness of Ms. Heliotrope had implied dominatrix to me.

The drop in tension seemed like a good opportunity to get out of the house before Brian said something else to piss me off. "I'm going out to get groceries. Do you want anything?" If I didn't ask, he'd probably raid the groceries I got for Des and me and complain.

Grabbing Des's list from the kitchen, I wrote down Brian's requests. The list quickly became a convoluted mess of food items I wrote down and then had to cross out as Des piped in to tell Brian he was no longer allowed to eat them. Between Brian stating he had to carbo-load and Des reminding him that carbo-loading was for marathon running, not weight loss, I couldn't tell if I was creating a list or a modern-art commentary on the complexity of American dietary habits.

"Come on. Can't I have at least one cheat?" Brian asked petulantly.

Des rolled his eyes and returned to his laptop. "One."

Brian did a little dance of triumph and stuck his tongue out at Des.

"I saw that," Des deadpanned.

"How could you see that?" Brian groused. "I'm right behind you."

Des turned and pointed to the screen of his laptop, which reflected everything behind him.

Brian finally decided on ice cream as his cheat, and I added it to the list. Then I sent him upstairs to take a shower, which he wasn't enthusiastic about. I reminded him that if he didn't bathe, he'd probably get a rash, and if his lack of bathing continued to be an issue, Des and I would hose him down in the front yard.

"Bye, Des," I said. He waved a hand in response as he used the other to type something into an email with surprising speed. He then seamlessly switched back to using both hands.

"Don't forget the ice cream!" Brian called from upstairs.

"Yeah, yeah." I left before he could run down the stairs and try to convince me to add more junk food to the list.

I happily drove to the store, relieved to be away from Brian. I just wasn't sure what we could do for him, outside getting him running again. Now that the safety buffer of being an irresponsible teenager was gone, he should have been able to make at least some basic responsible choices. If only we could find someone older who could help him learn how to be an adult better than Des or I could. Brian was a follower, so if he had the right person to follow, maybe that would help?

I pushed the thoughts aside as I pulled into the parking lot. Grabbing a shopping cart someone had left in the next space over, I walked toward the doors, thankful I had remembered my sunglasses. The bright sunshine seemed to exist only to mock me. The familiar whoosh of cool air as I entered the store made my arms break out in goosebumps.

I started in the vegetable aisle and wandered, grabbing whatever Des and Brian needed while considering what I could eat that might be enjoyable with my minimized sense of taste. Salsa? Something extra spicy might register with my diminished taste buds. I grabbed a couple of jars, along with some tortilla chips, figuring their texture, at least, might make them fun to eat. Turning a corner, I found the bread aisle. I was picking up a loaf automatically when I realized it would probably feel like eating a sponge.

Pulling away from the bread shelf, I looked over the food in the cart. I was calculating the total cost in my head when I heard a familiar voice.

"Mom, we can afford to buy blueberry muffins, especially when they're on sale. I will agree to eat only one a day, and if you and Dad eat them as well, that will be two for each of us and will last us two days. I think it makes sense."

I looked up to find Des's mom, Rhonda, and younger sister, Clarissa, standing in front of a display of muffins.

"Clarissa, if we're going to have muffins, I would prefer we get the ingredients to make them ourselves. Not only would they be fresher, but we could also make a healthier version that tastes just as good." By her expression, Rhonda was not interested in Clarissa's arguments.

"But, Mom, if we do that, you'll have to make the time to make them with me, and you know you work late at the hospital most of the time." It was hard to remember Clarissa was only ten years old when her arguments were so intelligently reasoned. While Jocelyn had followed in their mother's footsteps by becoming a doctor, Clarissa was well on her way to following in their father's footsteps and becoming a lawyer.

Rhonda's face fell. Making time for Clarissa was probably a sore spot for her. She loved her children and loved spending time with them, but her work as a surgeon often took her away from having as much family time as she wanted. Des and Jocelyn didn't resent her for it, but Clarissa would sometimes pull it out in arguments to get her way. Since it was a fairly successful strategy, she wasn't afraid to use it.

I walked over. "Hi, Dr. Adebowale! Hi, Clarissa! It's good to see you."

Rhonda smiled at me; I could tell she was relieved to have the argument interrupted. "Josh, you know you are always welcome to call me Rhonda." She gave me a quick hug, the smell of her coconut conditioner a familiar comfort. "It's good to see you. I heard you're dealing with a strange health issue?"

I nodded. "Yeah, but I'm sure we'll figure it out. Jocelyn's doing her best to help."

"Good. If you ever need anything, you know I'm happy to help out."

"You've already done so much for Dad and me over the years." She always invited us over for holiday meals and parties, helping to ease some of the stress that holidays tended to bring up for Dad.

"Think nothing of it. You're family, and you've always been a good friend to Des."

Her words made me think about Brian again. "Hey, do you know anyone who, like, helps people? Brian needs . . . well, you know what he's like. I don't know how much Des and I can do to help him pull his own weight."

Rhonda gave me a look I recognized. She liked me, but she wasn't fond of Brian, especially after a snide comment he'd made a few months ago about how she should be home taking care of the house instead of working.

She sighed. "I don't know, Josh. If he were younger, there would probably be programs he could be involved in. But now that he's legally an adult, it's harder. At this point, I'd recommend therapy. To be honest, I don't like that he's living with you two. Des doesn't talk about it much, but it sounds like Brian isn't contributing to the household at all."

I wasn't surprised she had come to that conclusion, but I didn't want to confirm it. That was a conversation she would have to have with Des. "Well, if you know anyone who could help him, would you let us know?"

"I could ask some of my colleagues if there are any local free or low-cost services he can use."

Clarissa cleared her throat, glaring at me to signal she wanted the conversation to be over. I took the hint. "Thanks. That's all I ask. I'll see you guys around!" I moved on to the next aisle.

I hadn't realized the next aisle over was pet supplies, so

I walked through it quickly. As I approached the end, I smelled something that made my mouth water furiously. My appetite had become so poor over the last few days, I was a little shocked to have such a strong reaction to any food at all. Though the scent was familiar, I didn't recognize it; I had never been so drawn in by it before.

I followed the delectable aroma until I found myself standing in front of the meat counter.

I blinked for a moment, surprised that the smell of raw meat had induced such a strong reaction. It would have been one thing if it were cooked, but I had walked past a display of rotisserie chickens in a hot case near the front of the store and hadn't had the same reaction. This, though—the raw meat smelled like warmth and life, even though it was clearly cold and dead.

Puzzled by my own reaction, I stared at the variety of meats as though hypnotized.

"Ahem."

The unfamiliar voice startled me out of my daze. I found a man standing next to me whom I didn't recognize. He lifted a pale hand to shove the bridge of his glasses back up his nose.

"Oh, I'm in your way." I started to move my cart.

"No, wait." There was a desperation in his tone that made me stop.

"Is there something I can do for you?"

He ran his fingers awkwardly through his messy dark hair and smiled. "You wouldn't happen to be Josh Buck-milter, would you?"

"Uh, yeah," I replied cautiously. I'd met too many strange, new people in far too short a time span for my taste. Was this going to be my life now, encountering strange people with even stranger secrets? While this guy looked relatively harmless in a nerdy way, I wasn't going to drop my guard if I could help it.

"Ah, I see. I'm Dr. Chen. I work with Jocelyn." He offered his hand a little too enthusiastically.

I remembered Jocelyn mentioning how he had rushed my tests. I stared at his hand for a moment. I wasn't sure if he was supposed to be talking to me outside the hospital. When he realized I wasn't going to shake it, he pretended he was examining his fingernails. Then he ran the hand through his messy hair once more and gave me a nervous smile.

"Okay," I said, still wearing my best poker face.

He turned to look at the selection of meat behind the glass counter. He spoke quickly, as if worried I'd just turn and walk away if he didn't get all the words out fast enough. "You know, considering your bloodwork, I recommend eating foods rich in iron, like red meat. A good rare steak or hamburger could help you feel a little better. Maybe even some blood sausage. It could be good on a pizza." He paused and looked at me uncomfortably. "Jocelyn mentioned you like pizza."

"Oh. Maybe that's why this smells good right now. Maybe my body is telling me I need to eat it. I just wish my bank account would let me afford that much meat." I shrugged.

"Well, you don't have to get steak. Hamburger is less expensive. And seriously, blood sausage may sound strange, but it's really good."

He was being a little too helpful, and I wasn't sure what to make of it. However, there was no way this guy was going to do anything to me other than give me food recommendations, so I decided it was okay to drop my guard a little. "I guess I could afford some ground beef."

"Here." He walked around me to the specialty section and grabbed a sausage—I assumed it was the blood sausage he had been raving about—and put it in my cart. "You won't regret this. You may not have much of an appetite right now, but if you find something you'll eat, then you might as well go for it, right?"

"Okay, okay, man, I'll get the sausage and ground beef." I was starting to get a little annoyed. It also seemed like there was something he wasn't telling me, like he was talking so much because he was hiding something. "Happy?"

"Oh, good. I think this will really help you. You won't regret it, I promise." He smiled and ordered some ground beef for me, putting it in my cart.

I walked away with a quick goodbye, eager to leave Dr. Chen behind. He returned it with a huge, toothy smile. Then he gave the butcher a huge order for a wide range of meats.

I wandered up and down the aisles accompanied by the mouthwatering smell of the meat as I grabbed everything else on the shopping list. As I reached the frozen section to snag some ice cream for Brian before heading to the register, I realized I had only really gotten Des's and Brian's food after getting the meat. Nothing else seemed appetizing to me.

I decided to just give up, buy the food, and go. If I got hungry, which was doubtful, I could come back another day. The normalcy I'd been hoping to find at the grocery store had been spoiled by Dr. Chen and my strange, new obsession with raw meat.

I was waiting in line at the register when a teenage girl behind me looked in my cart and sneered at me in disgust.

"Ew, you really shouldn't eat meat. Those were once living creatures, you know. How would you feel if someone raised you in a factory farm and then killed you for food?" The girl stepped closer with each word. I spotted a few pins on her messenger bag bearing slogans about being vegan.

I took off my sunglasses and glared at her. She must have been startled by my eyes, which I'm sure were in cat form because of the sunlight streaming in through the nearby windows. She nervously shoved a pamphlet about living animal-product-free in my cart, then backed away slowly.

I had to admit, maybe there were some advantages to these weird changes. I put my sunglasses back on with a flourish. I then went through the usual motions of emptying my cart onto the conveyor belt, paying the cashier, taking my cart out of the store, and loading my car up with all the groceries. At least that part felt entirely normal.

As I drove home, my right eye started to twitch, though not bad enough to obscure my vision. Between the smell of the meat in the back seat, the odd interactions with Dr. Chen and the vegan girl, and all the events of the past few days, my attempt at a normal life was falling apart. I rubbed my eye beneath the sunglasses as I made my way through the ordinary suburban streets, wondering what other abnormalities were hiding behind the pleasant-looking front doors. More BDSM scenes? More unusually attractive people with butlers holding strange parties where they mesmerized innocent pizza delivery guys? Maybe that steampunk woman with the guy on a leash was a neighbor as well?

I sighed. Maybe there was no such thing as truly normal. Maybe we were all just different shades and hues of weird.

Once home, I pulled up to the curb and sat for a moment with my sunglasses off, pressing the heels of my hands into my eyes to stop any further twitching. After a couple of deep breaths, I took off my seat belt and grabbed some of the groceries. Brian jogged down the front steps and opened one of the back doors to help bring the bags inside.

"Man, I'm glad you're back. I already lost a couple pounds over the past couple days, and I need food!" Brian held one bag open to examine the contents. "Ooh, good ice cream choice!"

"Yup," I replied a little sharply.

"Hey, you good?"

"Yup," I replied again, sarcasm coloring every word. "Everything's weird, as usual. I mean, I'm fine enough, I guess, except for the almost constant weirdness that seems to be following me around lately. At least nobody's dead. Hamburgers tonight?"

"Even if you can't taste . . ." Brian seemed to pick up on my mood then. "Sorry. We'll have burgers." I had a feeling Des had talked to him about being more sensitive while I was gone. I definitely owed Des one.

"Cool, cool." I followed Brian into the house, where he unceremoniously dumped the groceries on the counter, heedless of the fact that there were eggs in the same bag as the ice cream.

"Des is working on getting things set up for the *Midnight Murder Mansion* tournament at the con he's going to this weekend."

I didn't bother to respond. As I started to put groceries away, I carefully checked the eggs for cracks. Satisfied that they hadn't been harmed, I shoved them in the refrigerator. "Hey, Brian? Have you ever thought of getting some extra help? Like, since your parents kicked you out?"

He shrugged as he opened the ice cream and shoved a spoon into it. "I have you guys. Why would I need anyone else?"

"Yeah, I guess," was all I could say. Maybe he really did

need therapy if he thought Des and I could handle all his problems. All my life, I'd felt like I was just trying to keep my head above water. But that was the point. I was trying. He wasn't.

"You thinking of turning vegan?" Brian pulled the pamphlet out of the bag the ground beef was in. He looked at it with his eyebrow raised doubtfully as he handed me the plastic-wrapped tray of meat.

"No. Some girl shoved it in my cart." My mouth started to water as the scent of the meat reached my nose. Yeah, there was no way I was turning vegan.

After everything was put away, I vegged out on the couch, only to witness Brian polishing off the entire container of ice cream while playing some random first-person shooter game. Trying to find solace in the fact that Brian was probably the most depressingly predictable thing in my life, I got up and blended a tasteless smoothie full of stuff that was supposed to be healthy before returning to watch him yell at the screen as he shot up monstrous-looking aliens.

Des popped out of his office a couple of hours later. He made a beeline for the kitchen and examined the refrigerator. "Yo, time for Josh's kick-ass hamburgers tonight?"

"You know it!" I shouted from my lounge spot on the couch.

"You gonna make these anytime soon?" he joked. "I'm starving!"

"Yeah, seriously!" Brian chimed in, not moving his gaze from the screen.

"Fine, fine," I said. "Just don't get mad if it doesn't taste right because of my dysfunctional taste buds."

I reluctantly got up and trudged toward the kitchen. While I wanted to eat the burgers, part of me didn't really want to make them. But of course, if I didn't make them, I couldn't eat them and see if my taste buds would react the way my nose did.

Des looked at me. "If you need some help, I can pitch in."

I shook my head. "No, it's fine. If you want to make something to go with them, go for it."

"Salad it is."

"Nooooo!" Brian groused from the living room. "Fries!"

"Salad," Des asserted, his tone implying he wouldn't accept any arguments.

We traded a smirk as Brian groaned in the living room.

I pulled the ground beef out of the refrigerator and tore off the plastic. The tantalizing smell was even stronger now. Dumping the beef into a bowl, I added my secret concoction of spices, then mixed them in by hand and shaped the patties. As I did, I had the disturbing urge to eat them raw, but I kept my head and put the patties in the skillet. I usually preferred to grill them, but frying them up was faster.

As the meat browned, I realized the tantalizing smell was getting fainter. Deciding to eat mine rare, I took mine out early and put it on a bun before finishing up the others.

Des looked at the lightly browned meat on the bun. "Hey, man, you don't usually eat your burgers that rare."

"Yeah, but I feel like I want it rare today." I added slices of cheese to the tops of the other two patties so they would melt a bit, then put those patties on their buns as well.

Des had the table set for us. He always insisted we eat at the table. Sometimes, I couldn't remember if he was my friend or my substitute mom with his insistence on such things. We all sat down and dug in.

The moment the slightly bloody meat hit my tongue, I

nearly passed out in pleasure. I had never eaten a rare burger before that had tasted so good. It was like my taste buds had been saving their energy in preparation for this moment. There were subtle nuances to the flavor I had never noticed before. I was in heaven.

I opened my eyes once I'd finished the burger and noticed Des and Brian staring at me.

"You okay, dude?" Brian asked.

"Did you . . . taste it?" Des followed up.

I smiled. "Oh god yes! I could taste it. I mean, the bun didn't taste like anything, but the meat did. I feel like I've been starving for days and now I can finally eat. I'm going to make another one."

Getting up, I made a patty out of the last bit of hamburger in the tray and began to heat it up. Meanwhile, I wondered how Dr. Chen had known meat was the solution to my dietary woes. How was it that this really got my taste buds going when I could taste hardly anything else? I was tired of having so many questions, but at least now I had an idea of who I might go to for some answers.

DAY 6
WEDNESDAY

I had to be on the right track. My gut instinct told me that Dr. Chen knew something he wasn't telling me. Unfortunately, I didn't know how to approach him. I doubted the hospital would give me his personal information. Jocelyn couldn't help either. Apparently, she was booked back-to-back with appointments, so I had to leave a message.

With the answers I hoped for beyond my reach, I went about my day. I opened the second package of ground beef and had a rare hamburger for breakfast, which cheered me up a bit, and tried to figure out what to do with the blood sausage. Maybe I could get Harriet to make me a pizza with it. That idea lifted my spirits even more. Hamburgers were good, but I really wanted to taste actual pizza again.

I grabbed one of Des's Japanese sports drinks after my burger and enjoyed the slightly saline aftertaste. It was nowhere near as good as the hamburger, but I wasn't going to question it. I did start to wonder if any sports drink would do. I also wondered what about those two things made them easier for me to taste when everything else was so bland.

I decided to run by the grocery store again before work and pick up more varieties of sports drinks to see if I could figure out what exactly I was tasting. Maybe that would help me figure out the connection between the meat and the sports drinks. At least it might give me a chance to find some answers on my own since I wasn't sure how to start exploring the Dr. Chen angle. After fully stocking up on sports drinks, from Astro Charge to Zenergy—to the point where my trunk was nearly overflowing—I headed straight for work.

"Hey, kid," Gino said when he unlocked the door for me. "You're early."

I took a sip of one of the energy drinks I had brought in with me. It was supposed to be cherry flavored, and I could smell it, but mostly, I just tasted that same saline flavor. Was it the electrolytes, maybe?

"Yeah, I did some shopping beforehand and overestimated how long it would take."

Gino gave me an evaluating look. "You know, Josh, you're looking a little less pale. You feeling better?"

"I am?" I tried to catch sight of my reflection in one of the windows, but the light was passing through it at the wrong angle for me to get a good look.

"Let's hope this is good news. I don't want to lose my best delivery boy unless it's for a good reason." Gino patted me on the back as I took a sip of my drink. I nearly choked on a bigger gulp than I'd meant to take.

Gino walked behind the counter and started doing some cleaning, so I took a seat on one of the barstools.

"Hey, Gino, I was going to ask Harriet, but maybe I should ask you too: have you ever made pizza with blood sausage?" I had decided to get more when I bought my sports drinks, and I put the bag it was in on the counter.

"Hmm . . . I haven't, but I'm sure it's possible." He put down the cleaning rag and grabbed a tablet sitting next to the register. "You can put just about anything on a pizza."

The door to the restaurant opened, and I turned to see Harriet walk in. "Hey, guys! What are you two up to?"

Gino gave her a huge grin. "Josh thinks we should try blood sausage on our pizza."

Harriet put her things down on a nearby table and rushed over to look at the tablet. "Blood sausage? Huh. I did that once in one of my classes in culinary school. The assignment was to take a common dish and make it unusual. I did some research and found that blood sausage does get used on pizza. Often with pears and blue cheese."

"How did it work out?" I wondered if a pizza with blood sausage and a stronger-smelling cheese would help balance out my lack of taste for most foods.

Harriet smiled proudly. "It was great! The class loved it." Seeing her smile, I almost forgot what we were talking about.

"What about Muenster cheese?" Gino asked.

"Interesting. What are you thinking about?" Harriet asked.

"Well, *blood* sausage, *Muenster* cheese . . . Halloween is coming up soon."

Harriet nodded. "Good point."

"Want to give it a try?" Gino usually took the lead on creating new pizza combos, but occasionally, he would give Harriet the opportunity.

"Sure! I can give it a try now, before we start." Harriet pulled her hair back into a ponytail, put her Gino's cap on over it, tied on her apron, and began to wash her hands. "What made you think of blood sausage, Josh?"

"Well, I had a strange conversation yesterday that led to

me discovering I can taste rare meat. The person also recommended blood sausage, but I've never had it before, so I wasn't sure what to do with it."

Harriet stopped in the middle of washing her hands, the soap suds dripping down her arms and back into the sink. "Wait, you could taste rare meat? Josh, that's fantastic!"

Her enthusiasm was contagious. "Isn't it? I was so happy yesterday when I tried it and could actually enjoy what I was eating. I hoped that with the blood sausage—"

"You'd be able to enjoy eating pizza again?" Harriet grabbed my hands with her soapy ones and gave a little hop. "This is great! I'll be able to figure out some meal options for you while we solve the puzzle of what's happening to you."

I ignored the slimy soap on her hands. She was so happy, I couldn't help but grin back at her. "Awesome!"

She looked down at her hands. "Oh, I'm sorry. I forgot I hadn't rinsed my hands off." She took her hands back quickly and rinsed them, but honestly, if she'd continued holding my hands with her soapy ones, I wouldn't have argued at all.

Harriet grabbed a towel to dry her hands off. "You should probably rinse yours too, Josh."

"Oh yeah. Right." I jumped off the stool and walked around the counter to clean my hands off. She handed the towel to me and turned back to the counter to grab the bag of sausage I'd left there.

"Hmm . . . I wonder. I suppose it's the blood you're tasting? Maybe iron? I wonder if foods high in iron or other nutrients that are good for your blood would help. Maybe spinach, sardines, broccoli . . ."

I could see Harriet was in cooking mode and wasn't

really talking to me. I knew better than to say anything else, so I sat down to watch her experiment while Gino started setting things up for the evening. She carefully considered each item Gino placed in front of her with a critical eye, as though she were measuring out chemicals in a laboratory experiment.

Renato walked in and sat next to me. The high school was across the street and a few buildings down, so sometimes he came over for lunch. "Hey, has Harriet gone mad food scientist again?"

"Yup," I replied.

He chuckled. "You know, if my chemistry teacher was as much fun to watch as Harriet is when she starts experimenting, I'd probably get better grades in that class."

"Pay attention to your teachers," Gino chided.

"I know, I know. This is just more fun to watch. Besides, my teacher is a sixty-year-old bald man with a bad comb-over. Harriet may look nerdy, but she's a lot cuter than my teacher."

I felt a slight pang of jealousy, but I wasn't too worried. Harriet treated Renato like a little brother. There was no reason for me to be concerned. But then again, if she saw Renato as a little brother, how did she see me? I was younger than her too. Maybe I was just another little brother?

I pushed the thought out of my head and turned on my stool to look out the window. A familiar car drove by, and my heart suddenly lurched in my throat. It was that Porsche I had admired at the mansion. Long-Haired Dude was in the front seat, driving the speed limit. If I hadn't been so freaked out by seeing him again, I would have questioned how anyone could possibly drive a car made for speed so slowly.

I darted over to the window to watch as he drove to the

high school and entered the parking lot. There was something inherently wrong about the whole thing. What was
some rich guy doing wasting his time at the high school?

Long-Haired Dude turned his head to look directly at
Gino's. He smirked, and even though he was wearing sunglasses, I realized he could see me. My skin crawled, and I
ducked down beneath the window to hide.

"Uh, Josh? What are you doing?" Renato asked as he
approached me. "Pretending to be some kind of super spy?"
He eagerly looked out the window and, after a moment,
spotted the car. "Damn, that's a badass car! What I wouldn't
give to have one of—"

I pulled him down to crouch next to me. "Hey, have
you seen that guy at school before?" I popped my head up
to see that Long-Haired Dude's attention was now focused
on Mr. Costello, who was shaking his hand and attempting
to charm him.

Renato popped his head up to watch. "Nope. Never
seen him before. Ha! Costello is going out of his way to suck
up to that guy."

Long-Haired Dude pulled a satiny handkerchief out of
his pocket and wiped his hand while Mr. Costello admired
his car. He sneered at Costello as though he were a worthless
bug. When Costello turned back around, Long-Haired
Dude's expression immediately became more pleasant. They
walked to the sidewalk, where the school building offered a
little shade, and Long-Haired Dude took off his sunglasses.
He looked back at me and Renato with a grin, then turned
so he could look Mr. Costello in the eye.

Mr. Costello, who was usually fidgety, stood uncharacteristically still. The hair on my arms stood on end. Was
Long-Haired Dude some kind of hypnotist? Was that what
had happened to me? All of this felt so wrong. Sure, Mr.

Costello was a complete jerk, especially considering what he'd said to Des and Brian about me the other day, but with everything I'd been going through the past few days, I didn't think he deserved the same.

Renato chuckled. "I never knew Costello was such a brownnoser! Wait until I tell my friends."

I did my best to ignore him as I watched the interaction. The way they were angled made it too hard for me to read their lips . . . which probably didn't matter because I could not read lips anyway, but it wouldn't have hurt to try. I was starting to hate that I never went through a spy phase when I was a kid.

"What are you two up to? We have customers coming in," Gino said suddenly from right behind us. I jumped, startled and surprised that such a big man could be so quiet.

"Uh . . . nothing, Dad! Just, um . . . oh, hey, isn't that car cool?" Renato asked, trying to cover for us. "Maybe I can get one for my eighteenth birthday?"

Gino blinked. He looked out the window at the object of Renato's desire. "Are you kidding me? Do you know what kind of car that is? Do you know how expensive that is? No. Absolutely not. If you want a car like that, you'll have to buy it yourself."

"Aw, come on, Dad." Renato stood up and started pulling his dad away from the window. He gave me a thumbs-up behind his back as they walked away to let me know he was going to distract his dad for me. "You know that by the time I earned enough money to buy that car, I'd be too old to enjoy it. You and Mom can at least help out, right?"

I turned back around to look out the window one more time, only to see Long-Haired Dude getting back in his car and driving off. Mr. Costello waved as the car sped away.

Then he just stood there for a moment, blinking a few times, before he smoothed his suit jacket down and walked into the school.

I was disappointed I hadn't been able to figure out what the interaction was all about, but I was also quite happy that Long-Haired Dude was gone. It was my first time seeing any of the people from the mansion since the whole mess started, and my fight-or-flight instinct had kicked in a lot more strongly than I had expected.

I took a deep breath and tried to pull myself together. Wednesdays tended to be busier at Gino's, and this Wednesday was no different. My day would sometimes start earlier on busier days due to people calling in lunchtime orders, and I was almost immediately sent off on several deliveries. There was a quick break when I walked back in around three.

"A Hawaiian pizza with chicken for Roberta," Gino shouted back to Harriet, who quickly got to work.

"How's it going in here?" I asked. Almost all the tables were taken by high school kids hanging out after school.

"Pretty busy." Gino pulled out a plate and put a slice of pizza on it. "Here. Harriet made this for you."

I gazed at the mouthwatering slice of pizza, and most of the tension from seeing Long-Haired Dude drained away. He was still a nagging thought at the back of my mind, but the idea that I might be able to eat pizza again was overwhelming. Generous slices of blood sausage mingled with spinach, pears, and blue cheese on a thin crust coated with tomato sauce. It smelled amazing. I took a deep breath, hoping this pizza would taste at least somewhat as good as the hamburger.

It was now or never. I opened my mouth, took a huge bite, and began to chew. While I didn't really taste the pear and barely tasted the spinach, the blood sausage combined with the aroma of the cheese made my day. It may not have been what I was used to with pizza, but since I could actually enjoy it, it was good enough.

Harriet turned to see me eating the slice. She raised an eyebrow, to which I responded with a thumbs-up. She grinned and got back to work, putting her next creation into the brick oven. Gino placed another pizza in the oven while she continued on to prepare another order. It all felt so normal: me sitting and savoring one of Harriet's creations while watching their pizza-making dance in the kitchen.

"Is that the thing Harriet made?" Renato asked. "Should I try it? Blood sausage sounds weird."

I spoke with a huge bite still in my mouth. "It rewwy goot."

"Huh?"

I finished chewing and swallowed. "It's really good. It's not what I expected. Try it."

Renato grabbed a slice and took a bite. "Huh, it's not my favorite, but it's not bad." He took another bite. "Wait until I tell my friends I ate blood sausage. They'll probably freak out and start calling me Count Renato."

"Well, then call me Count Josh because I'll go vampire for this pizza," I joked back.

"We'd probably have to put it in the blender and have you drink it through a straw to make it authentic," Renato suggested.

"Yeah, but then it wouldn't really be much of a pizza, would it?"

"Yeah, not really."

"Hey, Renato, take these orders, then we'll take a break to get ready for tonight." Gino handed a few pizza boxes to Renato. "Do your homework when you get back."

Renato sighed. "Yeah, yeah."

"Don't 'yeah, yeah' me," Gino said. "I barely paid attention in school, and now I run a pizza restaurant. You're a smart kid. If you apply yourself in school, you could run a whole chain of pizza joints and never have to deliver another pizza again."

"Okay, Dad." Renato rolled his eyes at me before walking out the door to make the deliveries.

I stared at the door for a moment, suddenly thoughtful, then turned back to Gino. "You really care about your son."

"Yeah. Part of the reason I hired you was that you have drive. I was hoping it would rub off on Renato a bit."

Gino paused to grab a rag and started wiping down the counter slowly, pensively.

"Don't get me wrong, kid. I don't hold you responsible for teaching my son to have goals in life. It just seems like kids these days don't have dreams for the future the way we used to. I don't know what Renato wants at all. I want him to have things to look forward to in life. All he seems to want is the latest video game or to hang out and do nothing. I don't want him to think that having dreams means he can't achieve them, even if his father couldn't achieve his own." He looked wistfully at a photo on the wall of himself back in high school, wearing his football uniform.

I looked down at the greasy plate where the pizza I'd just inhaled had been moments before. What were my goals? At one point, I thought it was getting a good job, like being an accountant or working my way up some corporate ladder, marrying the woman of my dreams—Harriet, of course— and living the suburban life with a couple of kids and a dog or something. Now? I was starting to wonder if I'd be able to achieve even that simple a dream before whatever was going on either changed me to the point I was just too weird to have a normal life or killed me.

"Renato's a good kid. Even if he doesn't know what he wants yet, he'll figure things out."

Gino nodded. "I just wish he'd give me a few hints about what he was thinking."

"Don't worry, Gino. I didn't tell my dad what I wanted out of life when I was in high school either. I'm still not sure how to tell him anything about my life." I sighed. "Maybe Renato isn't telling you because he's worried he'll let you down or something."

Gino smiled wanly as he started cleaning the counter again. "He'll never let me down. I just want him to be happy."

The phone rang, and Gino picked it up. I heard Graziella's familiar tones, so I went to the sink to wash my dish, turning on the water to drown out the phone call.

"Hey, Josh," Harriet said as she joined me in cleaning up. "What you said to Gino was really kind. I'm sure what you're going through is messing with your own goals, but don't feel like your goals have to be about being responsible to others. Think about yourself a little too."

She had taken my advice to Gino and turned it back on me. Maybe she was right. Was what I wanted really about me or trying to create something I thought was normal? Maybe I wanted the suburban dream just so my dad wouldn't feel bad about not being able to give me a normal-looking life when I was a kid.

Did I need to have a normal life? Maybe it was okay that I was changing.

"Do you see yourself here for the rest of your life, Harriet?" I asked as I scrubbed a cup.

"No. Even though I love Gino's, this is practice. I want to open my own pastry shop. I'll make the typical sweets, like cakes and cookies and such, but I also want to make savory pastries. Working in a pizza place gives me the chance to build up my skills with savory ingredients." She smiled and nudged my hip with hers playfully. "You've had those bacon-cheddar-broccoli muffins I've made before."

"Yeah, those are good." She'd used me as her taste tester when she came up with the recipe back in high school. She'd brought different versions every day for two weeks and made me eat them at lunch. She hadn't accepted any feedback unless it critically looked at the combination of flavors, and once she was satisfied that I had told her everything I thought, she'd scribble down notes and take them home, only to bring a newer, tastier version the next day.

"Gino knows it too. He was thinking we could do a joint venture. Maybe he'll have Gino's here and then add on to the building so I could have my own shop next to his. People could get their pizzas here and their desserts at my place, or we could share delivery service or something. We're still figuring it out, but for now, I'm happy being here."

We continued working on the dishes in silence, occasionally splashing each other playfully. Then Harriet started to set up for the evening shift, while I went out to fill my car up with gas for the night's deliveries. When I came back, orders were already coming in.

"Hey, Josh, could you take this one?" Gino handed me a couple of boxes. "I know I usually send Renato to that area, but the woman who ordered sounded a little distressed. Maybe something's up?"

"Yeah, okay. I'll get the first order where it's going, then I'll get to that lady."

"Thanks, kid."

I took off, not really thinking much about what Gino had said. I remembered reading somewhere that food delivery was one of the most dangerous jobs. We never really knew what we were heading into.

I dropped the first pizza off to a group of kids who were studying for a test, then made the short drive down a familiar couple of blocks to a familiar-looking house. After I parked, I walked up to see a kid crying on the front porch. I immediately recognized him as the kid I'd grabbed the other day when he would have walked out into the street.

"Hey, Tommy, is that you?"

He looked up at me, his lips trembling and nodded. "Mommy!"

"Mommy?" I realized there was yelling coming from behind the front door.

My blood started to pump faster in my veins. I was already on edge after seeing Long-Haired Dude earlier, but my instincts told me this situation was bad. It wasn't just my nervous system being a little extra spicy. I pulled out my cell phone and called the local police department, hoping that would be faster than calling 911.

"Willow Springs PD," said a voice from the other end of the line.

"Hey, it's Josh Buckmilter. I'm delivering pizza, and I think there's a problem at one of the houses I'm delivering to." I gave her the details.

"We'll send someone right over. No matter what, don't try to go into the house. Just wait with the kid until we get there."

"Okay," I replied, even though it felt wrong. I was right there. I'd be able to do something sooner than the cops could. I looked down at Tommy, who was clearly terrified.

"We're just going to go down to the sidewalk, okay, Tommy?" I held out my hand, which he grasped tightly with his chubby and slightly damp fingers.

We began to walk down to the curb when I heard a crash from inside the house. This was more than just a verbal argument. I stopped walking and put my hands on Tommy's shoulders. "Don't go anywhere, okay? Stay right here. Some nice police officers are on their way, and they'll help us."

Tommy nodded, and I did exactly what the officer had said not to. I walked straight up to the front door and rang the doorbell.

"Shit, who did you call?" demanded a male voice tinged with fury. The words were met only with sobs.

"Pizza!" I said in a cheery voice, hoping I sounded as nonthreatening as possible.

There was a shuffling sound behind the door, and it opened a crack. "We didn't order any pizza," a large man said through the crack, clearly hiding what was going on in the room.

"Well, we got an order, and it's already been paid for with a credit card, so it's yours." I shoved the pizza toward the door.

The man opened it slightly wider, enough that I could have tipped the pizza box sideways to pass it through. "Just hand it to me like this," he said, clearly irritated.

"And ruin your pizza? All the cheese and toppings would slide down to the edge, and you'd just have a sloppy mess," I said, trying to get him to open the door even more.

"Listen, kid, I don't want your pizza," the guy growled. He jerked the door further open and leaned toward me menacingly.

Suddenly, I smelled it. That smell from the meat section of the store. It was coming from one of the man's hands, and more was wafting from the room behind him. Somehow, though, it smelled even better than it had at the meat section. There was something . . . I don't know . . . richer about it.

Something came over me then, and I shoved open the door, making the man stumble back. I caught sight of Tommy's mother on the floor, coughing up blood, before the man growled and launched himself at me, fists ready to take me out.

Everything seemed to move in slow motion then as a strange but not entirely unpleasant sensation started around my upper teeth. I began to both salivate and feel strangely thirsty, as though the inside of my mouth were both wet and dry. I saw the woman staring at me worriedly before I turned to see two beefy fists on the verge of connecting with my solar plexus. With a burst of speed, I easily evaded the man's flying fists.

After that, it was like instinct took over. By the time the cop cars pulled up, I held the angry man's arms in a tight grip behind his back with one hand. For some reason, I had his head tilted to the side with my other hand, my open mouth hovering over his neck.

"Let go of the man, Josh."

The words cut through the mental state I was in, but it took me a moment to snap out of it. I could still smell blood, but I felt a little more aware of myself. I let go of the man and backed away.

"I'm pressing charges against this kid!" the angry man shouted once he was free. "He shoved his way into my house. I want him behind bars!"

"Josh, come here," said the officer who had spoken before. I did as he said and walked down the porch stairs. Another officer came over and had me sit down on the lawn while the first walked up to the man at the door.

I must have been in shock by that point. I just sat there, barely registering anything. I knew Tommy was crying on the lap of a third officer while the officer who had had me sit down asked me questions, but I couldn't really answer them. I was so mystified by my own actions, I wasn't sure what was real and what was a product of my imagination. I was vaguely aware of giving Gino a call to let him know I had to go to the police station.

As one of the officers finally led me to a police car, I stared blankly out at the street and barely noticed Red Lipstick in a nearby car, watching as I was taken away.

DAY 7
THURSDAY

One week. It had been one full week since that strange night when I innocently delivered pizza to the mansion where Long-Haired Dude and Red Lipstick lived. One week since my body started changing. One week, and I found myself sitting on a chair in the Willow Springs Police Department after midnight, wondering if I was going to be arrested. I couldn't help but wonder what would be next. Aliens? Ninjas? Alien ninjas?

"Josh, thank you for waiting patiently," Officer Sullivan said as she sat down across from me at her desk. Though I was relieved it was her instead of Officer Monroe, who tended to be less diplomatic, I still felt like an angry swarm of bees had decided to make a permanent home of my nervous system.

"Um, yeah. Thanks, I guess." I hated that the adrenaline rush from earlier, which had made me feel stronger and more capable, was gone, leaving me exhausted.

"Josh, no charges are going to be pressed against you," Officer Sullivan began, much to my relief. "Mrs. Collins explained what had happened. She's pressing charges against her husband, and we'll be helping her and her son get support from a domestic violence shelter."

I nodded. I was happy to hear they were getting help. I still felt uneasy, though. I hadn't really been acting like myself through the whole ordeal.

"Josh, are you paying attention?"

"Yeah, yeah, I'm sorry. I'm just feeling kind of overwhelmed."

Officer Sullivan pulled her chair away from the other side of the desk and placed it closer to me, sitting down. "Josh, I want to explain something to you. While some of what you did was right, some of what you did was wrong. You called us directly. That was smart. It helped us get there faster. You sat with Tommy initially. That was also smart.

"What wasn't smart was leaving him alone, going to the house, and trying to play hero. You aren't trained for that. Domestic violence situations can be incredibly dangerous, and your actions could have escalated the issue into something far, far worse. Do you understand? Someone could have gotten seriously injured, and if a weapon had been involved, you could have died. Mrs. Collins could have died. Tommy could have died."

She sat back in her chair and looked at me critically. "I know you, Josh. You're a good person. You want to do the right thing. So next time, do the right thing, okay?"

"I will."

"Good." She patted me on the shoulder. "You're really lucky that fancy-pants lawyer showed up. Mr. Collins was shouting right and left about how he wanted to press charges against you. The next thing we knew, he was calm, asked that no charges be pressed against you, and said that he understood what he did was wrong. He confessed to abusing his wife. That lawyer is some kind of hero. I've never seen anyone flip that fast."

"What lawyer? I don't have a lawyer."

Then it hit me. Why would someone flip that easily, indeed? I had a feeling I wasn't going to like the answer.

"Well, you must have some kind of guardian angel of the legal kind because she seemed quite happy to represent you." Officer Sullivan stood up. "You can go home, but keep in mind that because you witnessed what you did, you'll probably be asked to testify in court in the near future."

"Wait, I can really go?"

"Yup. I think she said she'd drive you back to your car so you could take it home." Officer Sullivan looked over my shoulder and nodded to someone behind me. "She's here."

I turned around and saw her. Long legs, skintight navy-blue dress with a designer blazer, full red lips, and red hair twisted up into a fancy updo that seemed like it could only be created by magic. She was no lawyer. She was Red Lipstick—well, maybe that wasn't really her name, but it was her, nonetheless.

I didn't want to leave with her, but I wasn't sure I had a choice. She'd already told them she was my lawyer, and it wasn't clear whether they'd let me go without her. Even so, it would be idiotic to go with her. I had every reason not to trust her after what had happened last Thursday. At the same time, she had a magnetic presence, and I was so worn down, I wasn't sure I could resist.

It was a terrifying thought.

What scared me even more, though, was how I had managed to immobilize a man who had a good fifty pounds of muscle on me. Why had I been holding his head at that angle? Why had that been my instinctual response?

I followed Red Lipstick out of the police station like a

frightened, obedient puppy. Mr. Wellington, the butler from the night at the mansion, was standing next to a Maybach. When he saw us, he immediately opened the back door so we could enter.

"After you, Josh. A woman never slides all the way in when wearing a dress." Red Lipstick gave me a charming smile that carried a shade of menace behind it. I looked into her eyes and suddenly felt like I should do exactly what she told me to, even though I didn't want to.

Part of me tried to resist, but I couldn't muster the strength. I began to enter the back seat of the dark car. It was so black inside, it was like stepping into a void with no clue of what dark terrors would meet me on the other side.

"Wait!" called a somewhat familiar voice.

We all turned to see someone approaching from a nearby shadowed area unlit by streetlights. If I hadn't had such good night vision now, I wouldn't have noticed her there at all. With a peacock feather in her hair and a turquoise-and-green silk Victorian dress to match, Ms. Heliotrope stepped out beneath the streetlights.

Red Lipstick's face scrunched up into a scowl. It was a beautiful scowl, but a scowl nonetheless. It was clear she did not like Ms. Heliotrope at all, and I had a feeling the dislike was mutual.

"Genevieve," Ms. Heliotrope greeted sternly.

"Carolyn," Red Lipstick responded in disgust.

I looked back and forth between the two women, who seemed to be trying to stare each other down. I really wasn't sure who would win, as both were pretty intimidating in different ways. Red Lipstick—or rather, Genevieve—had an air of being in control of every situation, as though she could figure out every outcome and manipulate it in any direction she wanted. Ms. Heliotrope, on the other hand, wasn't quite as unflappable, but she came across as having some kind of influential status—not too dissimilar from Officer Sullivan, who was probably writing a report about tonight's incident right now. I literally felt stuck between a rock and a hard place.

Genevieve broke the silence first. "This is none of your business, Formalist. I've done nothing wrong tonight. If anything, I protected us."

Ms. Heliotrope raised the eyebrow that wasn't covered by the eyepatch, which I noted was a deep turquoise that matched the rest of her outfit. "You may have done nothing wrong *tonight*, but that doesn't mean you haven't been up to something." Standing with her arms crossed, she gestured toward me with her head. "I don't exactly remember you enjoying the company of pizza delivery boys."

"You know, I'm not exactly a boy anymore," I squeaked out. They ignored me, which left me feeling like the description of boy was more accurate than my technical status as a full-grown adult . . . who still played video games, read comic books, collected trading cards, and had a collection of action figures that I absolutely did not play with anymore. Nope, not me. Much too mature for that. Maybe . . .

"Oh, but Joshykins here is just such a cutie. Who wouldn't want his company?" Genevieve grabbed my face in an unexpectedly viselike grip with one hand and pulled me closer, wrapping her other arm around my waist. I felt that same goose-bumpy, arm-hair feeling I had when I saw Long-Haired Dude in the high school parking lot. She was much stronger than she looked. "What business of it is yours, anyway?"

"You know it's always my business if you or anyone else is up to no good. Look at him. Have you even explained to him what's happening yet? I know you and Danforth are up to your games again." Ms. Heliotrope put out a hand for me to take. "Mr. Buckmilter, you don't have to do anything she says. She's untrustworthy and will treat you like a puppet until she gets what she wants, then she'll discard you like so much trash on the side of the road."

Genevieve scoffed. "You have no proof of anything. Maybe I'm protecting this sweet child to guide him into a respectable position among our kind." She punctuated every few words by twisting my head slightly to one side or the other.

Their kind? They were being purposefully vague about everything, but they clearly held the answers to all my questions. Ms. Heliotrope may have been right about Genevieve, but with how little information she was giving me, I wasn't completely sure she was trustworthy either. "Can you two stop arguing and please just explain what the hell is going on?" I squeaked as I tried and failed to wiggle my way out of Genevieve's steely grip.

Genevieve let me go and tamed her angry scowl into a pleasant smile once she faced me. She spoke in a tone that was supposed to be cute and flirtatious, but I didn't buy it. "Sweet Josh, this woman is a stick in the mud, and she'll only serve to destroy our fun. You don't have to listen to her if you don't want to. Now, let me have Mr. Wellington drive us back to your car so you can go home to your little friends."

It was then I noticed something. The last time I'd met Genevieve and the Long-Haired Dude, I'd felt mesmerized, like I was halfway into a dream state. This time, it seemed almost like that was happening again.

"No."

My voice was weak as the word slipped out of my

mouth. I wasn't quite sure how I'd managed it. Something was a little different this time, though. I watched Genevieve blink. It was a subtle reaction, but I could tell she wasn't expecting me to say that at all.

"Well, you're not going with *her*, are you?" Genevieve gestured toward Ms. Heliotrope.

Whatever Genevieve had been doing to keep me under her control had dissipated. I spoke with slightly more confidence. "My car isn't that far from the station. I can walk there."

Ms. Heliotrope put one of her arms through mine. "See? Josh can make his own decisions without you."

"Ugh." Genevieve sighed, her lips pursed in a pretty pout. "Wellington, let's go."

"Yes, madam."

Genevieve smoothly sat herself down in the back seat of the car. Mr. Wellington shut the door behind her and got into the car himself, driving off down the street.

Ms. Heliotrope and I stood for a bit, watching the rear lights of the car fade away. When they'd disappeared, I looked at her, unsure if I was better off in her company.

"You made a smart choice, Josh."

"Did I?" I turned to face her. Being released from whatever power Genevieve had had over me suddenly made me blurt out all the questions I hadn't been able to ask while they were making decisions for me. "Are you going to give me answers? What's happening to me? What are you? What was it she called you . . . a formalist?" I sighed. "What the hell is going on?"

She tightened her grip on my arm, and yet again, I had the same skin-crawling feeling I'd had with Genevieve. Even her grip was similar to Genevieve's, though the position of her hand on my forearm didn't look like a grip at all. "Josh, I'm limited by the Conclave in what I can tell you, but I can give you some answers tonight, if you'd like."

"Wait, really?" I asked, keeping up with her steady pace as we walked side by side.

"It depends on what you ask, of course." Her left eye glinted in the light. I wasn't sure if she was doing me a favor or threatening me.

We walked a little ways saying nothing. I wasn't sure what question to ask first since I had so many. I was also terrified that if I asked the wrong question, she might easily pull my arm off. I decided to start with something that might give me a sense of who Ms. Heliotrope was. Maybe that would help me determine if I could trust her to give me real answers.

"So, what was it that Re—Genevieve called you? A formalist?" I asked cautiously.

"That's your first question?" She raised her exposed eyebrow, the only part of her somewhat stony expression that hinted she might be surprised. "Well, among our people, a formalist is an enforcer of laws, much like a police officer. It's my job to make sure our people follow the rules and don't cause problems. When they do break the rules, it's my job to bring them to justice."

"Our people?" I blurted out, then realized I'd asked too bald a question.

She tilted her head and looked at me as though she could see straight through me and read my inner thoughts. "I can't answer that. Not yet. But you'll know soon."

Her response irritated me. "Okay, then why do you dress up like that?"

Ms. Heliotrope laughed, breaking her serious demeanor. "This? I don't know. I've always had a bit of a flair for the dramatic, and since I became part of this . . . community, I suppose, I decided to take on a certain persona that seemed fitting. I rather enjoy it, in the very least."

I nodded thoughtfully, then broached a harder question. "So, if it's okay to ask, what happened to your right eye?"

She touched her eyepatch with her free hand. "This?" Her hard shell came back up. "Be glad you haven't experienced what I did when I went through what you're going through now."

I gulped at the dark tone that shaded her words. I wasn't sure how much longer she would let me ask her questions, but she had just confirmed that whatever was happening to me had happened to her. "You had a normal life before, didn't you?"

Her reply was soft and tinged with regret. "Yes."

Rounding a corner, we continued to walk in an uneasy silence. I had a feeling she had a story to tell but there was no way she was going to tell it. After a while, I spoke again.

"This change I'm going through—will I survive it?"

"Some people do; some people don't. The hardest part is dealing with . . . food." The pause between the last two words was odd, as though she wanted to use a word other than *food*.

"Yeah, a guy told me eating meat would help. Some lab technician at the hospital or something."

I could feel a slight pause in her step. It was almost imperceptible. "Did you meet Dr. Chen, perhaps?"

"Yeah. Kinda nerdy guy with glasses and messy hair? A bit awkward?"

She laughed unexpectedly, the sound tinkling like wind chimes. "He can be like that when he's worried about saying too much. But once you get to know him, he's okay. You're very fortunate. Things could have ended up much worse for you if you hadn't figured out what he told you soon enough on your own."

"Wait, is the fact that you know him related to why my tests came back so quickly?" I thought back to what Jocelyn had said about the speed of the tests.

Ms. Heliotrope responded with a hiss of air between her teeth. I had a feeling that while it was a question I shouldn't be asking, her lack of answer was confirmation enough.

I then remembered her "pet" from the other night. "Could I end up like that feral guy?"

She nodded gravely. "Yes. I've had to collect several people who ended up like that. Most of the time, the Conclave will end their lives so they don't have to suffer, but sometimes I find ones who clearly still want to live. It's not much of a life, but I take care of them the best I can, and they can be very helpful when we have to hunt down someone who defies the laws of the Conclave."

That didn't sound good. I wasn't sure I wanted to be anywhere near the Conclave, whatever it was. "I'm guessing you can't tell me what the Conclave is."

"No, not yet. But understand, they do work in all our best interests. They keep us in line so that everyone—our people and the normal people of the world—can survive in relative peace." She looked at me. "That's all I can tell you about them for now."

I sighed. I felt like every answer she gave me only brought me more questions. "Okay, so the light sensitivity, the cat eyes, the lack of taste, the super speed . . . all that stuff is part of this change I'm going through, right?"

"Right. And don't bother asking any doctors about it. They'll think you're either anemic, mentally ill, or both.

You're not sick." She dismissed the idea with a wave of her hand.

That was the only answer that was truly a relief. I wasn't sick. I probably wouldn't die. There was a chance I might turn into some kind of brainless feral weirdo, but probably not. "So I'm maybe going to be okay, but I'll be . . . different."

"Yes. You found the meat trick, so that reduces your chances of turning feral."

We turned another corner, almost arriving at where I had parked my car. "Is there a point when you will be able to tell me more and maybe explain everything instead of only some things?"

She turned to face me and put her hands on my shoulders. "Yes. There are things you will have to learn when the time is right. You may not realize this, but you're being monitored. Genevieve and her people have been spying on you over the past week. Just as I, and other formalists, have been paying attention. We need to see that you're trustworthy and capable of understanding why we need to keep an oath of secrecy before it's determined by the Conclave that you are safe. It won't take long before solid decisions are made about this situation."

Her posture changed in that moment, almost as if she had just run out of steam. "But, Josh," she began, her visible left eye serious and a bit sad, "I'll do my best to help you every step of the way. I owe you that."

"You owe me?"

But she had already disappeared. She must have had the same rapid speed I did because her sudden disappearance was accompanied by a rush of wind nearly strong enough to knock me over. I wondered how she managed to run that fast in that confining Victorian dress, but I was getting the picture that whatever she was—whatever we were—normal rules didn't apply.

I finally reached my car, got inside, and sat down to take a few deep breaths. It seemed like this was going to become a new habit of mine, sitting in my car and trying to pull myself together. With jittery hands, I drove the few blocks back home. I was partially disturbed, especially now that I knew I was being watched by multiple people, but at least I knew a little more than I had.

Once I checked in with Brian, who was heading to bed himself, I made my way to my own room and looked around my relatively sparse living space. I closed all the blinds so I could at least be guaranteed a little privacy in my own home. I even put a sticky note over my laptop camera and made sure my laptop was closed. Then I put a foam bandage over the mic so I couldn't be recorded. Satisfied, I got into bed and slept restlessly.

I woke up around noon, relieved that Des and Brian hadn't demanded I join them on their morning run. I flipped on a pair of sunglasses before leaving my room and made my way downstairs to figure out which of my limited breakfast options to eat.

"Hey, Josh," Des greeted from the couch. "Brian told me what you told him last night about that delivery gone wrong. You okay?"

"Yeah, I'm fine. It was just weird." I debated telling him what Ms. Heliotrope had told me about my health being just fine, but I wasn't sure whether it was okay for me to say anything about it. If she could get in trouble for telling me too much, what would happen to me? I decided to say nothing, though I felt like I was letting my friends down by not telling them anything.

"Man, you've had a rough week. I bet it feels like months," Des replied, typing on his laptop.

"Yup. That's a good way to describe it." I walked past the living room, into the kitchen. "You hungry?"

"No, I'm going out soon to have a late lunch with a developer in the city. We're prepping for a panel at the con this weekend."

"Right, how's that all going?" I pulled a blood sausage from the refrigerator. I figured frying it up like normal sausage would be fine, so I went ahead and did that while I listened to Des.

"The *Midnight Murder Mansion* tournament is all set up, which is good. Nothing to worry about there. But the lead developer on *Vastness of Time* is new—that's the game I've been playing through—and he's a little worried about getting everything perfect. It's just because he's new to game development and he wants things to go well."

Des walked over, perched his laptop on the counter, and sat on a barstool so he could still talk with me while I cooked.

"The game's great, though. They've already done a massive debugging, and the playthrough is pretty fun. You're a time traveler, and you have to go to various points in history to correct changes being made by another time traveler. You can choose to either set everything back the way it's supposed to be or change things how you want and see how the ending works out. It has multiple endings, which is great for repeated gameplay. They're really worried about nothing, in my opinion."

"Sounds good." I tilted the frying pan and slid the sausage onto a plate, then sat down on the stool next to him to see what he was working on. It was profoundly better than thinking about my own problems. "Is this the game?"

"Yeah. The cool thing is, it can be seen as educational because it involves real historical events, but it's not obnoxiously so. See? There are specific points in history you get to travel to, like World War II or the Crusades. You can choose whether your character is a warrior, a spy, a politician, or an assassin and play out historical battles while influencing the development of governments. If you play the game straight and try to maintain the current timestream, the ending has you battling the other time traveler as the final boss. If you play in a way that messes with the timelines, there are three other potential endings. In one, it turns out you were the villain all along, and you're battling yourself as the one who corrected all the timelines."

"That sounds pretty cool." I took a bite of sausage. It was a relief to just talk with Des about fun stuff. I felt a little less worried about my own well-being now, so it was a lot easier to slip back into the usual stuff we'd talk about. Maybe the reason I had been having a hard time finding normalcy was because I'd been looking too hard.

"You think you'll have time to come to the convention one day? Maybe Saturday?" Des suggested.

"Yeah. Saturday sounds great." I was a little surprised Des asked. Conventions were so commonplace for him now that he thought of them more as work. It was rare he'd ask Brian or me to come because he couldn't enjoy them with us.

"Good. I'll have a little free time on Saturday since the competition is on Sunday. I have a costume with a mask so

I can walk around, and we can hang out like we used to before my streams became such a hit."

"You inviting Brian to come along too?"

"Yeah, we should all go. I can get you guys passes and just say you're part of my entourage or something. Then we can just wander around the floor or check out some panels before I have to go to mine. Plus, if it's both of you, you'll be able to keep Brian out of trouble, and he'll be around to keep you entertained."

I had no doubt Des was remembering a past convention when Brian was a little too touchy-feely with a few cos-players and got kicked out. I wasn't too keen on having to babysit Brian.

I sighed. "We'll have to have a 'cosplay isn't consent' conversation with him before we go."

"Yeah. I told him after the incident that if he ever acted like that at a convention again when I'm there in a profes-sional capacity, he's not allowed to come with me anymore."

The front door opened, and a moment later, Brian popped his head in from the hallway. "What up, yo?"

Des and I traded concerned looks.

Des patted the stool next to him. "Brian, my man, come have a seat. We need to have a little discussion."

Brian sighed as he grabbed a paper towel and mopped sweat from his forehead. It was clear he had been doing some kind of physical activity, but he wasn't dressed for running. "What did I do now?" he groused as he sat down.

"What's with the grass stains on your jeans?" I asked.

Brian instantly perked up. "I got a job!"

"What?" Des and I exclaimed simultaneously.

"It's not a big deal. I'm just taking care of Ms. Oswald's yard. She saw me running yesterday, and we talked about me not having a job right now. She's one of Mom's friends, so she said she'd be happy to pay me to trim her hedges, rake her leaves, and mow her lawn every once in a while. It's not a lot, but it's something."

"That's great, Brian!" Des said. "Before you know it, you could have your own gardening business or something like that."

Brian looked a bit bashful. "I don't know about that. But it's nice to have a little spending money."

"Well, save that spending money for this weekend because you and Josh are going to come to the con with me on Saturday."

"Wait, what?" Brian stared at Des in surprise.

"Well, as long as you keep your hands to yourself and refrain from the sexist comments, it's all cool," I mentioned casually. I was still worried that even though we were trying to help him get back on his feet, we wouldn't be able to do enough to repair what was already broken.

"I wasn't that bad!" Brian complained. "Besides, if girls dress up in skimpy cosplay, what am I supposed to say?"

Des gave him a pointed look. "You say, 'Cool costume,' and leave it at that."

"But girls dress up like that because they want attention. You know they do."

"You're verging on incel territory again, Brian," I warned. "The way you act at conventions impacts Des's professional image. It doesn't look good for his friends to treat girls inappropriately at conventions when he prides himself on being a gamer who respects gamers from all walks of life."

"You don't know what it's like to get people to respect me for being a blerd," Des chimed in. "Being a Black man who's into nerdy stuff isn't always easy. It's hard for girls as well. Let's just try to keep the fandom community as welcoming as we can. That's all I ask."

I had a feeling Des was expecting too much from Brian. Or maybe he was expecting too much from me. I wasn't sure how well I could keep Brian's behavior under control.

Brian sighed. "Fine. I'll restrain myself. Can I tell you guys if I think a girl is hot?"

"As long as you're not obnoxious about it, it's fine," I said, my exhaustion clear in my voice. "There's nothing wrong with thinking women are beautiful. You should just be a little less . . . you . . . about it."

"Well, maybe if you were a little more *me* about it, you'd be much further along with Harriet."

"Not cool, Brian," Des said. "You know Josh is dealing with some tough shit lately."

"Yeah? Well, how do you think I feel? Everyone's always telling me what I do wrong and how I'm embarrassing people and making them uncomfortable." Brian slammed his hand on the countertop. "Why do you guys keep making rules for me I never asked for?"

"Brian, you don't do everything wrong; we're just trying to help you learn to be better than what you were taught. Just remember, if you want people to treat you with respect, you have to treat them with respect as well."

While Des still managed to sound patient, I was starting to feel that weird twitchy feeling in my teeth from last night. I really didn't want to do something weird again, especially to a friend.

"Well, that goes both ways," Brian retorted. "Do you guys think I feel respected by you? You treat me like I'm a loser."

I decided to try taking a page out of Des's book. "I'm sure there are people out there who think I'm a loser for delivering pizzas, but if I spent time worrying about the people who think I'm a loser, then I would be a loser."

Brian rolled his eyes, and the tingly feeling in my teeth grew stronger. If he didn't get his shit together, I wasn't sure what I would do.

"It gets better if you practice, man," Des said reassuringly. "Come with us this weekend. Instead of just reacting to people, watch how we interact with them. Maybe you'll find a way to make it work for you."

"Fine. I'm gonna go take a shower now." Brian climbed off the stool and headed toward the stairs.

I was starting to wonder if this convention was actually a good idea. Between Brian's bad attitude and my—whatever my thing was—this could end up being a recipe for disaster. Hopefully, this Saturday would go well, but I wasn't fully convinced.

DAY 8

FRIDAY

So Harriet's going too?" Brian asked as we helped Des get his car packed for the trip into the city. Des would be staying at a hotel because he had to be at the convention all weekend, and he had a couple boxes of promotional items he was taking with him.

One of the boxes held a full steampunk costume with a leather mask and goggles. It reminded me of Ms. Heliotrope and her feral friend from the other night.

"Uh, yeah, she's going," I replied absently, thinking about Ms. Heliotrope. "She said so last night at work. Gino's cousin is in town for the weekend and wants to start his own pizza place, so he's learning the ropes, and Renato and Graziella will do the deliveries. I think Harriet's wearing some kind of cosplay this time. She seemed really excited."

"I wonder what she's going to be," Brian said. "It's hard to think of plain old Harriet wearing something sexy."

Des walked over and lightly slapped Brian on the back of the head. "First of all, not all cosplay has to be sexy, and second, didn't we tell you to chill out on that?"

"Ooh, fancy words, Des," Brian snarked as he put a box in the trunk. "Maybe I'm just getting it out of my system now before the convention."

I hope so. I had my doubts.

"That's it," Des said. "I'm ready to go. See you tomorrow, guys. You know where to go to get your passes and everything?"

"Yeah," I replied. "Your mission briefing is currently in the mess hall and is dutifully being held in place by Officer Bunny Magnet. There's no possible way we could get confused or lost."

"You know I always need to make sure my friends are well taken care of," Des said with a smile. "See you guys tomorrow!"

"Yeah, see you," Brian replied, shutting the trunk. "Tomorrow's gonna be awesome!"

I wasn't as convinced. He might find it fun, but I had a feeling I'd end up chasing him around, putting out fires left and right. Some of them could be real fires, going by past experiences. Maybe I should consider bringing an actual fire extinguisher. Did I have a big enough backpack for one? Would they let me in the door with it? Maybe I should call ahead and see if that hippie candle lady would have a booth again. If she hadn't been right next to the booth selling snow cones, she would have lost a lot more hair.

At least the convention might be an opportunity to dig for info on what was happening to me. Who better than a bunch of nerdy fans to have info on supernatural creatures and strange medical facts? Ms. Heliotrope did say that medical doctors wouldn't be of any help, but nerds weren't often bound by the Hippocratic oath and the fear of malpractice suits. Hopefully, Brian would behave himself just enough that I could explore a little tomorrow.

"What are you doing for the rest of the day, Brian?" I asked as we walked through the front door.

"It seems I'm pretty popular with the old ladies. Ms. Oswald told all her bingo buddies about me working on her yard, and a bunch of them called me yesterday while you were at work. I'm booked for almost the entire day. I'll have so much cash for the convention!" Brian sounded so excited, I didn't have the heart to explain the importance of putting together a budget and contributing to household expenses.

"I have another night of deliveries, so I'll be pretty busy for most of the day too."

"Cool." Brian grabbed his jacket. "I'm heading out, then."

"Bye, Brian," I replied as he rushed out the door.

I had a few hours to kill before heading to work, so I decided to crack open my laptop and do a little searching. I put in the phrase *The Conclave* first, only to find loads of stuff about papal elections and some movie by the same name. I had a feeling the conclave I was searching for had nothing to do with Catholicism, so I continued scrolling for a bit. There were references to some books and tabletop role-playing games, as well as a comic book that looked interesting, but nothing that seemed related to what I was hoping to find. I moved on to *formalist* next. Still nothing that connected with Ms. Heliotrope, but at least I found out it was a synonym for *disciplinarian* or *enforcer*, which fit the sense of her I was beginning to develop.

I started researching some of the symptoms I had but couldn't find anything that connected all of them together in a clear way.

Finally, I gave in and started researching vampires, despite my doubts. I started going through the typical lists of what made a vampire a vampire and took note of the ones that didn't fit me. The first that came up was garlic. I snorted every time I saw it. If that one were true and I really were a vampire, I probably would have died in the front seat of my car with the pizza sitting next to me after my delivery to the mansion. I clearly wasn't having issues with combusting in sunlight. I didn't have some obsessive need to count items dropped on the ground. I didn't need to sleep in a coffin, though if I had, that would have made for a very interesting conversation with Des and Brian regarding why I needed one in my bedroom. I could see my reflection in mirrors, a daily reminder of how ordinary I looked. I could walk past the nearby church and the crucifix on top of it didn't bother me at all.

In searching deeper, I found some things that debunked those myths. Not all vampire myths included being vulnerable to sunlight but rather that they were just more active at night. Maybe they just tried to avoid daylight because it hurt their eyes. With the advent of sunglasses, that could easily be taken care of. The garlic thing was just a folklore concept based on garlic being a home remedy for various illnesses. Many of the ideas about vampires and coffins originated from people not understanding the decomposition process. Not all myths included the lack of a reflection.

By the time I needed to leave for work, I was more confused than I had been. I slammed my laptop shut and tossed it on my bed. What I really wanted to do was hurl it against the wall and have it break apart into tiny, satisfying pieces, but I didn't have the money to replace it unless I dipped into my savings. I was still holding out hope that I'd be normal enough to go to college at some point, and the thought of touching any of that money for anything else made me cringe, even though my laptop could use an upgrade within the next couple of years. Possibly my car too.

I pulled myself together and headed to work. It was a Friday, which meant fewer deliveries and larger orders for parties and get-togethers. I liked working Fridays, as people seemed a little happier to see me and sometimes gave me better tips.

Harriet was already prepping in the kitchen when I walked in the door. "Hey, Josh, looking forward to to-morrow?"

"Looking at you, I'm starting to question if I'm eager enough." She looked like she was almost vibrating in antici-pation. I walked over to the hook where my delivery uniform of Gino's jacket and baseball cap were hanging.

Harriet giggled. "I'm just so excited about this. It's my first time cosplaying, and I worked really hard on my cos-tume. I'm going to surprise so many people! I usually just go in jeans and some fandom tee shirt, but this time, I'm going all out."

"Any hints on what it's going to be?"

She seemed to consider it and looked really tempted to spill the beans, but she stopped herself. "Nope. It has to be a surprise. That's why I'm going alone instead of with you and Brian."

"Will we at least be able to recognize you?" Hopefully, we could find her right away. Maybe having Harriet around would be a good influence on Brian.

"Probably. I'm not wearing a full mask or anything. I won't be wearing my glasses, though. But that's all I'm telling you. We have our meeting place set up, right? You'll find out then."

"I'm sure it will be great."

I really had no idea what to expect. I thought about her past Halloween costumes, which tended toward gory, ama-teur monster makeup with regular street clothes, but with her state of excitement, I had a feeling this was going to be something very different.

As I put on my delivery jacket and hat, I decided to test something on my delivery runs tonight. I wanted to see if I could spot any of the people who were supposedly watching me, according to Ms. Heliotrope.

I took a walk around the restaurant before the first calls came in. Spotting the dumpster, I remembered my first meeting with Ms. Heliotrope and considered that others might find it a good spying spot. I went over to check it out, as well as the trees nearby. Thanks to my crazy cat eyes, I found a small video camera pointing at Gino's on one of the trees, and I immediately took it down. It definitely wasn't one of Gino's security cameras, and there was no other reason for one to be there unless someone was up to no good.

I looked into the tiny lens and waved hello. "Not this one tonight, friends." I crushed it under my shoe, then tossed what was left into the dumpster.

I also spotted a car I'd seen frequently in the parking lot over the past week and realized it was often parked so its rear camera faced the restaurant. I decided to leave it alone, as I didn't need to make another visit to the police station. Besides, the visibility from the camera would be pretty limited, as it pointed downward, and I could just as easily park my car far enough away to be outside its scope of vision. I finished my patrol around the restaurant and came back in.

"How was your stroll, Josh?" asked Gino. "You seemed a little obsessed with that car out there. Looking for something new?"

I was a little startled Gino had noticed. "Uh, yeah, at some point. I've always liked . . ." I looked out at the car, which was just the type of SUV a soccer mom would drive, the exact opposite of the kind of car I'd want. "SUVs. You know . . . because I would have more space for carrying pizza. And those rear cameras are great for safety, right?"

"I never thought I'd get used to those. Made it a lot easier to teach Renato how to parallel park."

"I'll bet," I replied, relieved that Gino had bought my explanation.

"You okay after the other night?" Gino asked. "You don't seem like your normal self—I mean, even less like your normal self than you have been."

"I'm okay. I'm really sorry about what happened with that delivery. I had no idea they'd bring me to the police station and keep me there for so long."

"No problem, Josh. I'd rather you do as the police ask than try something dumb and end up in more trouble. Besides, you did good, kid. You tried to help someone. I was prepared to pick up the slack, just in case."

"Oh, I see. You sent me to clean up the mess, right?" I joked weakly.

"I only send my best pizza deliverers on secret missions," Gino quipped playfully. "But no, I'm glad you're okay. You seemed to be running a little on autopilot that night."

"I'll be fine, I promise." I was about to say something more when the phone rang.

"Sounds like we might have our first delivery." Gino picked up the phone.

Harriet stood poised to get started the moment Gino handed over the order. While my Fridays might be easier in terms of deliveries, her and Gino's work was a lot harder. There generally wasn't a lot of time for talk when they had to make large orders, except to share directions about the orders. I decided not to distract them, so I sat back and waited until it was my turn to get into action.

Gino handed me a couple of larger-sized insulated delivery bags. "This one is for a party at the middle school, Josh."

"On it." I headed out to the car, staying alert for any signs of suspicious people.

As I drove, I started to feel a little stupid for being so paranoid. Why would anyone think my life was so interesting that spying on me would be fun? I could imagine it playing out like one of those wildlife documentaries.

"And here we have an average suburban eighteen-year-old. Notice his unremarkable plumage and secondhand car as he transports himself from his home to his mediocre job. And what's this? He's encountered a female of his species. Will he successfully communicate his interest in mating with her? Once more, he fails to inform her of his interest. Let us move on to a more interesting specimen . . ."

I arrived at the middle school parking lot and quickly made my way to the front office. I was nearly there when I heard the familiar pleasant voice of Ms. Perez, the school secretary, in conversation with a too-beautiful voice that made my skin crawl.

"Mr. Danforth, thank you so much for your donation. This will help us rebuild our multipurpose room this coming summer when school is out."

"Think nothing of it. One must always contribute to the community where one lives," said that rich, persuasive tone. There was something about the voice that made me think of a predator playing with its prey. "Oh, and call me Stephan."

"Of course, Stephan. One must always contribute to the community where one lives," Ms. Perez said, this time a bit flatly. I had a feeling the flatness was caused by Long-Haired

Dude—Stephan Danforth—using his mesmerizing voice on the secretary.

First the high school and now here? It made me nervous. What did Danforth have to gain by donating to the school? To make himself look harmless, like some upstanding member of the community? I was starting to wonder if it was an attempt to gain some sort of control over local government and businesses. I had a feeling he easily could. But why mess with a boring nowhere town like this?

My suspicions didn't really matter, though. I had to go into the very office where he stood, and I wasn't looking forward to it. But I had no choice. I had to do my job.

I took a breath and walked in, a big smile pasted on my face. "Pizza delivery! Where can I put these for you?"

"Oh, look, it's Josh!" Ms. Perez greeted cheerfully. She was one of the sweetest people I'd ever known. Even the fact she still remembered me after all these years meant a lot. It was part of why she was so loved at Willow Springs Middle School. It also made me angrier that Danforth might have used his mesmerizing voice on her.

"Ms. Perez! How are you?" I noticed Danforth observing me carefully and tried to pretend he wasn't there. I picked a pencil up off the counter and started twirling it between my fingers in an effort to focus less on the way he made my skin crawl. I only managed to make it spin a couple of times before it landed unceremoniously on the ground.

"I'm wonderful, thank you," Ms. Perez replied. "You've grown up to be such a handsome young man. Are you working hard?"

I smiled and bent down to pick up the pencil and put it back where I had found it. "Always. Where can I bring these pizzas?"

"Over to the multipurpose room, *mijo*," she said. "You

can bring them to the kitchen so they can be kept warm. There's a dance for the children in about an hour."

I handed her the receipt, and she signed the slip, then handed it to me. Glancing at the tip she'd written in, I realized it was thirty percent.

"Um, Ms. Perez, I think you gave me too big a tip. Are you sure the school can afford this?"

"Don't worry. This kind new member of our community has donated some funds to the school. We have a little to play with, and what better way to use it than to invest in our former students? You're still saving for college, right? You need that tip."

I was reluctant to take any money that might have come from Danforth's hands. "It's really okay—"

"No, none of that, *mijo*. I'm just happy to see you again, knowing you're working toward improving your future." She patted my cheek. "You were always such a good boy."

I glanced at Danforth, who seemed to find the whole exchange highly amusing. I didn't want to give him any more satisfaction, so I decided to just get the pizzas delivered and leave as soon as possible. "Thank you, Ms. Perez. It was good to see you again."

"You too, Josh."

I fled the office as fast as I could, hoping more distance between Danforth and me would ease the knot building in my stomach. I arrived at the multipurpose room in record time. Some students were there putting up streamers and balloons, chatting and giggling with each other.

"Oh, hey, it's that cool pizza guy!" exclaimed one kid.

Looking around, I spotted one of the kids who had made the prank call to Gino's last week. "Oh, hey! This time you get pizza with extra cheese and pepperoni at the same time, and you don't even have to pay for it."

"Oh, man, you guys make the best pizza. Can I have a piece now?"

"Sorry, no can do. These need to go to the kitchen. But you'll have some later, I'm sure."

Another kid approached, looking a little sheepish. She twirled a strand of hair around her finger. "Um, we should apologize. You know, for the prank call."

"It's okay. It was kind of fun. Besides, you called when we weren't busy, so it didn't cause us any trouble." I knocked on the door to the kitchen. "And you also ended up buying a pizza, so in the long run, you helped us."

"I guess so," the girl said, "but we didn't give you a tip."

The boy joined in. "Oh, yeah, we should have given you a tip."

"Don't worry. Your school just gave me a pretty nice tip, so that makes up for it." One of the cafeteria workers opened the door, and I began to hand her pizza boxes from the insulated carriers. "Just make sure you have a good time tonight with your friends and eat plenty of pizza so they order more next time you have a dance."

"Seth has a bottomless stomach," the girl joked, "so that won't be much of a challenge."

The boy looked irritated. "Shut up, Carrie!"

The girl sighed. "Seth, he wants you to eat more pizza. It's a good thing!" I had a feeling that between the two of them, she was the one with the brains.

"Oh, right." Seth gave me a salute. "I won't back down from my duty, sir!"

I tried to withhold my laughter as I finished handing the pizzas over. "Good man. Have a fun night."

"We will, if the boys actually dance with us," Carrie said.

I walked away, listening to them bicker playfully. It brought back memories of the first dance I had attended there. All the boys had been on one side of the room, and the girls had either giggled in the corners or danced with each other. Looking back now, we probably looked pretty stupid standing around like that.

I waved at Ms. Perez as I passed by the front office, noting that Danforth wasn't there anymore. Heaving a sigh of relief, I exited the school and headed toward the parking lot. My relief was short-lived, however, because Danforth was leaning against the driver's side door of my car, pushing his dark sunglasses back up the bridge of his nose.

"Joshua Buckmilter. You could use a new car. This thing looks like it's on its last legs." He gave the front tire a kick. The car responded with a groan.

I winced. He wasn't wrong. The tires were a bit bald. The rearview mirror didn't always stay attached. Sometimes it had a funny smell that had nothing to do with pizza. Then there was the time a bunch of wasps tried to make a nest in the crack of the back left door, which led me to "accidentally" denting the door with a baseball bat before Des could get the wasp spray from the garage. And the time a cat somehow got in and decided to give birth to kittens in the back seat, which left a stain I'd never been able to remove. I was still confused how that had happened.

"That's for me to decide." I opened the trunk to put the empty insulated bags inside. I was still scared of him, but I felt angry too.

"You're quite stubborn, aren't you?" Danforth said. "That's a good thing. We enjoy watching you squirm. A few people have already lost their bets, but they're still having fun."

I slammed the trunk shut. As if perfectly timed, the rearview mirror fell from its place inside the windshield. "What bet? Why are you all toying with me?"

"If I told you why, I'd lose the bet." He smirked. "Why would I want to ruin my chances?"

"Of course you won't give me answers. Nobody seems to want to tell me anything."

"Ah, did Heliotrope only give you half answers? Everything by the book with her, it seems. Thank goodness for that. At least she won't ruin the bet with her interference." He stepped away from the car. "Oh, and that camera you destroyed? It's already been replaced. There are plenty more too. We even have some up at your father's house and that girl's—the one who makes the pizza. That's been the most entertaining part of this: watching you get all nervous around the girl you like. You're quite the amateur."

I could feel that strange twitching in my gums again as my blood began to boil. I suspected he was trying to make me angry on purpose with his smug attitude, though, so I held back. "I need to get back to work," I grumbled, stepping around him to open my car door.

"A word of advice?" he asked nonchalantly.

"I have a feeling you'll give it to me whether I want it or not." I climbed into the front seat.

"I will. Don't get wrapped up in Heliotrope's plans. She's just as twisted as the rest of us."

He walked away. He painted such a dramatic picture, the debonair hero telling the victim they were putting their trust in the wrong place, then walking off into the sunset. But his words fell flat. Since he had never proven himself to be trustworthy, there was no reason for me to follow his so-called advice.

One odd thought did occur to me, though: maybe he was afraid of Ms. Heliotrope.

Something about that made me feel powerful. They were keeping information from me because they didn't want me to know what was going on, whether it was this bet of theirs or a much bigger, more sinister plot. And obviously, he didn't want Ms. Heliotrope knowing, if he felt he had to warn me away from her.

I drove back to work, thoughts swirling. After a while, I realized I wasn't paying extra attention to see if I was being watched, so I did my best to focus. I didn't really have much basis for figuring out who was watching me, so I just tried to make note of cars that seemed familiar or the faces of people who glanced at me while I was driving. I didn't like being this paranoid, but I didn't know what else to do.

When I got back to Gino's, I went out to the tree near the dumpster. Sure enough, there was another camera waiting for me. I spoke into the new camera. "I can do this all night if you want. It's your funeral."

I crushed that one as well and threw it in the dumpster to join the first.

The evening became a test of wills. Each time I went out to make a delivery, I would come back to a new camera in the tree. A couple of times, I found the camera in a slightly different place, and each time, I made a snarky comment. I was starting to feel bad about being so wasteful, but at the same time, I didn't want them to think I'd let them get the upper hand. I even searched my car during my break and found a camera hidden in one of the vents. It joined the others in the dumpster. After that, I was even more convinced there was probably a tracker on my car somewhere, but wherever it was hidden, I couldn't find it.

I came in from my break to find Harriet looking concerned. "Uh, Josh, what's going on?"

"What do you mean?"

"You've been kind of jumpy tonight. You keep going

out to the dumpster with nothing, then coming back. You searched your car during your entire break. I'm getting worried."

The concern on her face made me feel horrible. Up until then, I had been pretty honest with everyone about my weird changes. This time, though, I wasn't sure if I could tell her the whole truth. If I had been able to take down a man larger than me the other night, clearly Danforth, Genevieve, and the others could hurt Harriet too.

"Harriet, there are some other things going on with me. Not just the weird health changes. I don't know how to explain it, and I'm not sure I know enough that I can, but please trust me. I know things look strange, and I'm probably acting a little odd. I just want to make sure everyone's safe."

The doubtful expression on her face made me nervous. She must have noticed because she sighed. "Okay, Josh. I'll back off for now. But I want you to know that if you need help with anything at all, you can tell me. I'm your friend, and I want to help. I like helping you. So please, if there's anything I can do, let me know."

The hurt in her eyes broke my heart. "I promise, as soon as I know something I can tell you, I will."

"Okay," she said, still with a tone of doubt.

"I'm sorry, Harriet. I really do trust you, and I want to do my best for you." Harriet's reaction made me wonder if my behavior was more erratic than I'd thought it was. Maybe it wasn't worth it to keep searching for monitoring equipment. They knew I was aware of them watching me, and that might be enough. Seeing her worry made me feel guilty.

"I know you do, Josh." With another sigh, she hugged me.

With her hair smelling like garlic, pepperoni, and warm pizza crust, it felt like I was in heaven. I still felt bad that I couldn't tell her more, though.

She pulled out of the hug and poked me in the chest playfully. "Let's keep up the pace tonight, okay? No more random trips to the dumpster unless you actually have to take garbage out."

Remembering the boy from earlier at the middle school, I gave her a salute. "I won't back down from my duty, ma'am!"

She chuckled. "Okay, back to work." She ducked back into the kitchen and began to help Gino, who had another stack of pizzas for me to deliver.

By the end of the night, I was emotionally drained. Things were getting way too complicated, and I just wanted to enjoy my time with my friends tomorrow.

I brought the trash out to the dumpster and decided to check the tree one last time. The camera hadn't been replaced. It was a tiny victory, but a victory nonetheless. If I could just wear away at them, then maybe—eventually— everything would finally be revealed.

I walked back inside and found Harriet getting her jacket on. "You sure you don't want to ride with me and Brian tomorrow?"

"Nope! It has to be a surprise. Now go get to bed so you can get up early and arrive on time." To my relief, Harriet was back to her usual bright self. We walked out to our cars together.

"If you insist," I replied. "I'll see you tomorrow at the con, then."

"Tomorrow it is."

DAY 9, PART 1

SATURDAY

I was exhausted enough that I managed to get a decent night's sleep . . . which was good because it was a little over an hour to get to the city, and I would be driving the whole way. I knocked on Brian's door to wake him up.

"Ugh, I don't wanna get up," he groused.

"But the conven—"

Brian slammed open the door. "Let's get going!" He darted out of his room, still in his pajamas.

I blocked him from getting to the stairs. "Wait, wait, not so fast. We still have a little time to get ready. Get dressed. I'll get some breakfast together. Then we can get going."

Brian scratched his head. "Oh, right, gotta dress up for the ladies."

"No, got to get dressed so people don't think you're a weirdo who wears his—no, wait, we're going to a convention. If you go wearing pajamas, people will probably think you're in cosplay."

Of course, Brian hadn't heard me at all because he'd gone back into his room and shut the door to get dressed. I had to admit, I was happy about that. He was taking an interest in his appearance, which he hadn't for a few months now. Maybe I wasn't giving him enough credit.

Then I remembered that one of his favorite con shirts consisted of the faces of a bunch of anime girls looking like they were having orgasms. "Do *not* wear the ahegao shirt!" I yelled through the door.

"Aw, man, really?" came his muffled reply through the door.

"Really. You'll piss off too many girls without even opening your mouth if you wear that one."

He peeked his head around the edge of the door. "Hmm . . ." Then he closed the door.

I took a quick shower so I wouldn't smell like pizza, then got dressed myself. I found Brian sitting at the dining room table wearing a surprisingly presentable jeans-and-tee-shirt combination. Walking around the table, I saw the shirt pictured a mecha from an anime, much to my relief.

Brian gave me a slightly critical look. "I thought you were going to get breakfast ready."

I was tempted to remind him he was perfectly capable of making his own breakfast, but I didn't want to start the day on the wrong foot. "I am. I just didn't want to smell like pizza all day."

I walked into the kitchen and quickly pulled out ingredients for scrambled eggs for Brian and some blood sausage for me.

"That makes sense. I took a shower last night. Gotta impress the ladies."

I was worried about Brian's focus on "the ladies." I put a frying pan on the stove and walked over to Brian to make sure we made eye contact as I spoke. "It's not about impressing the ladies. It's about not offending them. Is that clear?"

"Clear as water!" Brian replied enthusiastically. I had my doubts, though, and his next words only confirmed them. "But if I impress them, that's even better, right?"

"I think it's best if we focus on keeping it simple. Be polite. That's all you need to do today." I went back to the kitchen and began making breakfast.

"Polite's easy. I can do that," Brian answered. "I practice all the time with the old ladies who have me work on their yards. Hey, did Harriet say what her cosplay was going to be?"

"She said it was a surprise," I shouted back over the sizzling coming from the pan "All she told me was she wasn't going to be wearing a mask and she wouldn't be wearing her glasses either."

"Huh." Brian sat down on one of the barstools at the kitchen counter. "I wonder why it's such a big surprise."

"I guess we'll just have to wait to find out." I brought over our food.

Brian dug in immediately and began talking at the same time. "I beh ih shomfik eky."

I finished a bite of sausage. "What?"

Brian swallowed his bite. "Nothing. I'm just going to focus on eating right now so we can leave faster."

"Okay." I ate my sausage as I considered Brian. He was a little too eager, and "eky" could have been him trying to say *sexy*, which worried me even more. I didn't want him saying anything to Harriet that upset her. I figured I upset her enough last night with my paranoid behavior.

After eating, I tossed a few things into my backpack: emergency sunglasses, emergency blood sausage sandwich, emergency hoodie, emergency first aid kit, emergency electrolyte drinks . . . It didn't take that long to put everything together, but Brian was breathing down my neck the entire time. It was like he had this aura of tense excitement oozing out of his pores. I was starting to wonder if he'd spend half the trip asking, "Are we there yet?"

"Okay, I'm set. You?" I zipped up my backpack, hoping I had everything I needed. I just wasn't sure what I would need. Should I have brought a straightjacket, in case I lost it like I had the other night during the pizza delivery?

Before I could turn around to face Brian, he was already out the front door, whooping. "Yes! Let's go!"

I grabbed the info Des had left on the refrigerator and followed Brian out to my car. The key fob no longer worked, so I had to manually unlock each door. I decided to tease Brian a little by taking my time settling into the front seat before unlocking the door for him.

While Brian hopped into his seat at record speed, I wondered about my sudden desire to poke at him. I had been feeling so ambivalent toward him lately, yet because the day was supposed to be fun, I wanted to capture part of what had made our friendship worthwhile since we first started hanging out together as kids. I realized our friendship had broken down significantly since we all moved in with Des, and I wasn't sure I knew how to have fun with Brian anymore when it was just him and me.

I drove for a while trying to figure out how to make this experience as fun as possible, while Brian messed with the radio. He pulled out a printout of all the panels and booths that were going to be at the convention and immediately started debating which were worth checking out. He must have noticed I wasn't paying attention because he waved his hand in front of my face.

"Earth to Josh! Did you hear me?"

"Oh, uh, yeah." I pushed his hand out of the way so I could see the road. "What panel were you talking about?"

Brian sighed. "There's this one about vampire folklore you should go to."

I almost sighed, too, when I realized what he was talking about. "Brian, there's no proof that what's happening to me is supernatural." Though I had similar suspicions, I didn't feel comfortable with Brian knowing what was really going on yet. He was the type to freak out and tell everyone, whether I was ready for that or not. And after what Ms. Heliotrope had told me the other day, I wasn't sure it was a good idea for the whole town to know.

"I know, but this one is a debate on what is fact and what is fiction. Even the description states they're looking at real medical conditions that used to be mistaken for vampirism. Don't you think that's maybe worth going to?" He poked at the description as though it proved his point.

He wasn't wrong. "Okay, I'll check it out. What about you? Anything you really want to see?"

"Well, you know, I'm all about the la—"

Brian stopped and sat up a little straighter, as if it would make him seem more mature. "I want to see Des's panel, of course, and maybe try a few prototype games. And there are a few panels about movies based on some games."

I noted the way he'd corrected himself. If he was this stuck on flirting with girls, despite our discussion earlier, I had a lot of work ahead of me. I was glad Harriet was going to be there, though; she could help keep him a little more contained on that subject.

Brian spent the rest of the trip reading off some of the panels and talking about games, only stopping occasionally to do air guitar or air drumming to the music playing on the radio. We eventually made it to a parking lot near the convention center and got into the will-call line without too much fuss.

"Damn, look at her!" Brian poked me as he pointed out a woman dressed as Corporal Westmoreland of PsyAgency from the *Rictus Horizon* gaming franchise.

I almost groaned and began to lecture him again when I took a second look. The woman's back was to us, so all I could see was red-streaked wavy brown hair tumbling over her shoulders, held back by a pair of futuristic-looking goggles. She wore a skintight black uniform with red piping. I honestly couldn't blame Brian for reacting the way he had. She turned to talk with someone in a similar uniform, and my jaw dropped.

"Harriet?"

She immediately turned and gave me a grin like a ray of sunshine breaking through heavy storm clouds. She said goodbye to the people she had been speaking with and ran over.

"Hi, guys!" She hugged us both. "Surprise!"

"Harriet, you look like a queen who needs my p—"

She squeezed Brian's lips together between her thumb and forefinger. "Brian, I know what you're going to say, and that's not appropriate. Now, I'm going to remove my hand, and you're going to do better, okay?"

Brian's eyes were wide as he nodded. Harriet let go, only for him to say, "—een."

"Brian!" Harriet and I said simultaneously.

"Come on! We're friends. It shouldn't count."

Harriet crossed her arms in front of her chest and gave him a stern look. "Brian, if I don't like it when other guys make crass comments like that, I'd rather not hear them from you either."

"It's just a joke," Brian grumbled.

"If you want to make jokes, please either keep them to yourself or make sure they're clean. People bring their kids to these things." I gestured to a nearby family with two bouncy kids dressed as characters from a popular cartoon. I then gave Harriet a smile. "You look great, by the way. Those goggles look so accurate to the game."

Harriet grinned. "I worked for months on them. I also had the boots custom made with pockets to carry a few PsyAgency gadgets." She reached down to a small zippered pouch on the side of her knee-high boots and pulled out one of the game's most common tools, a psychic amplifier that fit in the character's ear. "I don't have everything I want for the costume, but this is a good start."

I held up the detailed accessory to admire it. "This is really impressive, Harriet. Why didn't you tell me you were working on this?"

"Well, it's my first cosplay, and I wanted it to be perfect before I showed anyone." I looked back at her face and realized she was even wearing red contact lenses like the character did in the game.

I handed the accessory back to her. "Well, I'm impressed. You look great."

She gave me a huge hug, and I must have blushed because Brian rolled his eyes. Harriet didn't seem to notice, though.

Harriet must have made a lot of friends as a frequent convention-goer, as several people who knew her stopped by to say hello and talk about past events. I almost wished I weren't so careful with money and could go to these more often, just so I could hang out with her more. She introduced a few of her friends to us, and by the time we got to the ticket booth, we had already been invited to play a fantasy tabletop game, attend two parties in hotel rooms, and go out to eat lunch and dinner with various people.

Once we got inside the building, Brian stopped at the men's room. Harriet and I stood in the lobby to wait for him.

"You know, I can take over if you need a break from herding Brian," Harriet offered.

I smiled weakly. "Thanks. I might need it."

She fiddled with one of the zippers on her costume. "How are you, by the way?"

"Still weird, but I think I'm getting used to it, at least." I wanted to say more, but I remembered Ms. Heliotrope's emphasis on secrecy. The last thing I wanted was for someone to come after Harriet because I had said something I shouldn't have.

Harriet gave me a look that was difficult to read. It was kind, but there seemed to be a touch of fear or maybe worry. "Just remember I'm here for you, okay?"

I felt guilty for not spilling my guts about everything, so I hugged her instead. "Thanks, Harriet."

"What are you two lovebirds doing?" came Brian's voice from behind us.

We quickly pulled apart and looked away from each other. Brian had a way of making things feel awkward, and this was no exception.

"Oh, come on. I can at least make a joke like that, right?" He pulled out a map and started walking toward the dealers' room. "Let's go, guys. There's games to play and merch to buy."

I was relieved he'd changed the subject so quickly, and Harriet and I followed after. Almost immediately after entering the dealers' room, Brian stopped in his tracks, staring at a booth with an expression of utter surprise. In fact, he stopped so suddenly, Harriet and I both walked into him and nearly fell flat on our asses.

"Brian? You okay there?" Harriet looked at the display

of tiny armored knights sitting on the backs of different mythical creatures.

"It's—oh, man. Holy bananas wearing kilts! It's them!" Brian became absolutely giddy.

"Bananas wearing kilts?" Harriet whispered to me. All I could do was shrug.

Brian saw our confusion and immediately grabbed me by the arm. "You know! Remember that video game I used to play that nobody seemed to know a thing about? *Lazer Knights of the Cryptic Kingdom?*"

I furrowed my brow. The name didn't sound familiar, but I did remember Brian having a weird obsession with an obscure video game back in sixth grade. Neither Des nor I had played it with him because it was a single-player game and he'd refused to loan it out. "Maybe?"

He scoffed and grabbed Harriet's arm, pulling her along to join him at the booth. I followed. Whatever this was, it made Brian happy and kept him occupied, so who was I to complain.

"This one is Lord Grikton! He starts the game with a regular horse, but look! This one has him with Flurin the centaur! It's extremely rare! And here's Mistress Minton with her kelpie stallion. And—oh, no way! No way!" Brian gently picked up a knight riding the back of a hydra.

"Oh, you have a good eye!" said the guy behind the booth as Brian cradled the little figure as if it were the most precious treasure in the world. "That's—"

"King Octon and his hydra, Argon!" Brian finished.

Harriet and I traded confused shrugs.

Brian started crying. "This may be the best day of my entire life! I used to have one of these, and my dad threw it out as punishment for not eating my dinner one night. It was my favorite!"

Normally, I wasn't one to look down on someone else's fandom, but I had absolutely no idea what this was all about. But hey, if it made Brian happy, maybe he'd behave better for the rest of the day.

"Well, that one is on the rare side," the vendor explained, taking in Brian's somewhat slovenly appearance. "Not as rare as Lord Grikton, for sure, but it doesn't come cheap. Since the game wasn't popular, there weren't many of these made, so they're a pretty big collector's item."

"I'll take it!" Brian exclaimed.

"But I haven't told you how much it costs ye—"

"I don't care! It's mine!" Brian looked about ready to pop. He pulled out his wallet and handed it to the vendor. "Just take whatever's in there that will cover it."

Harriet immediately took the wallet back and made the transaction for Brian, whose face had shown more expression over this single tiny figurine than I'd seen him show in months.

"Uh, yeah, here's the box and a bag to carry it in." The vendor handed them to Harriet. Even he seemed a little overwhelmed by Brian's obsession.

"Thanks," I told the vendor as Brian carefully put the figure into its box. He made sure to place it in the packaging as lovingly and delicately as possible and then gently placed the box in his bag.

"No problem, kid. He's the first person who's recognized what these are. I wasn't sure I'd be able to sell any of them, compared to the rest of my stuff. Take a card. If he wants more of the collection, I'm happy to sell." The vendor gave me a card and a small catalog, which I tucked into my backpack.

The morning went well due to Brian's elevated mood. We all got to try *Vastness of Time*. Not only was it as cool as it had sounded, it even managed to keep Brian too distracted to act too inappropriately with anyone.

The best part was the panel for the upcoming *Rictus Horizon* movie. One of the actors spotted Harriet's costume in the crowd and complimented her on how accurate it was. When the panel ended, the actor asked her for a photo together so she could share it with the the cast who weren't there. Harriet inadvertently became a minor celebrity and kept getting stopped for photos after that.

About halfway through the day, I realized the panel on vampires was going to start. Brian and Harriet wanted to see some voice actors at another panel, so we arranged a meeting spot and I went to the panel alone.

"I disagree! It was simply people trying to explain obsessive-compulsive disorder!" said a voice as I opened the door to the panel, which had already begun. Three people sat on the stage, already arguing. I sneaked in and took a seat in the back. A couple of rows in front of me, a man wore an outfit covered with so many buckles, I wondered if they were a precaution against his clothes falling apart. His long gray hair hung down the back of the chair, and he kept laughing silently at the arguments of the panelists. A snicker broke free when they discussed vampiric aversion to religious symbols.

The longer I sat there, the more I focused on the strange man in front of me. There was something familiar about him, but at the same time, I couldn't recognize him. If he was someone I knew, his outfit was clearly very different from his usual clothing choices.

"What about walking in daylight?" asked one of the panelists. "Is that just a modern interpretation of vampires due to popular films, or does that go back further? Do vampires really combust in sunlight?"

The man in front of me outright laughed this time. I'd heard that laugh before. I was completely focused on him now, ignoring the panel.

"They don't combust. They just don't like daylight because it hurts their sensitive eyes," the guy said under his breath with a familiar chuckle.

Realization dawned on me. He was definitely wearing a wig because the last time I had seen him, he had short dark hair and glasses and looked decidedly less goth and decidedly more like a geeky doctor.

It was Dr. Chen.

I decided this would be a great time to play spy. If Ms. Heliotrope couldn't give me all the answers I was looking for, maybe he would slip up. Just the fact he was acting like a backseat expert at a vampire panel said a lot.

The panel continued to discuss other topics. Dr. Chen laughed again when they brought up a study that had calculated that life as we knew it would be over if vampires really existed. "They really don't need that much blood," he snarked. "Not even the young ones."

He must have thought he was safe from being overheard, as the whole back section of the room was empty aside from the two of us. He didn't seem to notice I had sat myself a little ways behind him and could hear everything he said. It helped that the seating area was dark, so the focus was on the well-lit stage.

I paid attention to every comment he mumbled. Every little bite of snark lined up with what I had been experiencing for the past week and a half. He even mentioned a few things I hadn't realized. Focused hearing was one of them, which was probably why I could hear what he was mumbling even though his back was to me and I was a couple of rows behind him. Most myths seemed to be based on people trying to explain things they didn't really understand, while the more practical, medical explanations made more sense. Everything lined up with the research I had been doing the other day.

Once the panel was over, the lights came on over the audience. Dr. Chen stood and stretched his arms over his head. "Well, that was entertaining."

"It was, wasn't it, Dr. Chen?"

He jumped, then turned and smiled at me nervously. "Who's Dr. Chen? My name is Wolfram. Wolfram von Raven."

He'd certainly gone all out on his costume; I would never have recognized him if not for his voice. He was wearing a long, artfully shaggy gray wig, and his glasses had been replaced with contacts. His outfit wasn't cheap either. The jacket looked and smelled like it was made of real leather, and the silk ruffled-collar shirt he wore underneath it looked like quality material. I was starting to wonder if maybe I should try studying medicine in college if he got paid well enough to afford it all. I could almost believe his name really was Wolfram von Raven and that he lived in a haunted castle in a distant land.

I glared, and he quickly conceded. "Fine, it's me. How have you been, Josh?"

I smiled knowingly. I didn't want to let on that I was still processing everything I'd heard and hadn't quite absorbed the idea that Brian was right and I'd been turned into a vampire. "Oh, I've been fine. Just, you know, turning into a vampire and all gives a guy an appetite." I felt that strange pressure in my gums that I'd experienced before and realized it was probably my canines protruding a bit. I gave him a bigger grin, hoping I was right and that it would freak him out.

Dr. Chen's face went pale with an expression of panic. "Oh, uh, just now? That's just . . . that was just me . . . joking, you know?"

I raised an eyebrow. "Really? I'll have to ask Jocelyn if you're normally the joking type . . . or maybe Ms. Heliotrope? I bet she knows you pretty well."

A strange, strangled sound came from his throat, then he sat back down. In unspoken agreement, we waited until the last of the audience members had left. Once they were gone, I spoke up again.

"It's true, isn't it?"

"You heard everything I said, right?" Dr. Chen pulled off his wig in a gesture of defeat. "Damn it! They're never going to turn me now, I just know it."

"I was a little late. I hadn't realized I had enhanced hearing, so thanks for letting me know that." I got up from my seat and climbed over the chairs in front of me to sit closer to him.

"Yeah, that one tends to build up over time, so it won't be at maximum until—" He suddenly stopped talking, dropped his wig to the floor, and reached for my shoulders. "You can't tell anyone I let that slip. Heliotrope would bring me before the Conclave, and who knows what they'd do to me." He shook visibly, and a bead of sweat trickled down the side of his face. I noted he also wore contacts that looked similar to the way my eyes looked in the sunlight.

"Do you know why this happened to me?" I hoped beyond hope I could get as much information out of him as possible before the next panel started.

"If I say anything about that, Genevieve and Danforth would definitely kill me . . . or worse. I'd rather face the Conclave." Dr. Chen reached up to wipe away the bead of sweat, only to smudge his pale makeup and leave a streak of his natural skin color showing. His hair was starting to come loose from under his wig cap, which only made him look even more the nervous wreck.

"So they're definitely the ones who changed me?"

He covered his mouth with his hands. "Damn, I shouldn't have said that. Forget I said that."

"Too late." I decided to push him. "What did they do exactly? And if you don't tell me, I'll tell Ms. Heliotrope, Genevieve, and Danforth that you were being less than cautious."

He gulped audibly, his eyes wide enough it looked like his contacts would pop out on their own. "Fine! Fine, I'll tell you! Genevieve and Danforth have been doing this for years. They find some unsuspecting average person, mesmerize them so they don't remember what happened, and then take bets. They take bets on whether the human will turn feral or survive the change and become a full vampire. They bet on when the human will figure out what happened to them and when they'll make their first kill." He sighed. "They're genuinely awful people. They do it because they're bored. Living for centuries can turn perfectly okay people into assholes."

I was stunned. Then I remembered Danforth mentioning a bet back in the middle school parking lot. "They did it as a bet?"

Dr. Chen nodded.

"What the fuck?" I was shocked. It was all a stupid prank. They'd destroyed my life for a stupid bet because they were bored. They'd torn my future apart for a cheap thrill. My canines twinged again.

"Josh, you need to calm down," Dr. Chen said placatingly. He leaned down to grab his wig and placed it haphazardly on his head. "When fledgling vampires get angry, they tend to attack others before they realize what they're doing."

It was like he'd poured a bucket of cold water over my head. That explained a lot about what had happened during the delivery trip a few nights ago. I'd attacked the man before I realized what I was doing. I sat back and grabbed the sides of the chair I was sitting in, hoping it would prevent me from grabbing anyone and trying the same thing again.

"Is that why you helped me at the store?" I asked as he struggled with his wig. One of the buckles on his sleeve had gotten caught in it, which only made him look more ridiculous.

"Yes, I'm kind of a human servant to the local formalists. I help them get blood so they don't have to feed off humans or other animals, and they help control the vampire population."

I got irritated watching Dr. Chen slowly become more and more entangled in his wig, so I reached out to help him. He flinched, but when I rolled my eyes, he gave in. I helped unravel the hair from the buckle, then got the wig straightened out on his head.

"So what does this all mean for me?"

Dr. Chen patted his wig a couple of times. "Well, as long as you behave yourself, they might let you live. They've been trying to catch Genevieve and Danforth for centuries without proper proof, so the Conclave will probably ask you to testify if they can make a trial happen. If you do, it's a lot more likely they'll let you live as thanks. Maybe."

"Well, I guess that's good?"

"Look, Josh, you have to keep this a secret, okay? You can't make it obvious you know what you've become. Maybe hold off for a couple more days and then let Heliotrope know that you know. That way, I won't get in trouble." He leaned closer. "I already did you a favor by recommending rare meat, right? Out of the kindness of my heart?"

I had to admit, he had a point. "Fine. I'll wait. I have another question, though. How often do they run these bets?"

"Eh, it depends. Sometimes it can be a few decades; sometimes it's a few weeks. Vampires tend to lose track of time since it's pretty meaningless to them."

"That probably makes it easier for them to avoid getting caught too. No pattern of behavior that law enforcement can follow."

"Right." Dr. Chen stood as several people started entering the room for the next panel. "I should go. Remember your promise, okay, Josh? I'll bring you some blood later this week if you do."

I didn't like the idea of drinking blood, but Dr. Chen looked a bit shaken and, honestly, a little scared of me. None of this was really his fault. He'd even tried to help me, so I couldn't really be that mad at him. "Fine, fine." I stood and started moving between chairs toward the exit.

Dr. Chen scrambled to follow. "Thank you, Josh. I knew you were one of the decent ones." He stopped me to shake my hand energetically. "It will be good to have you on the team."

He darted out of the room so quickly, I couldn't see a sign of his obnoxious wig anywhere once I made it out myself. It didn't really matter, though. I had answers now. I didn't like those answers, but at least I knew what was going on.

I walked down the hall a little ways before realizing I was going in the wrong direction. I turned around and walked back so I could head toward the meeting spot to find Brian and Harriet.

What was I going to tell my friends? What was I going to tell my dad? "Hey, everyone, I'm a vampire now" wasn't exactly a normal conversation starter. Plus, if I told them, would that get them in trouble? Would that put them in danger? On top of all that, Brian had been right. He had actually guessed correctly. If I told him the truth, he'd be so proud he was right, he wouldn't be able to keep it to himself. That would only cause more problems.

"Hey, Josh, you okay?" Harriet called from nearby. I turned and realized I had just walked past our meeting spot because I was so lost in thought.

"Uh, yeah, I'm good. The panel was boring enough it made me sleepwalk," I joked. "How was your panel?"

"Oh, it was so much fun! One of the voice actors had been on the panel for *Rictus Horizon* earlier, and he asked if I was interested in a career as a costume designer for movies."

"Yeah," Brian interrupted. "And get this: one of them said they had the same tee shirt as me."

I faked a smile so I wouldn't ruin their fun. "That sounds awesome! Hopefully the next panel I go to will be better than the last."

"It better be." Harriet took my arm. "You didn't come all this way just to take naps during panels."

I covered her hand with mine. A heavy weight settled on my chest as I realized I had no chance of a normal life with Harriet now. "I'm sure it will."

DAY 9, PART 2

SATURDAY

As I walked with Harriet's arm twined around mine, I was hit with the thought that this was all so epically unfair. If someone had asked me a couple of weeks ago how I would feel walking arm in arm with Harriet at a convention like this, I would have been over the moon. But now all I could feel was a dark chasm growing in my mind and every single thing I wanted out of my boring, simple life being chucked into that never-ending blackness, with no chance of retrieval.

I had never felt so completely alone. The idea that I had some weird medical issue had been bad, but it was nowhere near as isolating as the thought that I'd probably outlive every person in that cavernous room. They'd be ashes, and I'd still be an eighteen-year-old pizza delivery guy with no future. What kind of future could I have, really? Sure, I could probably go to school, get a degree, and work for a few years. But after that, what? People would start to notice I didn't age. While they got their first gray hairs, some laugh lines around their eyes, maybe a little arthritis . . . I'd be the same.

I wanted to cry and rage and scream. I wanted to get in

my car, drive back to Willow Springs, drive up to that looming mansion on Fairview, and destroy everything. I wanted to fall on my knees and beg them to take it back, to make me normal again. I wanted to ask them why. Why make me one of them when they could have taken someone like Dr. Chen, who was clearly far more interested in vampires than I'd ever been? He would have been happy to be Wolfram von Raven for the rest of his existence.

I just wanted to live a normal life, get married, have a few kids, and grow old. I had no expectations outside that.

Now it was just a pipe dream.

"Josh, what's Brian doing over there?" Harriet asked.

I looked up and saw him talking with two girls. I sighed. Part of me wanted to say, "Fuck it," and let Brian get himself kicked out of the convention like he had last time. But even though I felt like my world was ending, I knew that wasn't the right thing to do.

"Let's get him before he causes any problems," I told Harriet.

She let go of my arm and nodded. "Let's be delicate about it, though. I think it's better to let him at least try to practice better social skills before we cut him off."

I shrugged. "He has to learn sometime."

We approached the booth where he was talking with the girls. One looked a little put off, while the other looked like she was trying to be nice. As we got closer, I started to make out what he was saying over the noise of the crowd.

"Yeah, I used to run track in high school, but I kind of hit a low point and stopped. I'm working on getting back in shape, though, and I've already lost a few pounds. Just a few more weeks, and I'll have abs for days."

I cringed and listened to the nice girl's response. "Well, good for you. It's important to have goals."

It was clear she wasn't really interested in what he had to say. Her friend rolled her eyes as she pretended to look at some stickers on the table at the front of the booth.

Not picking up on their cues, Brian kept going. "You know, if you want, we can go get a room and have some fun on our own . . ."

Jesus Christ, Brian. I made a move to step in, but Harriet beat me to it.

"Hey, didn't we meet at another convention?" Harriet asked the nice girl, gesturing for me to grab Brian. "I think you were dressed as a steampunk version of Alice in Wonderland."

The nice girl immediately smiled at Harriet. "Yes, I did! You look vaguely familiar. Do you usually wear glasses?"

"Yes, I'm Harriet. That costume was amazing. Are you planning on wearing more cosplay this weekend?"

The other girl turned to face Harriet, and the three of them instantly began chatting like old friends. I took advantage of the situation to pull Brian aside. Once I'd gotten him a few feet away, he jerked his arm out of my grip.

"What are you doing?" he hissed, rubbing his arm. "Are you trying to twist my arm off?"

My already tempestuous mood must have made me grip Brian a little too hard as I dragged him away from embarrassing himself. "Sorry, Brian. You just—" I pinched the bridge of my nose. "Brian, you won't pick up any girls like that. You need to read their body language and stop talking about only yourself. That one girl was just being nice. She wasn't interested."

"And what makes you the expert?" Brian argued. "You can't even tell the girl you like that you like her."

"Maybe, but she was just holding my arm and she likes being around me. That's a lot better than one girl rolling her eyes when you aren't looking and the other leaning away from you like the Tower of Pisa."

"Well, what am I supposed to do?" Brian growled in a low tone. "Hell, they weren't even sevens, and I was talking to them anyway. I lowered my standards just to have some fun with them. They should be happy they got attention from me!"

I looked Brian over. His hair needed cutting, and instead of looking artfully messy, it just looked ragged. He may have been running again, but it had only been a week, and the gut he had was made more obvious by the fact that his jeans were a little too tight around the waist. He might have stood more of a chance if he were back in shape, but even then, it was obvious that his inability to have a normal conversation with those two girls was enough to make them back away.

"Brian—" I shook my head. "That doesn't—"

"Brian," Harriet interrupted, walking over. "You can't talk to women like that if you expect them to like you. One of them said you were just going on and on about having run track in high school. That's not the way to impress anyone. You have to ask questions about them and engage them in conversation, or they might think you're arrogant and self-centered." Brian looked away, but Harriet took his face in her hands and turned his attention back to her. "Brian, both those girls thanked me for interrupting you because they felt uncomfortable. You made them feel uncomfortable."

Brian forcefully yanked Harriet's hands away from his face. "Well, how am I supposed to get laid if the two of you come barging into my conversations?"

Seeing Brian treat Harriet like that triggered something in me. I felt that pressure in my upper gums, and my eyes felt a little more sensitive to the dim light. I had already been angry and frustrated and itching for a fight, but seeing the hurt in Harriet's eyes and the way she rubbed her left wrist after he had laid his hands on it broke the dam.

I grabbed Brian's shirt and growled menacingly. "You apologize to Harriet right now, or we're leaving."

His eyes grew big, and a few people around us stopped to watch.

Harriet took in the situation and immediately began to placate the small crowd. "Oh, don't worry. He's just reenacting a scene and practicing using his trick vampire teeth. It's all in fun."

At the word *vampire*, I immediately deflated. I let go of Brian's shirt and slumped against the wall.

"Uh, yeah, he was just playing around," Brian said unconvincingly.

Somehow, the small crowd bought it. One person asked Harriet where I had gotten the custom teeth and contact lenses. Realizing what I must have looked like, I turned to Brian. He looked as scared of me as I was of myself.

"I'm going to the bathroom," I mumbled and ran down the hall to the closest men's room.

Once inside, I looked around the room, which was fortunately empty, then looked at myself in the mirror. My usually brown eyes were amber with slitted cat pupils. My canines were elongated, and the tips were sharper than normal. I shut my mouth to hide them but only managed to bite my lip and draw blood.

I reached for a paper towel to wipe off the blood but then paused and looked at myself again. I was turning into a monster. I had lost my temper with Brian in front of Harriet, in public, and I could have hurt him. I stared at my reflection in shock and watched as a tear trickled down my cheek to join the trail of blood dripping from my lip.

How could I help Brian if I couldn't even help myself?

I crouched down and put my head between my knees. I sat there for a minute or so, trying to even out my breathing and clear my mind.

I didn't look up as the restroom door creaked open, even though the sound was accompanied by Harriet's voice. She was asking Brian something, and he seemed reluctant to comply, but he eventually relented and left. The door closed, dampening the sounds of the happy, enthusiastic crowd outside. I heard footsteps approaching, and I could tell they weren't Brian's.

Harriet sat next to me and rubbed my back until I was ready to sit up straight again. "This isn't just any old medical problem, is it?"

"No. It isn't." My voice didn't sound right. It was thick with sticky, awkward emotions I couldn't even name.

"Can you tell me anything about it?"

I shook my head. If I told her anything, I was afraid something might happen to her. Maybe Ms. Heliotrope would have to do something if she found out Harriet knew too much. I couldn't risk that.

Then I realized that if I wasn't careful, I could hurt her too, like I almost did with that abusive jerk the other day . . . like I almost did with Brian.

The thought broke me. I had believed that one day I'd work up the courage to tell Harriet exactly how I felt about her. It hadn't even mattered to me if she only wanted to be friends. I'd just always hoped I could someday stand before her and tell her I loved her. That I'd always loved her and no matter what, even if she couldn't return those feelings, I'd always do my best to help her know she mattered.

Now? There was no chance. How could I even hope to be with her if I couldn't control myself? I could hurt her in a fit of rage and not realize it until she was lying bloody and lifeless at my feet.

I began to sob uncontrollably. Harriet immediately curled around me and held me in her arms as the past week of fears and doubts and painful realizations finally came out.

"It's okay," Harriet said gently. "Brian's watching the door so nobody can come in. You can let it out."

"I'm sorry. I'm so, so sorry. I've messed everything up," I choked out between sobs.

"You didn't do anything wrong. We're here for you. All of us. Even Brian."

"But—" I stopped.

"But what? We all care about you. We all want you to be okay."

"I'm never going to be okay again."

"We'll find a way. You don't have to be alone."

But I am alone.

I ran my hands through my hair and took a deep breath. This probably wasn't the best place for a breakdown, especially since Harriet looked so incredible and she was in a men's bathroom. Somebody might get the wrong idea when they saw us leave, and I didn't want anyone to think of her as anything but the kind, decent person she'd always been. Sure, she could probably kick their asses with her background in martial arts, but they wouldn't know that at first glance.

"Let's . . . let's get out of here," I said, my weariness evident in my tear-roughened voice.

She held out her hand to help me up. "You don't have to rush, you know. You can take your time."

"No. Let's just go. We'll be late for Des's panel if we stay here too long. I want to be there for him." I took her hand and stood up, despite the feeling that if someone threw me into a lake, I'd probably sink to the bottom no matter how desperately I tried to swim to the surface. My limbs felt heavy, as if I'd been handed the weight of the world.

"Wait a second." Harriet grabbed some paper towels, dampened them, and wiped off my face. It felt like a strangely absurd gesture, like something a mother would do for her small child.

I laughed weakly.

Harriet gave me a small smile. "I'll get you a dry one."

"No, it's okay." I reached past her for the paper towel dispenser behind her.

I hadn't realized how close we were already standing; as I reached out, my face was suddenly only inches from hers. I could smell the floral scent of her shampoo. I suddenly felt extremely self-conscious, and my heart began beating a mile a minute.

It must have been a day for extremes; I had probably felt every emotion known to humankind in less than an hour. This feeling, though . . . I suddenly felt like being alone with her was better than trying to leave as soon as possible.

"Josh?" Harriet asked, her voice soft and gentle.

I turned my head to look directly in her eyes. They were a touch too gray to rightly be called blue, except for a few brighter flecks near her pupils. I never used to think about the different shades of color. Blue had been blue to me. Green had been green. But now, with my enhanced vision, I understood why one shade of blue might be called azure and another, turquoise. The sapphire flecks in her eyes might have been my favorite color.

I must have moved closer without realizing it because Harriet put her hands up on my chest. I didn't know if she did it to stop me or if she did it instinctively. All I knew was the feeling of her hands intensified my longing to close any gaps between us.

"Hey, guys, you might want to hurry up. Some people aren't quite buying my claim that the bathroom is flooded," Brian whispered loudly through a crack in the door.

The moment was ruined. I backed up and shook my head as though I were coming out of a dream. I covered my eyes with the palms of my hands and sighed. "Fine, let's go."

Harriet nodded, her face turned away from me. "Yeah."

It could have been wishful thinking, but it did look like she was blushing a little when I glanced at her after we'd sneaked out of the bathroom. The three of us made our way toward the main hall, where Des was going to talk about *Vastness of Time* and tomorrow's *Midnight Murder Mansion* tournament. I hoped Harriet's blush came from feeling at least a fraction of what I felt for her, but I was so numb after breaking down, it was a weak hope. It was much easier to think about Des and supporting him from the audience.

I decided I would deal with this tempest of emotions when we got home and I could be alone in my room. Maybe I could call Ms. Heliotrope. I wondered how she had felt when she first became a vampire. What kinds of changes had she made in her life? Had she needed to make hard choices like hiding the truth from her friends and family?

At least it was a plan. There was no way this feeling of dread was going to leave me anytime soon, but having a plan made me feel a little more in control.

We were right outside the doors to the main hall when I stepped aside. "Hey, guys, I have to make a phone call. I'll meet you inside, okay?"

"We're early, so we can find a good spot and save you a seat." Harriet looked like she might say something else but only nodded instead.

"Yeah, a seat," Brian said, still looking a little spooked. "Thanks."

I immediately found a private corner . . . or at least private enough, considering the crowds. Pulling out my phone, I scrolled through the contacts. I had put Ms. Heliotrope's phone number in my contacts after our talk the other night as we walked to my car. I found it quickly, took a deep breath, and hit the call button.

The time between each ring felt like an eternity, but after the fourth ring, she finally picked up.

"Hello?" came the voice I had been hoping to hear. Something about her tone was strangely reassuring, and I felt a little weight lift from my shoulders.

"Ms. Heliotrope? It's me, Josh. Something happened and . . . well . . . I know what I am now."

She was silent on the other end for so long, I started to wonder if she'd hung up.

"Where are you now?" she finally asked.

"I'm not in Willow Springs. I'm at a convention in the city."

She let out a soft sigh. "That's probably not the best place to be when you find out you're a vampire."

If circumstances had been different, I would have laughed. This didn't really feel that funny, though. "I was able to pass it off as some kind of vampire cosplay with the help of my friends since this is a convention where a lot of people dress in costumes, but I can't be sure of how people viewed it when my—my fangs popped out and my eyes went weird."

"Your friends covered for you?" Ms. Heliotrope asked sharply.

"Uh, yeah?"

Ms. Heliotrope went quiet for a moment. It hit me then:

if even I wasn't supposed to be completely informed, it probably wasn't good for Harriet and Brian to know anything either.

"I think I can explain that I had the teeth as a surprise. They already knew about my eyes changing, so I can't really cover for that. Maybe I could find a booth that sells fake vampire teeth and tell them that's what they saw?" Thank goodness I was at a convention where there would be booths like that. I hated lying to my friends, but I didn't want them to get in trouble for my lack of self-control.

"Thank goodness for small favors." The relief in her voice was palpable. "When can you get back home? I'm sure you have more questions."

"Yes. I won't be back until late. I still need to be here to support Des, and I'm the dri—"

"Josh, I understand you're a caring person, but you can't brush this off. If you stay, you need a plan. Do you have anything to eat that's meat or something like that?"

"Yeah. I made a sandwich with leftover blood sausage."

"Good, good. When you bared your fangs—was it pretty recently?"

"Yeah." I wasn't sure why the timing mattered.

"Okay, sometimes when a new vampire gets triggered, it's hard for them to calm down enough to control their thirst. You should eat that sandwich now, even if you're not hungry."

"Right." That made sense. I opened my backpack and pulled out my sandwich.

"Also, you need to come back as soon as possible, okay? Don't stay longer than you have to. If you can arrange for another ride for your friends, do that. The worst place for a new vampire is a crowded space. If you go on a rampage . . . well, we don't want that to happen."

I thought about her strange "pet." The last thing I wanted was to become like that guy. Was losing control part of how a vampire went from mostly human to a mindless beast in human form? I shuddered.

"Okay. Maybe Harriet will take Brian home or something."

"Good. I'll wait for you at your house." Her tone suggested she'd accept no arguments.

I couldn't help but argue anyway. "I'm not sure when I'll be back, though."

"Josh," she said, her voice stern. "I don't care when you're back. This is my job, and I'll wait if I have to. I don't want you turning feral, okay?"

Something beneath her stern tone struck me. It sounded like concern or something deeper. Protectiveness, maybe?

"Okay."

We talked a bit more about the possible timing of me getting home. I felt a little more confident as I took bites of my unpleasantly cold sandwich and went over possible scenarios that might prevent me from getting home faster. She even gave me a few pointers on how to stay in control until I could leave. Once we were done, she said something I didn't expect.

"Josh, I know this feels like the end of the world, but it doesn't have to be. I made some heartbreaking choices when I realized what I had become. Looking back, I probably could have made some less extreme choices and things would have been okay. There's a lot I regret, and I don't want you to feel the same way. Please take your time in deciding what to do. You have a lot more time than you might think."

It sounded like something my father would have said,

and I had to gulp back tears before I could respond. "Um, okay. Thank you."

"If you need to call me, I'll have my phone with me," she said. "Goodbye, Josh."

"Bye," I said, but it seemed like she might have hung up by then.

I downed the last of my sandwich and got up, making a beeline for the booths. I found one that sold convincing enough vampire teeth similar to what I had seen in the bathroom mirror. I made the transaction as quickly as possible. Des's panel was about to start, so I moved through the crowd at a slow jog and got into the main hall just before the audience lights dimmed. Looking around, I spotted Harriet and Brian easily with my improved vampire vision.

The seat they had saved for me was next to Harriet, who had clearly placed herself as a buffer between Brian and me. That felt like a good plan since I didn't want to spook Brian any more than I had. Once I'd sat, Harriet reached out and squeezed my hand. I gave her what I hoped was a brave smile but didn't say anything as the emcee started speaking.

I wished I were more enthusiastic about the panel for Des's sake. He and the other panelists talked about a lot of things, from basic info on *Vastness of Time* to the value of embracing diversity across fandoms. If I hadn't been dealing with my own personal crisis, I would have paid more attention. I mostly focused on how composed Des was and how well the crowd responded to what he said. I felt a little jealous of him for being able to stay calm, even when one audience member asked why people should care about diversity in gaming at all in a snarky tone. I had a feeling that if Des were turning into a vampire, he'd be able to handle it better than I was.

"Okay, everyone, thank you for your support! Our

panelists will be signing at the table outside in about ten minutes, and you can see a few of them participating in tomorrow's *Midnight Murder Mansion* tournament."

I blinked for a moment as the lights went up, surprised it was already over. Harriet and Brian stood, ready to take their backstage passes out to go see Des, while I still sat there stunned. I must have been so distracted by my own thoughts, I hadn't realized how much time had passed.

"You ready, Josh?" Harriet asked.

"Uh, yeah." I scrambled to make sure my backstage pass was visible.

I followed Brian and Harriet through the crowd to one of the event staff members, who ushered us back to where Des was talking with one of the voice actors from the game. The moment he spotted us, he gave his megawatt smile and waved to us.

"Over here, guys!"

Harriet gave him a hug, and Brian gave him a fist bump.

"That was great, Des," Harriet said. "I have to play the full game now. It's amazing!"

"Yeah, it's definitely one of those games that gets you hooked!" the voice actor said.

Des's brow furrowed as he looked at me, but he held onto his smile. He patted Brian on the shoulder. "Why don't you three talk for a moment. I have to ask Josh something."

Everyone nodded and cheerfully continued the conversation while Des pulled me aside.

"You seem off, man. You okay?" he asked once he seemed sure nobody could overhear us.

"I'll be okay. I just think I need to get back home earlier than I expected."

"Do you need me to call Jocelyn for you?"

"Do I really look that bad?" I joked lamely. From the

look on his face, I must have. "It's less a health thing and more a personal thing."

"Brian messed up?"

"Well, yeah . . . that's not what it is, though."

"Okay. I can have Brian stay with me tonight at the hotel, or maybe Harriet can bring him home instead. Just take care of you, man." He patted me on the back. "If you can make it tomorrow, that's cool, but don't feel like you have to. We all just want you to get better."

I was tempted to tell him there was no getting better from this, but I put on a smile instead. "I'll try to make it."

"Good. The fact you're here right now is enough already." He turned his head as someone called his name. "I gotta go out there to sign autographs. It sucks you can't stay since I'll have time after autographs to throw on my costume and walk around with you guys. Just tell Harriet and Brian I have everything covered and they can talk to me about arrangements for Brian."

"All right."

I watched him dart off to join the rest of the panelists, then walked over to Brian and Harriet. When I explained that I needed to go, Brian seemed relieved to see me leave and Harriet said she'd be happy to drive him home if he couldn't stay with Des.

I gave Ms. Heliotrope a quick text as I left to let her know I was on my way home.

I was grateful for the quiet drive home without Brian, but seeing his relief at not having to be alone in the car with me made me anxious. Was it safe for me to be living with Des and Brian if I lost control? I started to fall down the hole I had earlier, overwhelming thoughts and fears circling my brain. By the time I got home, I was almost back in the same state I had been in after talking with Dr. Chen.

The only thing that made me feel better was the now-familiar sight of Ms. Heliotrope in a steampunk outfit leaning against the front door.

"Hello, Ms. Heliotrope."

She nodded and stepped aside so I could unlock and open the door. "I'm glad you got back so early. Now it's time to do the real work."

DAY 10
SUNDAY

*H*ow well do you trust your friends?"

It was Sunday morning. Ms. Heliotrope had spent the evening investigating the entire house with the help of the strange feral man. Brian had ended up staying at the hotel with Des, which made it easier for them to get things done without having to answer questions. It was like watching a K-9 unit do a search for drugs. In this case, they had been looking for surveillance devices.

I was disturbed by how much they had found. Each room had had at least a couple of small video cameras and microphones. It was completely excessive, and I couldn't help but feel more paranoid. How amateurish I must have seemed the other day when I thought I was being so clever looking for monitoring devices around work.

If I couldn't trust the vampires and I was now one of them, maybe the right question wasn't whether I could trust my friends. Maybe it was whether they could trust me. Thinking about it realistically, a vampire with a couple of human roommates would make for either a wacky eighties sitcom or a horror film. Considering how I'd reacted to Brian at the convention, I feared the latter would be more likely.

I must have sat silently a little too long before Ms. Heliotrope spoke again. She sat a little closer to me on the couch and put her hand on mine. "Josh, I'm not asking whether you think you can control yourself around your friends. That's what I'm here to teach you. What I'm asking is if your friends will be able to handle this. From what you've explained to me, it sounds like they have some idea of what's going on. Do you think they'll talk?"

I hated to admit it, but out of all of them, Brian might. His lack of filter could be a problem. Then again, his lack of filter could also make him sound a bit unstable. If he spoke up about this, it might not be me who suffered for it. It could be him.

"I—I don't know. Maybe? I think if we talk with them and explained what was going on . . ."

"Josh, I couldn't even tell you a few days ago what you were becoming. Do you really think you will be allowed to tell them?"

I ruffled my hands through my hair and let out a frustrated sigh. "No. But what can I do? I need to live somewhere. I'm not exactly made of money. Who ever heard of a vampire working as a pizza delivery guy? In the books, they all seem to be super rich and living in castles or mansions or something. I'm living off tips."

Ms. Heliotrope laughed. "Everyone starts from somewhere, Josh. Sure, some people get turned when they're already wealthy, but some of us just have to work hard and invest for a while. I was hardly wealthy when I was turned. I'm not even all that wealthy now. Being a formalist for the Conclave helps, though. It pays well enough, at least."

"Are you telling me I should do what you do?" I asked, a little bewildered.

She shook her head. "No, Josh. You can make a choice. Becoming a formalist was my choice. Being a vampire doesn't mean removing yourself from society completely and only functioning within vampiric circles. However, if you intend to continue among humans, you do need to make sure you know how to control yourself."

So I couldn't act like I had yesterday. I was lucky I had been at a convention, where my behavior could be passed off as a cosplayer being a little too in character. What would have happened if Brian had pissed me off at home and Harriet or Des hadn't been around to keep me in check? How much of myself would I lose? I glanced at Ms. Heliotrope's feral creature, whom she had introduced last night as Doug. He was curled up like a puppy on the other end of the couch. I really didn't want to end up like him.

Ms. Heliotrope seemed to read my mind. "It's less likely you'll end up like him, Josh. Doug had addictive tendencies, and a vampire with addictive tendencies isn't going to be able to control themselves at all. That's why he's under my care. I can do a lot more to help you get stable, considering you're already starting out as someone with a sense of self-discipline. There's still a chance you could become feral, so I do need you to follow directions."

I thought of Brian again. It was probably better that this had happened to me than to him, if self-discipline was key. He hadn't been showing much lately, and any he had shown had been instigated by others.

"So where do we start?"

"First, we need to work on controlling your strength. Your strength hasn't fully manifested yet, so getting started on gentling your touch now will help as you continue to transition." She pulled a tennis ball from one of the plastic bags she had propped against the couch. "Squeeze this like you normally would."

I took the ball and eyed her dubiously. Tennis balls didn't exactly have a lot of give. She raised her eyebrows, as if to tell me to go on and do it already.

"Fine." I squeezed the ball with my left hand as hard as I could. The fuzzy exterior stayed intact, but the rubbery interior completely fell apart. I opened my hand and let the mangled ball fall to the floor. Feral Doug lifted his head to look at the ball. Then, with such rapid speed I barely saw him move, he grabbed the ball and curled back up on the couch to play with the crumpled mess.

I couldn't help but flinch watching Doug with the deformed tennis ball. Ms. Heliotrope must have noticed, because she didn't hand me the ball she was holding.

"What is it, Josh?"

"I know you said I wouldn't end up like him, but how long will it take me to get the control I need to not accidentally hurt someone?"

"I can't really say. You just have to keep practicing until it becomes second nature. I don't even remember how long it took me, but now I don't have to think about it. We can't all be like Mozart and be talented from the start."

I sighed. "Give me another ball."

This time I held it gingerly in the palm of my hand, slowly bringing my fingers closer to the ball until I held it in a featherlight grip. My fingers were barely a cage around the ball, but at least it hadn't fallen apart.

"Good, good," Ms. Heliotrope said. "However, people will find it strange if you grip things so slowly and obviously. You have to do it in a way that looks normal."

"How did you figure it out? Like, how to make it look

like a normal grip without breaking things, I mean?" I put the ball on the table in a small groove that would prevent it from falling off. Feral Doug eyed the ball like he wanted to pounce on it. He slowly reached out a hand to take it.

Ms. Heliotrope gave Doug a sharp look. He immediately whimpered and pulled his hand back. She picked up the ball, her grip looking perfectly normal. "I think of it this way: I want to hold it gently, as if it were my very own baby, but firmly, so I don't drop the baby."

"Hmm . . ." I wondered what Ms. Heliotrope's life had been like before she was changed. Had she had a family or kids? What would it have been like to have a baby and to be afraid of hurting it just because she didn't know how to control her grip?

We spent time practicing with tennis balls until Doug had so many broken balls, he couldn't decide which to play with first. Ms. Heliotrope was satisfied with my grip being light and convincing enough.

"Let's stop here," Ms. Heliotrope said, pointedly watching Feral Doug's failed attempts to juggle a few of the balls. "I have a couple more tubes of tennis balls here for you. I want you to practice your grip when you're feeling angry or frustrated. Those will be the hardest times for you to keep control, so it's even more important to know how to hold back your strength."

That made sense. "So what else do I need to work on? Do I need to start drinking blood?"

"No. Well, you don't need to drink blood from a living creature yet. I can see if Dr. Chen can get you some blood from the blood bank, but you should also continue eating bloody steaks and the like. That can help stave off the hunger. Once you get used to drinking blood, it becomes difficult to return to eating food. Since one of the ways you can hide what you've become is to show people you eat just like them, it's good to keep eating—especially food with garlic in it. We should thank the humans for that particular vampire myth. Their belief that we are averse to garlic when we aren't makes it easier to hide among them."

"Yeah, I noticed garlic hasn't done anything to me, which is good since there's garlic in just about everything at Gino's." It was a relief to know that being a vampire didn't prevent me from doing my job.

"Spend some time watching how your friends respond to you when they come back from that convention. Show them those fake vampire teeth. It can be okay to have some humans around who know what you really are, like Dr. Chen. He has access to donated blood, which makes him extremely helpful. But you need to be careful; if someone says something to the wrong person, the Conclave will take action, and that action can be brutal."

I wasn't looking forward to everyone coming back. Brian had already been a little touchy after what happened yesterday; he had been so quiet after I had calmed down with Harriet in the bathroom. I had no clue what he might have been talking about with Harriet and Des without me there. The last week and a half hadn't been rough just on me. It had been hard on everyone. What if they all decided they were done with me?

"Okay, I'll try to figure this all out . . . somehow." I started to clean up the balls that Feral Doug hadn't claimed for himself. He looked at me like a kid whose bag of candy had been taken away from him after trick-or-treating. It was weirdly pitiful, especially coming from someone so unpredictable and, frankly, terrifying. "You can have them, guy. I'm just cleaning up the mess."

Feral Doug squinted as though he didn't quite believe me, but he backed off as I loaded the balls into one of the discarded plastic bags. When it was full, I held it out with my arms as straight as possible, not wanting to get too close. He snatched the bag from me with both hands and held it open to check the contents. Once satisfied, he handed the bag to Ms. Heliotrope and grabbed another empty bag. He started picking up balls and putting them in the bag, just like I had.

"How much of him is still there?" His behavior seemed more human than pet when he was cleaning up. "Will he ever be normal again?"

"It's unlikely. Most ferals get hunted down and destroyed. If you were to let them go wild, they would hunt down a population until there was nobody left, then move on to the next place, and the next place after that. We keep our population under control so we don't end up in a world where there are too many vampires and not enough humans to feed from. That's why what Genevieve and Danforth are doing is so horrible. We always have to hunt down the subjects of their bets and either mentor them before they become feral or . . ."

Ms. Heliotrope gazed upon Feral Doug with pain in her eyes. "I had to get special permission to keep him and a few others to see if we could train them. Maybe they can somehow be valuable members of our society. Doug has proven himself valuable. He's like a trained police dog, in a sense."

"Do you think he's okay with that? Being like a pet?" I couldn't imagine wanting to live that way, myself.

"I honestly don't know, but he seems happy most of the time."

Feral Doug brought another full bag over, and this time he handed it to me with a goofy grin. "Thanks, man, but you can take all of them home with you. They're yours."

His eyes lit up as he gave a happy grunt, and he took the bag from my hands.

"I think you've made a friend," Ms. Heliotrope whispered to me from behind her hand.

"I could probably use another if things don't go well with the friends I have now." Out of nowhere, an image formed in my head of Feral Doug and me hanging out in front of a TV, playing video games. Or rather, I was playing the video game, and Doug was chewing on one of the controllers.

Ms. Heliotrope patted my shoulder. "I hope everything works out with them. I truly do. I did this all by myself when I first started to change. I was too scared I would hurt everyone, so I left them behind, and I still regret that choice to this day. If I had trusted myself and them more, things could be very different now."

"So I should be careful not to give too much away, but I should see if maybe they can handle it."

"As far as you can without giving anything away." She shrugged. "Besides, you'd have me, Doug, and Dr. Chen if you have to leave your friends behind, and that's a good start. Right?"

While an intimidating steampunk cop lady, a dude who was more pet than man, and "Wolfram von Raven" didn't exactly sound like the most conventional group of friends, at least they knew what I was going through. "I suppose so."

"Don't sound too excited. You might faint," Ms. Heliotrope quipped sarcastically. She turned to Feral Doug, who was trying to hold both bags of balls and hug them at the same time. A few of the balls started falling out, so he had to stop and put them back in the bag. "Let's go. We don't want to surprise Josh's friends."

I watched them leave through the sliding door into the

backyard instead of taking the front door. It was wise since the neighbors would probably lose their minds at the sight of the strange duo with the bags of mangled tennis balls.

I spent the rest of the afternoon before work cleaning the house out of sheer guilt. Maybe when everyone saw I wanted to make amends for my strange behavior, things wouldn't go over quite as badly. Everyone's clothes got washed, the refrigerator was thoroughly cleaned, and I even managed to move the appliances to clean under them. Things like that were definitely easier with enhanced vampire strength.

When it was time to head off to work, I took a quick shower and hopped in my car. I was almost too preoccupied while driving to notice Danforth's Porsche parked in a handicapped parking space, clearly without handicap placards, in front of the town hall. Standing nearby on the steps was Genevieve, speaking with the mayor. She was wearing a suit similar to the one she had worn at the police station when she was posing as my lawyer. I slowed down and watched as she flirtatiously grazed her neck with the tips of her fingers and laughed at something the mayor had said. In the meantime, the mayor looked dazed and sweaty, his balding head showing his blush as easily as his cheeks.

This was weird. First, Danforth at the middle school and high school. Now, Genevieve was at the town hall. I even thought back to when Genevieve had come for me at the police station. My instincts told me something was definitely up. I decided to keep it all in mind as I sped up again. Ms. Heliotrope might want to know about it.

When I arrived, Gino was already bustling around in a frenzy, Graziella, Renato, and Gino's cousin following after. They were attempting to help him get everything in place but clearly weren't as skilled as Harriet.

After a couple of minutes, Gino noticed I was there. "Hey, Josh, since Harriet isn't here, things will be a little crazy tonight. I'll need you to step things up."

"Aye, aye, captain," I replied, and not sarcastically. I pitched in and began to prep pizza boxes. As I folded cardboard flaps, I thought about the tennis ball experiment and tried to see if I could use some of that super speed to make the process go a little faster.

"Firm but gentle, like holding a baby," I muttered as I slowly increased my speed.

"Hey, you're getting those done pretty fast," Renato noticed.

I slowed down a little bit. "Yeah, just trying to get things ready now so it's easier later."

Renato looked at me strangely. "Uh, yeah, of course."

I wasn't sure if his response came from me moving faster than I should have or from how nervous I sounded. I hoped it was the latter, and I had a feeling it was when Renato just shrugged and went back into the kitchen.

"Hey, Dad," I heard him shout. "Josh doesn't need any help. What else do you need?"

I might have gone a little overboard. I'd managed to assemble a floor-to-ceiling stack of boxes, and several others were strewn around me. While my hands may not have been a blur of speed, I still needed to be more careful with how I used my abilities. I stacked up the rest of the boxes and headed back to the kitchen, where Gino was wrapping up the rest of the kitchen prep with his cousin and Graziella had just finished tying a scarf on over her hair and was reaching for an apron.

"Josh." Gino came up behind me and slapped me lightly on the back. I jumped slightly as he walked past. "Harriet called. She said she'd be in later to help."

I gulped. I was nervous about seeing her and the guys again. I thought I'd have a little more time before interacting with any of them. "Uh, okay," I said, my voice pitching slightly higher than usual.

Graziella chuckled. "It's so cute how you young people can be so awkward about the people you have crushes on."

While she was completely off base about why I was being awkward, I was mortified she had said anything about how I felt for Harriet.

I sighed. "Everyone knows."

"Yup, even Harriet knows," Renato said. "You have to know that, right?"

Graziella smiled gently. "Just tell her how you feel. She's waiting for you to be confident enough to tell her. She knows you need to be the one to say it."

"Do you—do you think she feels the same way I do?"

"It's up to her to tell you that," Graziella replied.

The bit of hope I felt was suddenly dashed when I realized my being a vampire was going to be a major wrench in the works. There was no way I could have a normal relationship with anyone as a vampire.

Graziella must have noticed my change in energy, because she squeezed my shoulder reassuringly. "You can do it, Josh, when you're ready."

If only I could explain to her what the real problem was.

Before I could really think things through, the Sunday evening delivery rush started up. I made a point to grab a couple more boxes than I usually would for a delivery, just to speed things up a little.

Nobody seemed to notice, but it did help things go a little more smoothly. I realized that most people didn't really pay much attention to what was going on around them unless it was exceptionally strange. Although, if my love for

Harriet was obvious enough for people to notice, I had to wonder about people's priorities. I mean, here I was, a vampire of all things, but it was my inability to voice my feelings to the woman I loved that everyone noticed.

I blamed reality television.

About halfway through the night, Harriet showed up. Things were too busy for us to exchange anything more than a quick hello before she started making another pizza and I had to leave for another delivery. I usually liked how busy Sunday nights were, especially because the tips were great, but tonight I just wanted it to be over so I could talk with everyone and figure out what they thought was going on after yesterday.

When the last pizza had finally been delivered and the restaurant was officially closed, I suddenly found myself filled with dread. As much as I wanted to talk with my friends and get it all over with, my mind had started playing out worst-case scenarios.

Harriet cornered me after I threw the trash in the dumpster. "Hey, Josh. You doing okay?"

"I think so. What about—are you—are you okay? And the guys?" I asked nervously.

"I think you should talk with them. Brian's kind of freaked out. He didn't say much, but he started writing stuff down in a notebook and bought some weird things at the convention. Des just thinks you played an ill-conceived practical joke. I didn't tell them what happened in the bathroom."

"Th-thanks for that. What about you?"

I sounded like an idiot. It was just so hard to figure out what words to use. She'd seen me completely break down, and I wasn't sure if I seemed like an emotional wreck, a cruel practical joker, or even a monstrous threat.

"Well, I'm more worried about you." She came closer and put her hand on my cheek. "This illness is really getting to you, isn't it?"

Part of me was relieved she had used the word *illness*, and I relaxed briefly.

"But," she continued, "putting on fangs and threatening your friend isn't okay, Josh. Brian may be hard to deal with, but he didn't need to be scared into behaving better, and I think you know that."

I was relieved she had automatically thought I was wearing fake fangs. She was off base about the motivations behind my behavior, but right about how bad I felt.

"I do need to apologize to him, and I plan to. I already cleaned the whole house today as an apology. That's not going to be enough, but I wanted to do something. Make a gesture, you know?"

"That's a good start. Do you want me to come with you? In case you need me to explain that I saw how upset you were?"

I didn't really want her to elaborate on my bathroom breakdown, but I thought it might be good to have everyone together at once so I could see what they thought was going on.

"Maybe that's a good idea. We could all get on the same page or something."

"Good. I'm glad you're trying, even if your behavior yesterday wasn't great." She turned and walked ahead of me down the hall to get her jacket. "If you can wait a moment, I'll follow you to your place."

"Sure." I grabbed my own jacket.

Harriet had a quick conversation with Gino and grabbed a couple of pizzas for us to take home. "You ready?"

I took the boxes from her and gave her a thin smile. "Yeah, let's go."

We waved goodbye to Gino and went to our separate cars. As we caravanned to my house, I tried to listen to music and prevent my sweaty palms from slipping off the steering wheel.

I parked in front of the house and took a few deep breaths. My nerves were getting to me. If they'd figured out too much, I was afraid of what Ms. Heliotrope and the Conclave would do.

I jumped slightly when Harriet tapped on the window. Pulling myself together, I nodded at her, pulled the keys out of the ignition, and opened the door.

"I'll take the pizzas," Harriet said.

I handed them over and got out of the car. The lights were on in the kitchen and in Brian's room. It was now or never.

Harriet smiled encouragingly. "Let's go. We have a peace offering." She held the pizza boxes up higher as though they were the answer to all our problems.

There was something so cute about the way she held up those pizza boxes that I couldn't help but laugh. Some of my tension bled away, and I felt better about going inside. I followed her to the front door and unlocked it.

"Hey, guys, we're here with pizza!" Harriet shouted as we walked in.

Des turned away from the TV, where he was playing an old sixteen-bit video game. "I'll join you in just a second." He then shouted toward the stairs, "Brian! Food!"

Brian's feet pounded down the steps, but the moment he saw me, he stopped.

"Brian, I'm really sorry about yesterday. Can we talk? I brought pizza."

He sighed and finished walking down the stairs. Harriet put the pizzas on the dining room table, and he made a beeline for the food. I noticed he gave me a wide berth.

"Don't eat that without plates," Des warned as Brian grabbed a slice and began eating without a napkin in sight.

"I'll get them." Harriet ducked into the kitchen while I took a seat at the table as far away from Brian as possible. I didn't want to spook him again.

"I'm just going to take this upstairs," Brian mumbled, attempting to make his escape.

Des blocked his way. "No, we're sitting and talking about this." He gave Brian a shove toward the table and pulled out a chair. "Sit."

Brian sat down and ate while Harriet passed out plates to everyone. Once everyone was settled, I began to speak.

"I really want to apologize. I didn't mean to scare you, Brian. I handled that really badly."

"Can you explain what happened?" Des asked. "I feel like I'm still fuzzy on the details. Brian keeps saying you're a vampire, and Harriet says you were just stressed out and played a stupid prank."

I almost sucked in a sharp breath when Des said *vampire*, but I took a deep breath to buy myself some time instead. I had to make this convincing, and the most convincing lies were usually based on the truth. I hated lying to my friends, but this was the only way.

"Brian was rude to Harriet. She was trying to explain to him why the way he was talking to girls at the convention made them uncomfortable. With all the stuff I've been dealing with, I kind of snapped. I-I tried to scare Brian a bit. I had some really good vampire fangs and put them in, and with how weird my eyes have been looking, I must have freaked him out more than I expected. I was trying to play on the fact he had said I was turning into a vampire. It was stupid, and I immediately regretted it, which was why I ran to the bathroom."

It was almost the truth, and I hoped the details were enough to keep them from asking too many questions.

Brian narrowed his eyes. I could tell he wasn't completely convinced. Des seemed to accept the explanation, though, and Harriet as well.

"That sounds pretty much like what happened," Harriet said.

"Of course you would take his side," Brian groused.

"Brian, this isn't about taking sides," Des stated. "This is about how on edge everyone is and how we need to find a better way to deal with it."

"He's a vampire!" Brian insisted. "There's no way he put in vampire teeth that quickly. There's no way he's just sick! Who gets sick and develops super speed or weird cat eyes? This isn't normal." Brian gave me a pointed look. "You're not normal."

"Brian, that's not appropriate," Harriet interjected. "You know he's going through a lot right now."

"See! I'm the one who got attacked, and you're defending him, even though he was the one who attacked me!" Brian stood from his chair.

"Brian, please calm down," Des said.

"Look, I'll give you space, okay? I won't bother you. I'll stay out of your hair." I didn't know if that would be enough for him, but it was the best I could come up with.

Brian crossed his arms and glared at me.

"Brian, he's really trying his best here," Harriet said.

Brian sat down again. "Fine, but he's not allowed in my room. You may not think he's a vampire, but I'm not convinced he's not."

I had to roll that sentence around in my head for a moment to process what he'd said. Essentially, Harriet and Des were fine with my explanation, and I probably didn't have to worry about them thinking I was a vampire. Brian, however, was going to be a problem, and I'd have to do whatever I could to convince him otherwise.

"Okay, your space is yours. I'll respect it, no matter what." I took a bite of the tasteless slice of pizza in front of me, just to remind him I could eat food, just like him, and didn't need to take my meals in liquid form.

"Good," Brian said.

"I'm sorry about all the trouble I've been causing everyone. I think I'm starting to feel a bit better, so things should be getting back to normal again," I said, hoping it would be the final apology of the night.

Des and Harriet reassured me everything was fine, and Harriet left for her place.

I felt like a partial load had lifted off my shoulders, at least. Exhaustion took hold after the busy night, and I trudged up the stairs to bed, too tired to call Ms. Heliotrope about seeing Genevieve at the town hall.

DAY 11
MONDAY

"Uh . . . what?"

I stood in front of Brian's door, perplexed.

Des clapped me on the shoulder. "Yeah, I'm with you on this one, Josh."

We tilted our heads sideways to the left, then sideways to the right to better understand what we were seeing.

"Since when is Brian religious?" I asked.

Des reached out and touched the paint, rubbing it between his fingers. "Um, it's pretty fresh, so maybe he converted sometime this morning?"

"You want to knock, or should I?"

"I guess since I'm technically the landlord, I should be the one to ask. I got this." He knocked on the door. "Brian? I have a question."

The door opened slightly. "Is Josh with you?"

"Yeah, I'm here."

"Then you can talk to me through the door," Brian said.

Des offered me a shrug. "Okay, then. Why did you paint a huge cross on your door?"

"Because Josh is a vampire," came Brian's muffled voice.

Des raised an eyebrow and crossed his arms over his chest. "I see. So you think painting a big red cross on your door will keep him away."

There was a guilty pause, then an awkward response. "Yes?"

"You know, Josh is standing right here and looking at the cross. It doesn't seem to bother him at all."

Brian opened the door and peered out. "It doesn't?"

I reached out and put my hand on the cross. "Well, it's still a bit wet, and it's going to be annoying to clean off, but otherwise, no."

"Okay." Brian closed the door, then opened it again to hang what looked like a lei of garlic over the doorknob.

"You know I work at a pizza restaurant, right?"

"Damn it!" Brian cracked open the door once more to remove the garlic. Then he sprayed something on the doorknob instead.

"What do you think that is?" I asked Des.

"Maybe holy water?"

"Ah, right." I reached out and put my hand on the doorknob. Nothing happened, other than my hand getting wet.

"Yeah, that didn't work either, Brian," Des said. "Wait, when did Brian have a chance to get holy water?"

"Shit." Brian threw a handful of rice out the door and closed it again.

"You know you're going to have to vacuum that up, right?" Des asked.

"But is he counting them?" Brian asked.

"Counting what? The rice?" I asked.

"Yeah!" Brian shouted. He was starting to sound desperate.

"Not really?" Des looked at me uncertainly. "You're not counting the grains of rice, are you?"

"Why would I count grains of rice? I have better things to do." I was a bit perplexed by that one before I remembered it was one of the more obscure bits of vampire folklore: to distract a vampire, throw beans or rice at them, and they'd have to stop and count each bean or grain of rice before they could continue the chase.

"Damn it!" Brian opened his door completely. He stood there with a cross and the lei of garlic around his neck. "What's going to work, then?"

"Brian, I said I wouldn't go into your room, so I won't. Isn't that enough?" I sighed and rolled my eyes.

"But you're a vampire! How can I trust you if you're a vampire?" Brian's voice went up an octave, making him sound like he was going off the deep end.

"He's not a vampire!" Des said. "Obviously, something weird is going on, but clearly, he's not a vampire."

I didn't say anything. I didn't like the idea of lying by omission, but in this case, it felt safer to let Des tell Brian I wasn't a vampire than to say it myself. I was still on the fence about accepting or embracing the label for myself when I felt like I was, as a person, pretty much the exact opposite of a vampire. I wasn't cool. I wasn't suave and confident. I wasn't devastatingly handsome or filthy rich. I was just some average guy with relatively bland ambitions that seemed realistic.

"Well, I don't trust him," Brian said stubbornly, his stance firm.

Des sighed. "At least clean the paint off your door. It clearly doesn't do anything to Josh."

"Why don't you kick him out?"

Des and I both stared at Brian, shocked. We had been

friends for so long, yet Brian was taking things that far? He really thought our friendship was that disposable? Maybe I shouldn't have been surprised. Things had been going downhill with increasing speed, and there might not have been much to salvage from the wreck as it hit bottom. That didn't prevent it from feeling like he'd just stabbed me in the heart.

Des took a deep breath, but when he spoke, his tone still verged on anger, like a wolf growling a warning. "Brian, what you just said is taking things too far. Josh is our friend. I'm not going to kick him out when he's done nothing wrong. He's allowed to be upset and frustrated right now after all he's been through. Also, I should add that between the two of you, he's been paying rent regularly and helping out around the house a lot more than you have."

"But I . . ." Brian's voice emerged weakly, his eyes wide with fear. It was clear by his sudden flip from confident and angry to scared and unsure that he hadn't expected Des to get so angry.

I was surprised too. Des wasn't one to lose his cool.

"I hate having to point this out, but this is my house. I let you live here. If you're going to suggest someone gets kicked out, make sure you're being a better roommate than the other person." Des turned around and walked away.

Brian's shoulders slouched as he opened and closed his mouth like a fish out of water.

I couldn't blame him for being in shock. Even though I didn't like the person Brian had turned into, I felt sorry for him. It must have been hard to live in a world so vastly different from what he had expected. Still, I was surprised by the words that came out of my mouth next.

"He's not completely right. I have done something wrong. I should never have treated you the way I did at the con. I may never stop apologizing to you for it. I lost your trust, and I understand why. I'll do my best to give you space."

I turned and walked away. Maybe this friendship had run its course. It wasn't just that he was so inappropriate and misogynistic at times. I had played a role in it too. I'd let my anger at his behavior build up. If I hadn't, I probably could have controlled my vampiric urges better and prevented that mess at the con from happening. Holding back my frustration had done neither of us any good.

Brian's door closed as I walked down the hall. I needed someone to talk to about how horrible this all felt, and as I ran through the names of people in my head, the only one I knew I could be completely honest with was Ms. Heliotrope. Everyone else was too involved and in the dark about all the details that had led to the situation.

I pulled out my phone as I took the stairs and sent her a text.

Hey, do you have time to talk today?

I reached the bottom step and slumped onto the couch to wait for her response. Luckily, it came quickly.

Yes. Do you want me to come to your house?

Considering what had just happened with Brian, that would be a no.

No, I think we should talk somewhere else.

I waited for a couple of minutes before she texted me an address. Standing up to leave, I almost bumped into Des, who had come up behind me.

"Oh, sorry."

"No worries, my bad," Des replied. "Going somewhere?"

"Yeah, I have this new . . . mentor? I think that's what I can call her. I've been talking to her about some of the stuff that's been going on. She's been helping me a lot." I was glad I didn't have to lie to explain.

"That's great! That's really good." Des's enthusiasm seemed a little forced. I could tell he was still a little on edge.

"Hey, if I need to leave . . . I mean, if there are any problems or if things get bad, I don't want you to worry. I mean, I know I can get back on my feet. I don't know if Brian can. If I have to make the sacrifice—"

"You don't have to leave," Des interrupted. "I'm sure, someday, we're all going to want our own places, but I won't make you leave."

I nodded. "I just wanted you to know that if it had to happen, I'll be okay." I wasn't really sure I'd be okay, but I had a feeling Ms. Heliotrope wouldn't leave me out in the cold.

"Got it," Des said. "I know you can handle some tough shit."

I knew he was referring to growing up without my mother and having to mature a little faster for the sake of my dad. We shared an awkward silence for a moment.

"I should go. She's waiting for me . . . my mentor, I mean."

Des snapped out of his thoughts. "Yeah, don't let me keep you. See you later."

"Later." I grabbed my jacket and sunglasses and darted out the door, relieved to leave the tension behind for at least a little while.

As I drove, I made a game of guessing where I was going. Was it Ms. Heliotrope's house? Was it a Conclave location? I didn't recognize the address since I'd never delivered anything there, but I had a general idea of where it was.

After several minutes of driving, I found myself in front of a Victorian-style house, similar to ones I'd seen in photos of San Francisco. It seemed a little obvious that Ms. Heliotrope, with her steampunk style, would live in a Victorian house, but if she wanted to go for a motif, she might as well do it for every aspect of her life.

I walked up to the door and knocked. I heard a brief scuffle and an unfamiliar voice making excited noises. I wondered if it was Feral Doug or some other feral vampire Ms. Heliotrope had hanging around. How many did she keep, anyway?

Ms. Heliotrope's familiar voice projected through the door. "Doug, back off. You know better than that."

A disappointed groan was followed by dragging sounds that faded away. Then Ms. Heliotrope opened the door.

"Hello, Josh, please come in," she said with a welcoming gesture.

I stepped into a surprisingly normal house. I had to admit, I had been expecting something stranger, like furniture by Jules Verne. Instead, the furniture was modern and unremarkable, aside from a handful of what appeared to be antiques. Feral Doug was the only sign the place might not be as normal as it seemed. He looked at me with huge eyes, made an excited, strangled noise, and charged me.

"Doug! Stop that at once!" shouted Ms. Heliotrope, who somehow managed to grab his collar before he could fully tackle me.

Feral Doug immediately went limp and flopped to the floor in defeat.

I felt bad for him, so I bent down on one knee and held out a hand. "Good to see you too."

Doug looked at my hand, then glanced at Ms. Heliotrope as if to ask permission to accept the gesture. She nodded slightly, and he immediately got on his knees, took my hand with both of his, and shook it enthusiastically. I had a feeling that if I hadn't had vampire strength, he'd probably have ripped off my arm.

"Very well, Doug. Josh and I need to have a conversation. If you will give us some space?"

Doug backed off and went to sit on the couch. On the way, he found one of the damaged balls I had practiced my grip on yesterday. He sat with his legs crossed in front of him and sniffed the ball, then started pulling at a bit of loose fuzz.

I sat in an easy chair near him.

"Would you like some tea, Josh?" Ms. Heliotrope offered.

I didn't really want tea, but it seemed wrong to say no. "Uh, okay."

"I'll be right back, then." She left the room, and I spent a couple of minutes watching Doug slowly peel the fuzzy cover off the tennis ball with an excruciating attention to detail. I nearly took the ball from him in frustration to peel the fuzz off for him, but Ms. Heliotrope returned with a tea tray. She placed it on the coffee table, set a cup and saucer in front of me, and poured the dark amber liquid from the teapot into the cup.

"Thanks," I said. Maybe it was the way she dressed, or just the way she handled herself, but something about being around her made me feel obligated to be polite.

She took a seat on the couch with Doug and poured her own cup. "You're welcome, Josh. Now, tell me what's going on. You don't seem quite yourself."

I almost snorted sarcastically. I hadn't been "quite myself" for about a week and a half, and things just kept getting weirder. I took a sip of tea instead. It didn't taste like anything, but at least it smelled nice.

"Did you have a talk with your friends?"

I put the cup back in the saucer. "Yeah. It went *mostly* okay."

She raised an eyebrow. "Mostly?"

I explained Brian's reactions from last night and what he had done this morning.

"I see." She relaxed further in her seat and tapped her fingers against her chin. "This could be a problem, but possibly not."

"What do you mean?"

She leaned forward and managed to give me the impression she could stare directly into both my eyes at the same time with her single eye. "Do people take Brian seriously?"

Her unwavering gaze made me nervous. "No? Not really. He's kind of an idiot."

She relaxed slightly. "Good. Although I have to question why you're friends with someone like that, his suspicions and laughable beliefs about vampires will make it easy to make him look foolish and unstable. As long as you behave yourself in front of him, his accusations will make you look even more innocent of vampirism than if he said nothing at all."

I wasn't sure if I liked where this was going, but she wasn't wrong. I didn't know why I felt guilty using Brian's fears about me when he had tried to convince Des to kick me out of the house this morning. He'd clearly throw me under the bus, and here I was, feeling like I was doing the same. What had happened to the friend I had as a kid? We used to spend Saturday afternoons sharing comic books while eating his mom's homemade cookies. Now he was a depressed mess of a person. Was it bad that I felt sorry for him, even though he kept being infuriatingly awful?

"Josh, unfortunately, your friend . . ." Ms. Heliotrope paused. "You may not even have a choice in this matter. If the Conclave finds out—and they will—they'll, shall we say, disappear him unless he can be made to seem mentally ill. He will have a greater chance of survival and a relatively normal life if we make him look paranoid."

I stood and began to pace. "This is . . . this is really screwed up."

"Vampires aren't known for their empathy and compassion, Josh. The older they get, the more removed they are from human nature. I know this is disappointing, but there is nothing gentle about being a vampire." She gave me a tender look, like that of a parent telling a child a difficult truth about the world.

I looked at the stripped and broken tennis ball in Feral Doug's hands and had to agree.

Ms. Heliotrope stood and slapped her hands against her legs. "Let's take a walk. Some fresh air will help you feel a little better."

I wasn't convinced it would do much of anything, but the concern etched on her face made me hold my tongue. If older vampires had no empathy or compassion, did that mean she was a younger one? She was stern and imposing, yes, but she seemed to care more than she let on. "Okay."

"Good. Doug, you'll be staying here," Ms. Heliotrope stated firmly. Doug looked disgruntled but got up, stuck his hand between the couch cushions, and pulled out another broken tennis ball. He sat back down and began to petulantly peel off the fuzzy cover.

"Come," Ms. Heliotrope said from the door. I felt a jolt of surprise. I hadn't realized I was so distracted by Doug.

We left the house, and she locked the door behind us.

"Are you sure he'll be okay?"

"Doug? Oh, no, he'll be fine. He knows he can only go out in the daylight under strict conditions. He's just not human enough to avoid unwanted attention." Ms. Heliotrope walked down the front steps. "Let's head to the park."

I followed her. She was only a few steps ahead of me, but even though I was taller and had longer legs, her determined stride was quick. It took me a moment to catch up.

"There's a small rose garden in the park I'm fond of," Ms. Heliotrope stated. "I'll show you."

We walked down into the park a ways before I remembered what I had seen at the town hall the other day. "Hey, Ms. Heliotrope, do you think more is going on with Danforth and Genevieve than this stupid bet?"

"What makes you ask?"

"Well, I saw Danforth talking to Mr. Costello—the high school principal—a few days ago, and then at the middle school the other day, he was offering a donation at the front desk. Then I saw Genevieve at the town hall, talking with the mayor. It all seemed strange. Suspicious, maybe. I mean, sure, it's a small community and people all know each other, but . . ." I shrugged. "I just thought you'd like to know."

She stopped walking for a moment. "That doesn't sound like their usual behavior. They rarely get involved in anything to do with local infrastructure, and they're hardly prone to spontaneous acts of charity."

I stopped awkwardly. "What do you think they're doing?"

"Not sure, but this is concerning . . . especially if they're getting involved with town government." Ms. Heliotrope began to walk again, her gait quick and agitated.

I scrambled to keep up. "I'm glad I remembered to tell you. Genevieve was also pretty chummy at the police station."

"I'll contact the Conclave this evening. It's good you told me this, Josh. This isn't normal. Our kind usually do our best to keep under the radar. And when we let ourselves be known . . . it's never good for anyone."

"Josh!"

Ms. Heliotrope and I turned in the direction of the familiar voice.

"Hi, Harriet!" I waved as she ran over.

She smiled as she caught up to us. "Hi, Josh! How are you doing today? Feeling a little more like yourself?" She looked at Ms. Heliotrope and offered her hand. "Hello, I'm Josh's friend Harriet. I don't think we've met before. I think I'd remember someone with so much style."

Ms. Heliotrope was wearing a brown bustle skirt with a crisp white shirt and dusty-blue fitted vest. It was more reserved than her usual steampunk vibe, but just as memorable.

Ms. Heliotrope gave Harriet a firm-looking shake. "It's a pleasure."

"Ms. Heliotrope is my . . . life coach," I said awkwardly. "I met her just the other day, and she's been helping me deal with . . . stuff."

"Ah, yes. I've been offering Josh some complimentary personal coaching as I try to establish my coaching business."

"That's great! I know Josh has been working hard, trying to save money for tuition." Harriet turned her attention from Ms. Heliotrope to me. "I'm glad you're still thinking about the future even though you haven't been feeling well."

"Well, you know . . ." I always felt a little awkward when Harriet praised me.

Ms. Heliotrope seemed to watch us closely, which knocked me even more off-kilter. "I'm sure Josh will be feeling fine soon. He seems to be fairly resilient so far."

Harriet's phone buzzed, and she pulled it out of her

pocket. "Oh, no. I'm sorry. I have to leave. I have to go pick up my brother from his activity group. I'll see you at work, Josh!" She ran off almost as suddenly as she had shown up.

"Hmm . . ." Ms. Heliotrope once again began walking down the path.

"'Hmm' what?"

"You're quite enamored with that young woman, aren't you?" Ms. Heliotrope teased.

I stopped walking and stared at her. "How does everybody know?"

"Well, it's kind of obvious. Your tone of voice is warmer, you blush when she compliments you, and when she left, you looked like someone just told you your dog had died."

"Do you think she knows?"

Ms. Heliotrope smiled slyly. "Oh, most definitely."

I sighed. "Ugh, that's what Graziella said. I must look like a complete idiot to Harriet at this point. I've had a crush on her for years."

"Josh." Ms. Heliotrope took hold of my arm and guided me toward the garden she'd told me about earlier. "Do you really think Harriet would have gone out of her way to say hello if she didn't like you back at least a little?"

"I dunno," I groaned as we walked along a stone path, heading to some rose bushes. "Maybe she's just being nice?"

"Very well. Believe what you want. However, you have a complication. You're one of us now. You'll never be able to have a normal relationship with a human. There's simply no way you could hide your condition from a human you're that intimate with. She seems like a smart girl; she would figure it out."

We stopped within a little circle of rosebushes of varying colors. They were all a bit limp, dry petals and leaves falling off at the slightest hint of wind. I sat on the small bench in the middle and put my head in my hands. I felt as wilted as the flowers. I'd wasted so much time not being direct and telling Harriet how I felt. Now . . . well, now I could probably never tell her. Brian's suspicions about me being a vampire were one thing. But if Harriet figured it out—and she eventually would—she'd be in danger from forces I probably couldn't protect her from.

Ms. Heliotrope sat down next to me. "Josh, if circumstances were different and I were actually your personal coach, I'd tell you to tell her how you feel. You wear your heart on your sleeve, and when it comes to her, it's clear your heart is absolutely certain how it feels."

"But I can't, can I?" I picked up a pink petal with browning edges.

"Do you want to keep her safe and happy?" she asked.

"Yes. Yes, I do."

"Then you have to let her go. If another vampire sees how obvious your feelings are toward her, they'll see it as a weakness, and they may try to exploit it. You already have enemies in Danforth and Genevieve, and they've been spying on you. Doubtless, they know about Harriet and your friends, and they will use that against you. It's only a matter of time, really. Just distance yourself a bit. You'll have to work on building a bit of an outer shell so people can't read you so easily."

"I've loved her for so long." I watched the wind blow petals off a yellow rose that had looked solid a moment before. A late summer butterfly that should have moved on a month ago landed on a leaf nearby.

"In a way, it's in your favor that you haven't told her yet. When I was changed, I was married. Having to leave was horrible, knowing I had to break the heart of the person I had given mine to. I still regret it to this day, except I know he's still alive and well."

I reached out my hand to see if I could get the butterfly to perch on my finger, but it flew away before I could get close enough. "I'm sorry you went through that."

"I'm sorry you're having to make a similar tough decision. You do have another factor in your favor, though."

"What's that?" I had a hard time believing there was anything that could make this better.

"I had to figure things out and make all those decisions alone. You, on the other hand, have me to help. I know it doesn't sound that great right now, but it should make things a little less lonely, maybe."

She sounded less confident than usual, and I glanced over. Her downcast expression made it clear she was carrying a heavy weight on her shoulders.

"You're right." I stood up from the bench and stretched to get some of the tension out of my shoulders. "I can't keep holding on to something that could hurt someone I love."

Ms. Heliotrope had a faraway look on her face as she also stood.

"I should head off to work soon. Let's head back."

We walked back to her house. Though part of me felt better knowing I wasn't in this alone, I also felt like my heart was breaking, and I didn't know if I could handle that much pain.

I managed a relatively low-key night at work. Harriet explained that my somber mood was probably related to the argument with Brian, which Gino accepted without question. Mondays weren't usually very busy, fortunately, so it was easy to go through the motions until closing.

I returned home to find Brian and Des having a conversation in the living room. They were so deep into it, they both jumped when I walked in.

"Hey," I said self-consciously.

"Hey, Josh," Des said. "Come join us."

I put the pizza on the kitchen counter and walked over, a little apprehensive. They both seemed really serious, and I wasn't sure what to make of it. I perched on the armchair and looked back and forth between them. Brian had a somewhat odd expression on his face that I couldn't quite read.

"So, Josh," Des said. "Brian has something to say to you."

That felt ominous. "Okay, what's up?"

Brian turned to me. "I'm sorry, Josh."

"You're sorry?" Where did this sudden change of heart come from?

"Yeah, well, I felt like you were getting all this attention, and I felt kind of left out," Brian said, his voice eerily calm. "And earlier, when I was on my way out to work on some yards, Des mentioned you got someone to be your mentor. I thought that was a good idea, so I decided to find someone who could mentor me in running a business. I went on my rounds and talked to a few people and found someone who was willing to help me."

"That sounds good." If he was going to finally take action to improve himself, maybe that was for the best. I had a lurking suspicion, though, that it wasn't all it seemed.

"It's awesome!" Des smiled. "Now we're all on our way to doing some good adulting, right? Who did you get to help you out?"

Looking at Brian, I realized part of the reason his expression was so strange was he wasn't blinking as much as a normal person should, which worried me. "Is it one of the business owners in town?"

He gave me a weird, calm smile. "Oh, he said he knew you. It's that guy who lives on the hill in that huge mansion? You know, Mr. Danforth? I can't wait to learn everything I can so I can be cool like him."

DAY 12
TUESDAY

When this all started, I thought things couldn't possibly get worse. Not being able to taste food felt awful. Being sensitive to light was frustrating. The speed thing was kind of cool, but having to hide it was hard. Being a vampire, which seemed cool in theory, was a series of annoyances.

That wasn't what hurt anymore. I sat at the dining room table, my head in my hands. Too many things had finally piled on top of each other, and the worst of it was, I had to give up Harriet and Danforth had managed to infiltrate my friends. I should have left before this could happen. I should have left the moment I realized what I was turning into.

Brian . . . what could I do about Brian without giving away what was really going on? Would he even be able to believe me, or was he so far under Danforth's control that it was hopeless? Having cameras and various monitoring devices all over the house and at work was one thing. Those could be removed or destroyed. I couldn't do that to Brian, though.

As for Harriet, what could her life possibly be with me?

She loved to cook, and I really couldn't eat much at all. She'd grow and change, and I'd stay the same indefinitely. She deserved to have the choice to get married, have children, and live a human life. She couldn't have that with me.

And if I found a way to make her a vampire like me? She wouldn't be able to taste the food she made. How could she be a chef if she couldn't even taste her creations to make sure they were just right? But if I wanted to stay with her and I didn't make her a vampire, she'd be in greater danger.

I had to fix this. I had to fix all of this. I'd had my chance to leave, and now . . . Brian may have been a complete jerk, but he didn't deserve this. I had to stay and try to fix things for my friends. I wanted to do the right thing.

"Hey, Josh, you okay?" asked Des.

I couldn't bring myself to lift my head to look at him while my heart was tearing itself into pieces.

"Josh? You can talk to me. Or I can call Harriet. You shouldn't be—"

I grabbed his hand. "Don't call Harriet," I rasped.

"So it's about Harriet." Des sat down and tried to pull his hand away from me. "You can let go of me now, Josh."

"Oh, sorry." I let go. I hoped I hadn't held it too tightly. When I glanced over, Des wasn't rubbing at his wrist, and I took that as a sign I'd managed to at least get that right.

"So what is it?"

He waited patiently as I pulled my thoughts together. There was only so much I could tell him without giving away everything. I couldn't get away with bullshitting him, so I had to tell him just enough of the truth—and just enough of a lie—to be convincing. I didn't want to lie to him, but I had no choice.

"I've decided to move on. I've spent all this time wanting to be with Harriet and doing nothing. I probably would have eventually told her how I feel. I probably should have long ago. But now I think I need to focus on taking care of myself. I need friends right now, but I can't invest myself in a relationship when I'm dealing with this mess."

I sat there hoping that was convincing enough. It really wasn't far from the truth at all. It was also interesting enough that I could leave my fears about Brian out of the conversation. I wasn't even sure how to approach that situation.

"I see." Des sat back in his chair and laced his fingers behind his head. "Have you considered how Harriet might feel about this?"

"Usually, I would, but I can't be a guy with a crush on a girl anymore. I need to make a decision. I'm a mess right now. Maybe it's not time for me to have a girlfriend." I rubbed my face with my hands and then crossed my arms and leaned on the table.

We sat there for a little bit in silence. Then Des laid a bomb on me.

"So, would you be okay with it if I asked her out sometime?"

I sat bolt upright and stared at him. "Wha . . . ? Huh?"

"I've always liked Harriet, but I've always held back because I knew how much you were into her. I mean, look at her. She's smart, kind, and down-to-earth. She's also pretty hot when she feels like putting some effort into it. She's a good person, and anyone would be lucky to be with someone like her."

Would I be okay with that? Would I be okay with Des asking her out? Would it break my heart to see them together romantically? I had no idea. Part of me was furious at the idea, but another felt like it would give me a convenient out. Des would treat her right, without a doubt. If I couldn't be with Harriet, I'd rather she be with someone like Des.

Brian walked past us into the kitchen. "Hell, I'd do her. Especially after seeing her in cosplay."

Des and I both turned to glare at him.

"What?" Brian shrugged and continued to the refrigerator.

Des pulled off his sock and threw it at Brian's head. "What's wrong with you?"

Yeah, better someone like Des than someone like Brian. But then, Harriet was too smart to fall for anyone like Brian.

My phone buzzed in my pocket, so I pulled it out to answer it. I figured whoever was on the other end would require a much less intense conversation than trying to give Des an answer.

"Hello?" I said as I watched Brian throw Des's sock back at him.

"Hey there, Josh," my dad said from the other end of the call. "You want to come by the store and have lunch with me before you go to work?"

"Yeah, sounds good." Then I wondered how I would hide that I wasn't really eating. "I'll probably eat at work, and I had a late breakfast, so I'm not hungry, but I'll come see you anyway."

"I'll get you a soda while I eat, then." My dad sounded pretty happy, and to be honest, it was a good excuse for me to get out of the house before I had to answer Des's question.

I got the details from him and made my goodbyes. As I shut off my phone, I got smacked in the face with a stinky sock. Des and Brian now had a couple of socks they were throwing around, so I wasn't sure whose foot belonged to it. I wasn't sure I wanted to find out.

I dropped the sock to the table in front of me. "Guys, I'm going to go see my dad. He wants lunch."

Des caught the sock Brian threw at him. "Yeah, okay. Tell him I said hi."

I had a feeling Des wanted me to give him an answer but was being polite. I'd probably have to decide soon, though, and it wasn't a decision I wanted to make.

I got up from the chair and grabbed my jacket, sunglasses, and car keys. "I'll probably go to work right after. See you later."

As I exited the house, I heard a sock hit someone, accompanied by some colorful language from Brian.

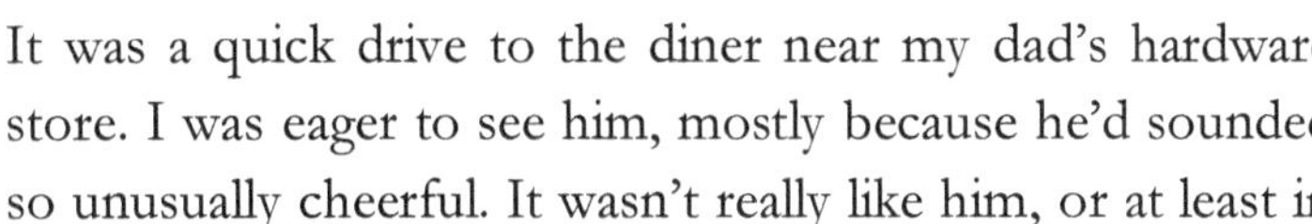

It was a quick drive to the diner near my dad's hardware store. I was eager to see him, mostly because he'd sounded so unusually cheerful. It wasn't really like him, or at least in my experience, it wasn't the Dad I was used to. I'd heard that when he was younger, he was pretty boisterous, but I'd never had a chance to experience that myself.

"Hello, Josh! Here to join your father?" asked the waitress. I realized she was someone from Harriet's grade back in school.

"Rebecca, right?" I hoped I got her name correct.

"Yeah! Your dad's this way." She gestured toward the booths so I'd follow her. As we walked, she whispered, "Between you and me, I've never seen your dad this happy. Has he met someone?"

I shrugged. "Your guess is as good as mine. I hope it isn't something too weird." These days, weird was dangerous.

"Hmm . . ." We passed by most of the booths before she stopped. "Have a seat, Josh. Here's a menu."

She placed it on the table and left, but I didn't sit down as I stared in horror at the sight before me. My dad was there, looking relatively normal despite his unusual joyfulness. That wasn't what disturbed me. What made my stomach drop was who he was sitting with.

On the opposite side of the booth was a familiar man with long hair and a far too recognizable redheaded woman with her signature red lipstick.

"Josh!" Dad exclaimed. "Have a seat! I'm glad to see you. We have much to talk about."

"Oh, Joshy, I didn't know Carl invited you!" Genevieve said dramatically.

Yeah, I'm sure you didn't. The thought dripped with more sarcasm than I would have been capable of had I said the words aloud.

"Look, honey," Genevieve continued. "It's our favorite pizza boy. What a pleasant surprise!"

"It is a surprise." Danforth held his hand out for me to shake.

I almost ignored it, but I had a feeling my dad would ask more questions than I felt comfortable answering if I didn't. I took Danforth's hand and squeezed it hard while I glared at him through my sunglasses. He smirked knowingly as he squeezed back.

"Good, good," Dad said. "Have a seat, son. We have a lot to talk about."

I sat down, leaving my sunglasses on, partially so I could hide that I was glaring at the two vampires across from me. They still had their sunglasses on as well, but on them, it looked like a fashion statement. Like they were wealthy big-city investors with a plan. I probably just looked like a gangly guy in my late teens, trying too hard to seem cool.

Dad smiled. "Now, son, don't you think it's rude to wear sunglasses at the table?"

I nearly jumped as he reached out to take them off my face. "No, Dad. I have a headache right now. Do you mind if I keep wearing them?"

"Oh, Carl, please. Let the poor boy wear his sunglasses. We're wearing ours after all." Genevieve smiled as she tapped her own sunglasses with one long, French-manicured fingernail.

"Of course, Ms. Danforth," Dad replied almost flirtatiously.

"Uh, uh, uh! You know I asked you to call me Genevieve, Carl," she flirted back.

I nearly groaned in disgust but held back. Danforth continued to smirk at me while the flirtation between Genevieve and my Dad continued.

Once I'd had enough of the simpering conversation, I interrupted. "Hey, Dad, I wasn't expecting there to be anyone else eating with us."

"Oh, did I forget to tell you? I invited you for a reason," Dad began. "Mr. Danforth here remembered you from when you delivered pizza to his place. He guessed you were my son when they came into the hardware store today, and of course, I had to brag about how proud I am of you and your hard work."

"Your father couldn't stop talking about how highly he thinks of you," Danforth interjected before taking a sip of water.

"Exactly!" Dad patted me on the shoulder. "So we got to talking, and Stephan—I mean, Mr. Danforth here—came up with an idea."

"Yes, I'm always looking for hard workers to mentor."

Of course you are, I thought. *You just stole my friend. I'm sure you're happy to find anyone else you can control.*

"I told your father I could pay your entire college tuition—even graduate school, if you'd like—as long as you work as my intern during your breaks. Then, if all goes well, I might be able to offer you a job at the end. If not, I can give you a stellar reference and help you find a position somewhere else."

The veiled threat under his pretty words was obvious. He wanted to control me just because he could. He wanted to manipulate me just because he could. He'd already done it to Brian, and he probably knew I was already aware of that. Sure, if I cooperated, I could have those nice things, but they'd come at a price, and I already knew the price would be too high.

"Isn't that fantastic, son? You won't have to deliver pizzas anymore to make ends meet. You'll get a free ride through school with a guarantee of work at the end."

Luckily, Rebecca came back for our orders before I could give a sarcastic response. "What will you folks be having today?"

"I'll have my usual, Rebecca," Dad said. Then he looked at Genevieve. "Oh, that was rude of me. Ladies should always go first."

"Please don't worry, Carl," Genevieve replied demurely. She faced Rebecca. "I'll just have a diet soda. A lady has to watch her figure, after all."

Rebecca, who had always been a little chubby, wilted at the words, but she pasted a smile on her face and wrote down the order. "And you, sir?"

Danforth handed her his menu. "A hamburger . . . rare."

"Would you like fries with that, or a salad?" Rebecca

asked, her discomfort visible. I wanted to tear the two vampires apart for how uncomfortable they were making her. I didn't know Rebecca well, but she'd always seemed like a nice person.

"Fries are fine," Danforth replied, clearly not interested.

"O-okay," Rebecca stammered. "How about you, Josh?"

I smiled sympathetically. "I'll have a cheeseburger. Rare, too, and with fries. And a chocolate milkshake." I wasn't going to eat much of the meal other than the rare burger, but I felt bad for her, so I wanted to give her a worthwhile order.

She gave me a more genuine smile. "Okay, Josh. So that's a usual for Mr. Buckmilter, a diet soda for the lady, a rare hamburger with fries for the gentleman, and a rare cheeseburger with fries and a chocolate milkshake for Josh. Anything else?"

"That's it. Thanks, Rebecca," Dad replied.

"And I'll take the check when we're done," Danforth stated.

"That's not necessary, Mr. Danforth," Dad began. "You're already offering us so much. At least let me cover your meal."

"Nonsense! I'm happy to pay." Danforth glanced at me over his sunglasses. The mirth in his eyes was hardly friendly.

"Thank you, Mr. Danforth."

"Ah, remember, that's Stephan to you, Carl," Danforth corrected. "We're all friends here."

It took all my self-control to not laugh in his face.

"Yes, Stephan, of course," Dad replied. "If you'll all excuse me, I need to use the men's room."

I stood so my dad could slide out of the booth. Then I sat back down and watched until he walked through the door to the bathroom. This was my opportunity to find out what they were really up to, and I was definitely going to take advantage.

I leaned forward and whispered harshly, "What the hell are you trying to pull?"

Genevieve laughed. "Oh, Joshy, why would you think we're up to anything?"

"You, not up to anything? Don't make me laugh," I growled. "I know what you did to me."

Danforth perked up. "Oh, you know now? Tell me, when did you realize what you are? We know that formalist creature got rid of the bugs we'd set up around your house. You're making it very hard to keep track of all your milestones for the bet. It's quite . . . disappointing."

"Well, you can stay disappointed because I'm not telling you. And stay the hell away from my dad and my friends," I hissed between clenched teeth. I could feel the itch in my gums as my fangs started to protrude.

"Better be careful, little Josh," Genevieve said. "You don't want your little friends to see what you are now, do you? And if they find out, the Conclave will send their formalist after you instead of us." She gave me a toothy grin, her bright-red lipstick highlighting her perfect, white teeth.

"Me, be careful? Don't make me laugh. I know the two of you are up to something, and it's not just this stupid bet either. Whatever you're doing, stop and leave my town." I dug my fingernails into the table, and splinters began to pierce the pads of my fingers.

Danforth laughed. "Too late for that, Josh. You are right, though. This isn't all about you. You're a distraction. There are processes in play that your small-town mind can't begin to fathom. So why don't you play along, let us know how you're doing, and stay out of our business."

"Sorry, sorry," Dad said as he rushed back to the table. "I hope you had a good talk about the offer?"

I couldn't respond since Rebecca returned with our orders. She placed each order correctly in front of us, then backed off. "If you need anything else, let me know." Despite her singsong statement and smile, her eyes shifted back and forth nervously. She was apparently intuitive enough to know there was danger at our table.

"It's fine, Rebecca. Thank you," I said. She gave me a look of relief and went off to help other customers.

I took a bite out of my cheeseburger and chewed it slowly, deliberately, so I wouldn't have to speak.

Looking at my dad, I realized he was kind of glassy-eyed. It was the same look I'd seen on too many people now. Had Genevieve or Danforth glamoured him like they had me when they changed me that night almost two weeks ago?

"I'm sure my boy will need some time to think it over," Dad said after he took a bite. "He's very independent and determined to work hard."

I swallowed the mostly tasteless bite. "It does seem too good to be true." I took another bite and glared at the two vampires, despite my sunglasses.

"Don't be rude, Josh." Dad laughed. "These are good people! Everyone in town has been talking about how much they've donated to the schools and volunteered to help out with town business."

They had definitely glamoured him. I swallowed my second bite—this one even more tasteless due to my fear of how smoothly these two monsters had integrated themselves into the town. Why would they need to get so involved with a small town unless their intention was to . . . control it? I nearly dropped my burger. Was that what they were up to? I thought about all the innocent people in the town who could—who would—be hurt by having unscrupulous vampires in control of their lives.

"I'll think about it," I said in as neutral a tone as possible, trying to hide my terror. What I was going through was just a test run. I was thankful for the sunglasses. At least they might be able to hide the fear in my eyes.

Genevieve smiled brightly. She looked like a model in a toothpaste ad. "Excellent! We look forward to hearing from you soon."

Danforth suddenly looked at his watch. "Oh, look, darling. We really must be off. That meeting?"

Genevieve nodded. "Yes, we should get going. Until next time, Carl, Josh." She gave me a pointed look.

They both hurried out of the booth and walked to the register to pay for the meal. I watched as Rebecca nervously took the jet-black credit card, swiped it, and handed the card and receipt back to Danforth, who signed the receipt with a dramatic flourish. Then he held out his arm for Genevieve, who took it, and they walked out the door full of cool confidence.

In the meantime, I was just barely keeping myself from exploding in fear and rage. They had screwed me over, but there was no way in hell I'd let them screw my dad over, or the people of Willow Springs. But what could I do? I was just one person—one vampire—and a weak one at that. They had the advantage all around. I could only hope Ms. Heliotrope had some reinforcements.

I chewed my burger, hoping I could at least let off some steam that way. I didn't care what it did or didn't taste like.

"Josh, why don't you move over to the other side so I can see you?" Dad said.

I looked at him, startled out of my reverie. "Uh, yeah, sure."

Pushing my plate to the opposite side of the table, I sat down in the cold seat. I pushed aside Genevieve and Danforth's untouched food and watched my dad take a bite of his bacon cheeseburger. His eyes were definitely glassy.

"Dad, are you okay?"

"Hmm? Why do you ask?" He took another bite.

"You aren't really acting like yourself today," I ventured cautiously.

"I'm not?" He looked genuinely confused.

"No, you're not. You don't usually act this cheerful, and you don't get this chummy with people you barely know. I mean, you're nice to people, but this was weird." I took another bite.

"It was?" He seemed a bit dazed.

"Yeah. How do you feel right now?"

"Okay. I mean . . ." He put his burger down, his brow furrowing. "I feel a bit fuzzy, though. Maybe I'm coming down with something? We're covered at the store. I think I can take the rest of the day off."

He blinked a few times, and his eyes seemed a little less glassy.

I put my burger down and looked at him intently. "Do you remember the people we were just talking to?"

His eyes took on that glazed look again, and he gave me an unnatural-looking grin. "Yeah, the Danforths! They're good people!"

"Who told you they were good people?"

He blinked again. "I don't know. They seem like good people, I guess."

"Dad, I know they seem like good people, but they're not. I want you to stay away from them, okay?" I took his hand and squeezed it gently to emphasize the urgency of my request.

"They're not?" he asked in almost childlike confusion.

"No, they're not. They might look nice on the outside, but I've met them before. They aren't trustworthy. You've always told me to trust my instincts, right?"

The glassy look in his eyes faded. He looked more like his usual, subdued self. While I hated bringing him down from the unusual cheerfulness, he wouldn't want someone else controlling his state of mind. "I trust you, son."

"Thanks, Dad. I'll see what we can do. Just try to avoid them." I took another bite, just to go through the motions while Dad finished his meal.

"Are you feeling any better?" Dad asked.

"Yeah, I'm feeling a lot better. I've had to change my diet a bit, but I'll be okay. I made a friend who has the same health issue, and she told me what to do." I figured it was true enough, if vague. I didn't want the Conclave to think Dad knew anything.

He smiled. This time it felt more genuine—more like him. "Good. I'd hate to lose you."

"I'd hate to lose you too, Dad." I offered him a brave smile, but the thought of anything happening to him because of me made my heart ache.

We sat in silence for a while, leaving all our deeper feelings unsaid as we finished our meals.

Rebecca came over to take our plates when we were done. "How was everything?"

"It was great, Rebecca," Dad replied.

She'd turned to leave when I touched her arm. "Hey, did they tip you enough?"

"No, those cheapskates," Rebecca mumbled. Then she gasped. "Oh no, I'm sorry. Forget I said that!"

"It's okay. I'll leave a tip for you. Those of us in the restaurant business need to look out for each other."

She smiled warmly. "Definitely. You know, Harriet always said nice things about you at school. She was right. You're a good person."

I tried not to flinch at the mention of Harriet.

"I did my best to raise him right," Dad said.

"You sure did, Mr. Buckmilter," Rebecca said. "See you again soon!"

Dad and I left our booth and waved at the cook in the kitchen before exiting. For a moment, we just stood outside, and then I gave Dad a slightly awkward hug.

"What was that for?" he asked.

"I love you, Dad." It was pure instinct. I wasn't sure what kind of son I could be to him now that I wasn't human anymore, but I at least wanted to make sure he knew I appreciated everything he did for me.

"Love you too, kid." He patted me on the back. "I'll just check in at the store, then head home. See you soon."

I nodded and watched as he walked away. Once the door to the hardware store closed behind him, I let out a deep breath and looked around. Something felt . . . strange.

I closed my eyes. Ms. Heliotrope had told me my instincts would become stronger, so I tried to pay attention to them. Opening my eyes, I looked across the street at a chain coffee shop. Ms. Heliotrope sat in the window, looking not at me but at the door to the hardware store.

That seemed odd, so I crossed the street and went in to see her.

I sat down next to her. "Hey, Ms. Heliotrope?"

"Josh! Hello. What are you doing here?" she asked, uncharacteristically flustered.

"I just had lunch with my dad. Look, I need to talk to you. The . . ." I hesitated, uncertain what I could say in public.

"I saw them. Tell me what happened."

I explained how the conversation went, as well as my concerns. She nodded when I was done. "This is the worst-case scenario I had imagined. We have to work, and fast."

"If there's anything I can do to help, let me know."

"I'm not sure, but . . ." She paused. "Keep your dad safe. Your friends too. If Genevieve and Danforth are doing what I think they're doing, it could mean trouble for the entire town, and that will only be the beginning."

"Do you think I should call off work today?"

"No, no. You're in a useful position with your job. You get to see what's going on in the entire town with all your deliveries. If you see anything else strange, let me know immediately. I'll be contacting the Conclave to see what they recommend."

"Okay. I should head off soon anyway. Good to see you, Ms. Heliotrope." I stood to leave.

"Josh?"

I turned to look at her. "Yeah?"

"You're doing good work. I'm really proud of you. And from what I've seen of your father today, I think if he knew what you were dealing with, he'd be proud of you too."

"Thanks." I gave her a warm smile and left the coffee shop.

I was too distracted to think about Harriet now. As I hopped in my car and drove to work, I thought carefully about all I had witnessed. Something was coming to a head, and it was far bigger than me being turned into a vampire. I only hoped it wasn't too late to fix things so nobody else was harmed.

DAY 13

WEDNESDAY

"Have you guys noticed anything . . . weird today?" Dr. Chen asked.

I had arrived at Ms. Heliotrope's house early to avoid the guys—Brian because I was worried my every action would be reported to Danforth and Des because I wasn't sure I wanted to give him an answer about Harriet yet. Plus, training with Ms. Heliotrope seemed like a good excuse. The more I practiced self-control, the better, right?

It was around noon when Dr. Chen came over to drop off some donated blood for Ms. Heliotrope. They chatted a bit about some new app that allowed people to track the blood they donated. Apparently, it was making it harder to hide blood that was being co-opted for . . . other uses, so to speak. That in itself was interesting; there were clearly some intricacies I had to learn about getting blood. However, Dr. Chen's question caught my attention even more.

"Everything seemed normal when I drove here this morning. People were driving around and stuff," I offered. "Why? What's going on?"

Ms. Heliotrope leaned in a little closer. The question had apparently piqued her interest as well.

Dr. Chen seemed surprised by our intense focus. "Um . . . uh, well . . . nobody was driving around, I guess?"

"What do you mean, nobody was driving around?" Ms. Heliotrope encouraged.

"The streets were empty. It was like a ghost town. While Willow Springs may be a small town, you usually see people around at lunchtime—running errands, getting lunch, stopping to chat on the sidewalk—that kind of thing. But on my way down Shady Avenue and onto Main Street from the hospital, there were no cars on the street—driving or parked—nobody was walking on the sidewalks, the stores looked empty . . ." He shrugged. "But then I passed by the high school, and the parking lot was jammed full of cars."

I gave Ms. Heliotrope a searching look, and she nodded. "Something must be going on, Dr. Chen. We think the new vampires in town are up to something. They seem to be glamouring all the local merchants and civil servants. They could have gotten to more people than we were aware of, much faster than expected."

I remembered our conversation yesterday. This sounded really bad.

The worry I was feeling must have been obvious, because Ms. Heliotrope continued. "This kind of thing has happened before, unfortunately. Usually with more grandstanding—taking a town or city with the intent of turning it into a center of power. This is more subtle than usual, but all the signs are there."

I wondered if she'd seen this happen before herself. I mean, I had no clue how old she really was—how long she'd been around. But Willow Springs? This town wasn't exactly a place of any significance. It was just an average town that wasn't too far from a big city. In fact, it was far enough away that having some kind of control over the place didn't seem like it would be valuable.

Just as I was about to question Ms. Heliotrope, my phone rang. I pulled it out of my pocket and answered it when I saw it was Des.

"What's up?"

Des sighed. "You know how weird Brian has been the past couple of days?"

"Isn't Brian always a little weird?" I asked, extra cautious not to say something wrong in front of Ms. Heliotrope.

She perked up at my mention of Brian for some reason. Considering what Dr. Chen had told me at the convention, I realized she could probably hear everything Des and I were saying.

"Yeah," Des said, "but extra weird. Like he was terrified of you a couple days ago, and then he just kinda wasn't?"

Because Danforth and Genevieve got to him.

"Okay, what's going on, then?" I asked.

"He invited me to some weird event today. I told him I'd think about it, then just kind of ignored it. A little while ago, he brought it up again, and I said I wasn't interested. He tried to convince me to go, then got pretty mad and said something about how the whole town was going to be there and I'd be stupid not to be there too. Of course, after that, I pretty much told him to fuck off. It was, you know . . ."

"Weird?"

"Weird," he confirmed.

Ms. Heliotrope gestured to get my attention.

"Hang on a sec, Des." I leaned toward Ms. Heliotrope. "What do you need?"

"Can you put it on speaker? I could hear some of the conversation, but I'd like to speak to him as well. I spoke with the Conclave last night, and they advised me that, should things get to this point and I needed to deputize a few trusted people, I could. We might be able to use your friend's help."

I nodded and put the phone in speaker mode. "Hey, Des, you're on speaker now. Ms. Heliotrope wants to talk with you too. We heard that something strange is going on at the high school. Do you think that's what Brian was talking about?"

"Yeah, Brian said it was going on at the high school," Des said. "You think these people can help us figure out what's going on with him?"

"Has anyone else spoken with you about this meeting, Desmond?" Ms. Heliotrope asked.

"No, but I've been really busy for the past couple of days with stuff related to the convention this past week-end—getting prizes ready to send out to fans and video editing and stuff. I've only really seen Brian and Josh."

Ms. Heliotrope looked deep in thought. "Desmond, would you be willing to do a little spying for us? From what Josh has told me about you, you have audio and video equipment. Do you have anything small that you can hide on your body?"

I immediately remembered one of Des's convention videos, where he walked around with a hidden camera and microphone. "Do you still have the stuff you used for your video at the convention last year?"

"I think so. Why, do you want me to go and see what's up?"

"Yes, if you please. We'll meet you a couple of blocks from the high school. You won't be alone." Ms. Heliotrope glanced over at Dr. Chen. "If you'd be willing to help too? I know you don't have a long lunch break, but if you can go in as well, we could probably collect more information."

"Okay," Dr. Chen replied. "I have about a half hour or so left on my break since I came straight here."

"Good." Ms. Heliotrope nodded. "Desmond, Dr. Chen will also be helping with this."

"I'll meet you on Oak Street, then?" Des asked. "Next to the mini mall?"

"Sounds good."

"Okay, we'll see you in a few minutes. Bye." I hung up.

Ms. Heliotrope grabbed a jacket and headed for the door. She turned when she saw Dr. Chen and me still sitting. "Well? What are you waiting for? We'll need to take both your cars so Dr. Chen can get back to work after."

"Oh, yeah, right." I scrambled to catch up as she strode out the front door, with Dr. Chen close behind.

Ms. Heliotrope hopped in my car with me while Dr. Chen took his own. I wasn't sure what she was planning, so I couldn't help but ask a few questions.

"What's going on? Wouldn't it be more obvious if Des and Dr. Chen showed up at the same time? Do the other vampires know who Dr. Chen is?"

"Dr. Chen is an anomaly of sorts. When it was discovered he wasn't vulnerable to glamouring like most humans, along with his, shall we say, interest in vampire culture, he was assigned to me as a kind of attaché. He helps procure blood and brings me information in exchange for being around vampires, with the possibility of being turned one day for his services. I want Chen there to make sure your friend Desmond doesn't get glamoured."

"Oh, that makes sense." I turned onto Oak Street.

"I don't want anything to happen to your friends or

your father, Josh." Ms. Heliotrope's tone was thick with intensity. "You'll need them, and the more people we have on our side, the better. The moment Genevieve came here with Danforth and they started involving themselves in human affairs, they escalated this from a vampire issue to a human one as well."

I pulled into the parking lot at the strip mall and nodded as Dr. Chen pulled in next to us. Her serious tone made me nervous. What would they do to us? What was it about those two vampires that had Ms. Heliotrope worried?

"Des is like my family, Ms. Heliotrope. My mom left when I was a baby, and my dad wasn't okay for a long time after. Des's parents always welcomed me into their home. They're my family now too. I don't want to see them suffer. Gino, Graziella, and Renato as well. They're my work family. Even Brian—he's being a complete asshole these days, but I don't think he deserves to be a plaything for vampires. And my dad and Harriet. I may have to move on once being a vampire becomes a problem, but I don't want anything to happen to them. There are so many good people here . . ."

I felt like this whole mess was my fault, even if it wasn't really.

"Josh, you haven't done anything wrong," Ms. Heliotrope replied. "I'll do my best for you. I promise."

Her expression was pained. The guilt I felt was nothing compared to the agony on her face. I wondered what she'd been through, what kinds of hard choices she'd had to make to be the person she was now.

My thoughts were interrupted by a tap on my window. I looked up to see Des waving at me, so I opened the door.

"Hey, man, you ready?" I asked.

"Yeah, I already wired myself up. I'll get that doctor guy wired for sound too." He handed me his laptop and a headset. "There's something familiar about him. He reminds me of this total vampire nut I saw at the convention." He laughed. "You can monitor us on this."

As I took the laptop, it suddenly hit me: This wasn't right. He was going into a situation where he didn't know all the factors at play. "Ms. Heliotrope? Can we—I mean, he should know what he's dealing with."

Ms. Heliotrope climbed out of the car and walked around to join us. "This is my responsibility. The Conclave will have your head if you're the one who tells him." She glanced around to make sure there was nobody nearby in the deserted parking lot, then returned her attention to Des while Dr. Chen walked over. "Desmond, what I am about to tell you is extremely top secret. You cannot tell anyone, understood? This knowledge can put you and your loved ones in danger if it gets out."

Des glanced at me questioningly. When I nodded, he looked back at Ms. Heliotrope. "Okay."

"Good. Your friend Josh was made a vampire two weeks ago."

"Wait, so he's really . . ."

"Yes, all the strange symptoms he's had—he's not sick; he's been changing."

Des nodded thoughtfully. "You're not pulling a prank on me, right?"

"That would be a pretty elaborate prank," Dr. Chen assured, "considering what you'll be walking into in a moment."

"He's right, Des," I said. "Brian was right. It's just that vampires aren't really what the folklore says."

"Desmond, we don't have much time, so we must be brief. The people who changed Josh are up to something. We think they're trying to take over the town. You will be going into a situation where you may be in danger of being bitten and fed from or even turned." Ms. Heliotrope looked him directly in the eye with her single eye. "Desmond, do you still agree to do this?"

"The town is in danger? My friends could be hurt? Of course! If I can do anything to help, I will," Des replied. "I'm still not sure I completely believe all this, but I'd have to be an idiot to not see something weird is going on. And Josh has never steered me wrong."

Ms. Heliotrope gave Des an icy glare. "Know that if you say anything—anything at all—our governing body will not hesitate to end you."

Des gulped. I couldn't blame him. Ms. Heliotrope could be frightening when she made the effort. He nodded. "Understood."

"Let's get set up and get you and Dr. Chen to the meeting." Ms. Heliotrope took the laptop from me and let me help Des get Dr. Chen wired up.

We sped through everything as quickly as we could, then headed over to the high school. Dr. Chen and Des walked through the crowded parking lot and entered the building, while Ms. Heliotrope and I hid around the side near the tables where my friends and I used to hang out during lunchtime. It was oddly empty considering it was a weekday and the tables should have been filled with hungry students. Where were all the kids?

"We're getting something," Ms. Heliotrope said.

We had managed to attach a small camera to Dr. Chen's thick-framed glasses. We saw the inside of the hallway and heard a buzz of noise over the microphones attached to both Dr. Chen and Des. They followed the sounds and ended up in the lobby outside the auditorium. It was crowded with familiar people from all over town. As Dr. Chen moved his head to take in the mass of people, I spotted Gino and Graziella. My palms started to sweat. I didn't see my dad or Harriet there, but the crowd was so thick, they could have easily been there as well.

"They got to them too?"

"Take it easy, Josh." Ms. Heliotrope put a comforting hand on my shoulder and gave it a gentle squeeze.

Dr. Chen and Des split up, walking through the crowd to make small talk and get info. Des fell out of Dr. Chen's sight pretty quickly, which meant we could only hear audio from Des. I anxiously listened, hoping he'd be safe. A familiar voice soon came through the microphone.

"Des? You decided to come after all?" Brian sounded half surprised, half smug.

"Yeah, I thought about it, and it seemed important to you," Des replied in his usual amiable tone. "You know me, I can't turn my back on a friend."

"Good. These people are going to make us part of something big, I just know it," Brian enthused.

"You ask Josh to come too?"

"There are other things planned for Josh. Besides, he's . . . well . . . I think he's a lost cause, Des. You know, with that weird health thing he has. I think he might be losing it. We have to stick together."

Brian's words gave me chills. What did they have planned for me?

Ms. Heliotrope focused on Dr. Chen's video feed while the blood drained from my face. These monsters had just gone in and manipulated Brian into their tool. Would it even be possible to salvage what was left of him now?

"Look." Ms. Heliotrope pointed at the screen, where Dr. Chen was walking into the auditorium. I saw Des slip in near him, and they found a spot near the back. The seats filled in quickly, and once everyone was settled, the lights went down over the audience and a spotlight shone on the stage. "Danforth and Genevieve were always ones for amateur theatrics."

Danforth walked onstage and took up position directly in the middle of the spotlight. Genevieve joined him from the other side of the stage. Danforth looked every bit the refined businessman in his tailored suit with his long hair tied back neatly, while Genevieve's skin shone like pale moonlight, which only served to accentuate her dramatic red lips and sparkling green eyes. Though their collective beauty made them mesmerizing even without the use of glamour, all I could feel upon looking at them was disgust.

I hoped beyond hope my father had managed to avoid the gathering after he seemed to shake off the glamour yesterday. I'd hate to see him looking upon these monsters with the almost religious fervor of the crowd we were looking at.

"Welcome!" Danforth's voice was clear and resonant. "This is a time of great import. You have all been chosen to help begin a new era for Willow Springs, and the benefits you reap will be immense."

A round of applause followed his words.

"We arrived in Willow Springs with the hopes that you, the fine people of this town, would be forward thinkers. That you would be ambitious and thrive on setting trends, rather than being followers," Danforth continued in his mellifluous voice. It seemed unfair that someone so warped could be allowed to have that much charisma. "So are you followers, or are you leaders?"

The crowd erupted in applause and shouts of approval once more. It made me want to vomit. What did he plan on doing? Turn some of the townspeople into vampires that served him, and the rest into blood cattle?

"Now, there are sacrifices that must be made, of course," Genevieve spoke up once the applause died down. Her perfect Cupid's-bow lips curved up into a smile that didn't quite meet her eyes. "But you can't make an omelet without breaking a few eggs, right?"

The audience laughed. They had no idea what they were dealing with. Those sacrifices were likely to break them. I thought again about the fact there were no students around. They weren't in the auditorium among the business owners and town officials. Sure, one teenager or two might skip lunch, but all of them, including the entire football team? I had a bad feeling about this. What was actually going on? Where were the kids? The entire campus was far too quiet for a school day.

"Ms. Heliotrope, do you think the eggs she's talking about breaking are the kids?" I asked as horror dawned.

She looked at me sharply. "Glamour the adults, raise the children to be cattle before they know that life could be different . . ." She shook her head in frustration. "It could end up being the start of them expanding out too. The Conclave could lose control and . . ."

She didn't finish her sentence, but she didn't need to, as my imagination could easily see where it was leading. I returned my attention to the screen and listened.

"Now, most of you were invited by us personally because we know you can make a difference," Genevieve stated. "However, I believe a few of you may be guests. Please stand and let us know who you are."

"Oh, shit, oh shit," I blurted out. "We need Des and Dr. Chen out of there."

Ms. Heliotrope was on it before I finished speaking. "Desmond, Chen, get out of there now."

I watched as several members of the audience began to

stand. I hoped Des and Dr. Chen's position against the back wall of the auditorium would help them escape the room quickly. The video feed started shifting, and it looked like Dr. Chen was moving. The camera turned to Des, who had started to follow him, when it caught the image of someone who could ruin everything. Brian had stood and was obviously scanning the crowd for Des.

"Yes, let's have you all come to the stage so we can meet you personally," Genevieve continued. It was clear they were going to make sure everyone in the room would be under their thrall.

"Des, you go first," Dr. Chen whispered as he pushed Des ahead of him. "They can't glamour me."

Ms. Heliotrope and I watched with bated breath as Des went ahead to the auditorium doors. Just as Des made it out, Dr. Chen pulled back. He turned to find Brian there.

"Hey, you're new, right? You should head up to the stage." Brian looked toward the auditorium door, which had just swung closed behind Des. "Hey, you didn't see my friend, did you? Tall Black guy? Kinda good-looking, I guess—at least the girls seem to think so."

"I'm not sure," Dr. Chen replied. "I was just heading to the bathroom; my work break is almost over."

Brian gave him an appraising look. "Well, you should go say hello anyway. It won't take long. I'm sure a couple minutes late won't be a problem."

"Okay." Dr. Chen followed Brian down the aisle and got in line to go onstage.

Brian turned and scanned the room again. Fortunately, the audience lights were still off, or he probably would have left the auditorium to look for Des.

In the meantime, Des was making his way through the hall. I didn't want anything bad to happen to Dr. Chen, of course, but I felt much less tense knowing Des was on his way out of the building.

Until a familiar and unwelcome voice came through Des's mic.

"Mr. Adebowale?"

Tension hit my shoulders again. "Shit, it's Mr. Costello. I know Danforth has talked to him. We can't trust him."

Ms. Heliotrope put her finger in front of her lips to hush me. We both leaned in to listen.

"Mr. Costello, how are you?" If there was one quality Des had that I severely lacked, it was the ability to be so calm under pressure. He was cool as a cucumber, while I wasn't even in the hallway with him and I was shaking like a leaf. The likelihood of Des getting away easily was slim.

"I'm quite well," Costello replied. "And you? Why aren't you at the meeting?"

Think fast, think fast! I thought, hoping Des could somehow read my mind and come up with something clever. I certainly had nothing.

"Well, I realized nobody from my family was there," Des offered smoothly. "I thought that was strange, so I wanted to call my parents and Jocelyn. Shouldn't they be involved too?"

I laughed. It was brilliant. Costello certainly loved to find ways to milk money out of the Adebowale family or at least gain some kind of prestige from being associated with them.

"You're quite right, young man! They should be here. It's rather surprising they're not. Good thinking!"

"They must have been really busy, what with Mom and Jocelyn being doctors and Dad being a lawyer. I heard they're a little understaffed at the hospital because one of the doctors is out on vacation. And Dad has that big divorce case—" Des gasped. "Oh, wait, I shouldn't have mentioned that."

"Divorce case?" Costello asked. "What divorce case?"

"Let me be honest with you, Mr. Costello. Can I call you Frank? We're on similar footing now since I'm not a student anymore, right?" Des may not have had a vampire's ability to glamour people, but he could be convincing when he set his mind to it.

"Uh, yeah, sure. Frank is fine." There was a note of nervousness in Mr. Costello's voice.

"Your wife knows," Des said in a conspiratorial tone. "She's known for a while. She just made sure to hide it from you so she could get my dad as her lawyer before you could. It was smart, too, because you'll either have to go out of town to find a decent lawyer or settle for the law offices of Brown, Ayala, and Stern, and we all know they couldn't win a case against my dad if their lives depended on it."

"It was that Buckmilter kid! I knew he couldn't keep a secret!"

"No, no, not Josh," Des replied calmly. "Your problem wasn't with him at all. She knew long before then. Remember when she went on that cruise with her girlfriends to the Bahamas? Well, when she and her friends came home, it was during the day while you were at work. They all went to your house first for some tea and cookies and found it a little unkempt. Her friends all helped her tidy up the house."

"Oh, no," Mr. Costello said in a small voice.

"Oh, yes. You know how Mrs. Johnson likes to snoop. Well, she found a box full of some . . . rather unsavory objects. And some photos. And a little book with some phone numbers in it." Des paused. "Frank, I hate to break it to you, but you've been caught. The only reason you still have a job is that your wife swore everyone to secrecy so she could find a way to take everything she learned about your extracurriculars and work it in her favor."

"No, no, no, no, no."

"I highly recommend you do some searching for a good lawyer," Des continued, "because things don't look too good for you right now."

"Okay. I'll . . . I'll go to my office and do some research. You won't tell anyone about this?"

"I won't tell a soul," Des said.

"Thank you, my boy. Thank you!"

There came the sound of an office door slamming. Mr. Costello likely wanted to escape the conversation, completely forgetting about Des and the meeting in the auditorium.

A minute later, Des joined us outside.

"Hey, I made it," he said breathlessly, coming up behind me and Ms. Heliotrope.

I wanted to laugh so hard, but I was afraid we might be caught if we made too much noise. Instead, I gave Des a huge grin, and we gave each other a high five. "Was all of that true?"

"No clue," Des replied. "But I did overhear Mrs. Costello when I went out shopping the other day. She was telling someone she wasn't satisfied with her marriage and was looking into getting a divorce. I remembered a few details from the conversation and dropped them in to make it more convincing. The rest of the stuff was just made up."

"Hmm . . . I wonder if you maybe messed things up for her."

Des considered that. "I hope not. But it was the only thing I could think of in the moment. I don't think I'd want to be stuck married to a Mr. Costello type for the rest of my life."

Ms. Heliotrope gave Des an approving smile. "You're a clever young man. It was wise of you to distract that man before leaving, or he might have followed you out and caught us."

Des crouched down next to us to see the computer screen. "Did Dr. Chen make it out?"

"No, but fortunately, he'll be fine. He's trained on how to act like he's been glamoured." Ms. Heliotrope watched the screen as Dr. Chen went up on the stage. "Dr. Chen is good at making himself look submissive and harmless, but he's an incredibly intelligent and determined man. It's fortunate he's working for our side rather than theirs."

Her assessment made me consider Dr. Chen in a new light. Was he a dorky idiot who played at being vampire on his days off, or was that just a ruse? It made me wonder how often I judged people without really seeing them. I glanced at Ms. Heliotrope with a smile as Dr. Chen left the stage.

She gave me a quizzical look. "What is it, Josh?"

"Oh, nothing. I'm relieved. I think this will work out. We should probably head back to the cars and go as soon as Dr. Chen gets out of there."

"Agreed. No need to linger." Ms. Heliotrope nodded and observed the screen until Dr. Chen pushed open the auditorium doors. "I'll have a report to make to the Conclave. Josh, if you're not working tonight, we can continue your training. And Desmond, please remember you'll need to keep this all confidential. The well-being of your town is at stake."

"Of course," Des said. "I can't have anyone hurt my family and friends, can I?"

"Good man."

Dr. Chen was making good time through the hallway,

judging by the video. "Let's get him and head back to the cars," I said.

I shut the laptop and handed it to Des, along with the headphones. Ms. Heliotrope took off ahead of us, giving Des and me a chance to talk.

"So, this is why you've given up on telling Harriet how you feel?"

I nodded.

"You don't think you can try to make it work?"

I shook my head. "No. It wouldn't be fair to her. I love her, but I don't own her, and she should be allowed to have the life she chooses."

We walked quietly for a moment. "What if . . . what if she would make the choice to be with you anyway, Josh? You could tell her, like you told me."

"I can't. Ms. Heliotrope only agreed because it was necessary, not because you're my friend. What you know now can put you in danger, but your knowing is justified. I doubt me telling Harriet because I love her would be enough to satisfy the vampire powers that be. They might kill me or her or both of us or anyone else they think she might tell."

"She may have to find out anyway, considering what those creeps are doing right now." Des turned his head, and I followed suit to see Ms. Heliotrope walking over with Dr. Chen and sped up.

Maybe he was right, but if I was going to tell Harriet, it had to be at the right time. But when the hell was the right time? Life suddenly seemed unbearably complicated. Things were much simpler when all I had was a crush on a kind girl who used to share her lunch with me in school.

Ms. Heliotrope threaded her arm through mine. "Let's get back to my house and make our report."

"Okay," I said.

Now wasn't the time to think about Harriet, as hard as that was for me. There were more immediate problems to address.

We said our goodbyes to Des and Dr. Chen, then drove back to Ms. Heliotrope's house. As she made a report to the Conclave over the phone, I wondered what would happen when I got back to work. Gino and Graziella had been there at the auditorium today. What would they be like tomorrow when I got to Gino's? Would they act like everything was normal, or would things be different?

The world seemed like it was closing in, but I had a feeling that soon everything was going to explode.

DAY 14
THURSDAY

I woke from a dreamless sleep. My brain must have decided everything had gone so desperately wrong, so completely unbelievably strange, that it just couldn't process anything.

I blinked a couple of times and realized something felt . . . off. Jolting up in bed, I looked over at my desk chair. Brian had draped himself over the chair so he was sitting on it backward, his head leaning over the back. He stared at me with eyes so hauntingly empty, my skin crawled.

I wrapped my blanket around myself; the strange expression on Brian's face gave me a chill that had nothing to do with the temperature.

"Brian," I said, my voice still a little heavy from sleep.

He tilted his head to the side, his expression unchanging.

I cleared my throat and spoke louder. "Brian. What are you doing here?"

He blinked a couple of times, then stretched his arms slowly, making his back crack. He remained seated.

"Oh, you're awake," Brian said, his voice void of emotion.

"Uh, yeah, I'm awake. You were sitting in my chair and staring at me." Did he even know what he was doing? Was that how I had looked two weeks ago, when the vampires glamoured me for their little game?

"Okay. I'll go now." Brian stood and walked to the door as though his presence in my room were a completely normal thing.

As I watched him leave, I was overcome by an internal debate. Was Brian my enemy now or simply a pawn like half the town? Did Danforth and Genevieve make him promises they never intended to keep, or were they grooming him to be a bigger opponent?

In two weeks, my friendship had disintegrated into a complete farce. Now, I pretended I wasn't suspicious of Brian, and he pretended he was still my friend to my face while talking about me behind my back, just like Mr. Costello had done.

Should I leave? Would it be better for me to move out? Would that leave Des in danger and make things worse for Brian? As much as I felt like my friendship with Brian was over, I wouldn't want to curse anyone with what had happened to me.

I stood, feeling strangely sluggish. I gave the clock a quick glance. Judging by the time, I should have gotten enough sleep. Maybe the lack of dreams was the issue. I decided to take a quick shower to help wake me up.

I stood under the tepid water for a few minutes, hoping the cooler temperature would help me wake up. Instead, I just felt tired and wet. I finished washing as quickly as I could manage, then went to my room, got dressed, and walked downstairs.

By the time I reached the bottom of the stairs, I was smelling something that perked me up. It was like high-quality salted caramel but better. I walked toward the smell, my mouth watering. I could barely keep myself from drooling as I followed the appetizing smell through the living room to Des's recording room.

I knocked on the door and walked in without waiting for an answer. Inside, Des sat in his gaming chair, a first aid kit on his computer desk. He was hunched over, cleaning his knee with a cotton pad.

I quickly crouched in front of him, my hands on the armrests so he couldn't escape, and stared at the red droplets on his scraped knee. I slowly moved closer, smelling the alluring scent.

"Josh, what are you doing?" Des's voice sounded like it came from far away, a distant sound with no meaning to my ears.

I darted forward and licked the blood off his skin. Once all of it was gone, the skin healed quickly—too quickly, I wanted more.

I opened my mouth and felt my canines grow, much like they had at the convention. Before I could do anything else, a fist collided with my face.

I let go of the armrests and fell back on my ass. Using one hand to prop myself up, I rubbed my cheek with my other.

"What was that for?" Whatever daze I had been in was gone, and I was suddenly much more clearheaded.

Des stared at me, horrified. "Josh, do you realize what you just did?"

"Huh?"

Des stood up. He was trembling as he backed away toward the door. "Josh, you just licked the blood off my scraped knee. You looked like you were about to attack me for more."

"I did?" I ran through the memory. It felt like I was watching a movie rather than remembering something I had been present for. It dawned on me then. This was the first time I'd drunk human blood since the change. "Oh my god, I'm sorry, Des. I'm so, so sorry. I didn't know what I was doing."

Des ran a nervous hand through his locs. "M-maybe you need to call Ms. Heliotrope and Dr. Chen."

"Y-yeah. That's a good idea." I could tell he was just as jittery as I was. "Oh my god. I can't believe I did that! I—what if I had—I'm sorry."

I had forgotten rule number one of being a vampire: vampires drink blood from people. These past two weeks, while I'd been agonizing over all the changes I was going through, I'd been reacting to it as though I were going through puberty a second time. Even getting mad at Brian at the convention and my meltdown afterward hadn't been enough for me to fully comprehend that I was dangerous. I was a danger to my friends and family. My ability to hold on to my sanity was balanced on the edge of a knife.

I couldn't stay here anymore. I had to help save Willow Springs, and then I had to leave. My friends weren't safe with me here anymore.

"I'm sorry. I'm so sorry," I whispered as I held my head in my hands and hunched over my knees. Was this what Feral Doug had gone through? The taste of human blood was so addictive, he had completely forgotten his own humanity?

"Here, give me your phone," Des said from nearby. The shakiness in his voice made it clear he was thinking along the same lines. "I'll make the call."

I looked up at Des, who now stood a few feet away. I was surprised he trusted me enough to stand as close as he was. He was right, though. Dr. Chen brought Ms. Heliotrope blood all the time, and she clearly had enough blood to drink that she didn't instinctively attack anyone.

When I gave him my phone, he speed-dialed Dr. Chen and put the call on speaker. Every ring felt like an eternity.

"Josh? This is a surprise. Is something wrong?" Dr. Chen's cheery voice was completely at odds with my desolate mood.

"This is Des." Des backed farther away from me. "Josh just tried to attack me for blood. We don't know what to do. Can you help him?"

Dr. Chen was silent for a moment before responding in a reverent tone. "I'm so incredibly honored that you called me for help. You're going to be fine. I can bring you some blood every day to help you stay fed and in control, just like I do for Ms. Heliotrope."

"But what about right now?" I was too scared that I might not be able to control myself even if he brought me blood today.

"Is there a room you can be locked in?" Dr. Chen asked.

Des and I looked around his small studio. We both seemed to have the same idea. "I can lock him in my recording studio. It doesn't have any windows, and I can put a lock on the door from the outside."

"Good. You do that, and I'll bring you blood as soon as possible." Then Dr. Chen hung up. He seemed to understand this was business and it wasn't time to be his usual talkative self.

I stayed in the studio while Des got some tools from the garage. I listened to the whir of his electric screwdriver while I cowered on the floor, fearing that if I moved even an inch,

I'd attack him again. After a time, the whirring stopped, and I heard the click of a padlock. Then Des tested the door. I didn't have the heart to tell him his padlock might not work since I now had increased strength.

"Um, is your knee okay?" I asked through the door.

His voice, when he answered, sounded sad. "Yeah. I think you actually healed it. It's completely fine."

I lay down on my side in the fetal position. "Oh, I guess that's kinda good. I'm so, so incredibly sorry."

"Look, are you going to be okay?"

"I don't know that I'll ever be fine again, to be honest. When Dr. Chen brings blood, it will probably help, I hope. It's probably safer for me to leave, though. Maybe Ms. Heliotrope can help me out."

Des took in a sharp breath. "Josh, you're like my brother. I'm sure we can figure things out. You didn't even hurt me. You actually healed me. My knee probably would have hurt for days and—"

"It's okay," I interrupted. "I'll do whatever works best for everyone. If I need to leave for everyone's safety, I'll leave."

Des sighed. "Whatever you choose, I'm here for you." I heard him lean against the door and slide down it.

"I know you are. I know." I stared at my hands. "And can you look out for Brian, maybe? He was in my room this morning, staring at me. He's definitely not okay."

"Yeah. He left for work already, but I'll keep an eye on him. That whole thing at the high school was really bizarre."

I smiled weakly. "Thanks."

We continued in silence for a time. I took a few deep breaths and finally sat up, then walked over to Des's computer. "Hey, Des, do you want to grab my laptop? Let's play a game."

Des burst out laughing. "Sounds perfect."

We pulled up *Midnight Murder Mansion* and started playing. It felt so normal to zone out for a few hours of gameplay, I allowed myself to be fooled into believing everything could be okay. Everything could go back to normal . . . until the front door rang.

"I'll get it," Des said through the door.

I heard the front door open and a rush of activity.

"Des!" Harriet yelped. "Have you seen my brother? Have you seen Neil?"

Neil was Harriet's younger brother. He had special needs, so him going off on his own wasn't ideal. I pressed my ear to the door. I wasn't sure I should say anything since it would probably seem strange to Harriet that I was locked in Des's studio.

"What happened?" Des replied.

"I don't know. He went to school like normal, but when my mom went to pick him up early for an appointment, he wasn't there. Nobody was. The entire school was empty. Mom and I have been looking for him everywhere, but we don't really have any idea where to start. The police aren't doing anything. They were acting weird with Mom on the phone, and when I drove to the station, nobody was acting normal. They kept telling me not to worry and that everything was fine, but they didn't do anything. So I left, and my family has just been wandering the streets, going door to door, calling his name." She sounded on the verge of tears. "I don't know what to do."

"Hey," Des said. "We'll do what we can. Should we call Gino's and let them know you won't be coming in tonight?"

Harriet sounded even more worried when she responded. "Gino? I already called him, and he was acting weird too. He closed the restaurant for the night."

"That's weird. Josh always complained that Thursday's one of your busier nights."

As I listened to their conversation, I fumbled for my phone. I looked through my notifications, and sure enough, there was a text from Gino saying he was closing shop for the night.

People were missing, Gino was acting out of the ordinary, the police were doing nothing, and the whole town of Willow Springs seemed like it had been invaded by body snatchers. I was relieved Harriet was still Harriet, but how long would that last?

This whole situation had gone too far. Harriet's brother was missing, the high school kids probably were too, and if what Ms. Heliotrope had said yesterday about keeping kids as blood cattle was true . . . I didn't want to think about it. Now was the time to act. Everyone who hadn't been glamoured by Danforth and Genevieve needed to know, and they needed to know now.

I texted Ms. Heliotrope.

Things are getting worse. Kids and teenagers are going missing. I'm telling Harriet everything. I don't care if the Conclave punishes me. Come over to my place.

The response was quick and brief.

Don't say anything yet. On my way.

I shoved my phone into my pocket. "Don't leave yet, Harriet!"

"What?" Harriet exclaimed. I heard her walk over and knock on the door. "Josh, is that you?"

"Yeah, it's me," I said in a rush. "Stay here. There's something going on. Ms. Heliotrope—"

"Wait, why are you locked in Des's studio?" Harriet asked. I heard her lift the padlock outside the door. "Des, why is Josh locked in your studio? Is this some prank?"

"No!" Des exclaimed. "No, it's . . . it's . . . I mean . . ."

"Ms. Heliotrope will be here soon. She might be able to help find your brother, Harriet," I explained.

"Why do you think she can help?"

"I can't say yet. But I think I know what's going on, and I think she knows too. We were at the high school yesterday, and there weren't any students there at all. It was Wednesday. Everyone should be in school on Wednesdays."

A couple of minutes later, Ms. Heliotrope arrived. I heard Des open the door. "Where's Josh?" she asked, all business.

"I locked him in my studio. Dr. Chen thought it was a good idea."

"Dr. Chen?" Harriet asked, clearly bewildered.

"Is Brian home?" Ms. Heliotrope asked, ignoring Harriet's question.

"No, he left for work already," Des said. "This is Harriet, by the way."

"We've met," Ms. Heliotrope told Des. Then to Harriet, "It's good to see you again."

"Josh said you might be able to help find my brother?"

"Yes. We need to get Josh out of that room first." I heard the padlock move on the door again.

"But what if he . . ." Des trailed off, probably afraid to say anything in front of Harriet.

"That's what I'm here for. Now open the door," Ms. Heliotrope demanded.

I heard the click of the lock and a few more sounds, then the door opened.

I saw Ms. Heliotrope first. She looked a little frazzled, as if she had run over using her vampire speed instead of driving. She pulled a backpack off her shoulders and handed me a pouch full of red liquid.

"Is that what I think it is?" I asked.

"Drink it. You look especially pale right now. You've hit the point where eating raw or rare meat isn't enough anymore." She gave me an uncharacteristically gentle pat on my cheek. If I hadn't known better, I'd have said her expression was one of parental concern. "This is the vital point where you need to stay fed or you could go feral, Josh. You need to drink."

I took the bag and almost gagged before I caught the same scent from when Des had been bleeding. I desperately tore open one of the tubes at the top and started gulping it down. While part of my brain protested, the rest of me suddenly went from tense to relaxed, as if I were sipping a tropical umbrella drink in a lounge chair on the beach.

"Okay, what's going on?" Harriet demanded, fear and frustration clear in her voice. "Why did Josh need to be locked up? What do you know that could help me find Neil?"

"Can we tell her?" I asked after taking another sip of blood. It had the same taste as Des's blood, like salted caramel but better, though not quite as fresh.

"I spoke to the Conclave," Ms. Heliotrope said. "They agree that things have moved too fast and gone too far. We need to enlist local help. We might not get enough formalists here fast enough for us to take care of this on our own."

I got up from the chair, still sipping blood, and followed her out of the room. Des still looked a bit jumpy and gave me a wide berth. Harriet looked completely disturbed by the blood bag.

"Is that what I think it is?"

"Yes," Ms. Heliotrope answered. "Please have a seat. After I explain what happened to Josh, I can get into where your brother might be."

We all piped in and gave Harriet as quick a rundown as we could. I let Des cover what had happened this morning, as I was too embarrassed to talk about it. By the time we were done, I'd finished my blood bag, and Ms. Heliotrope handed me another.

"I think I'm fine," I said, refusing the bag.

"Josh, we need you at your best and under control. Being well fed will help with that," she insisted.

"Wait, wait. This sounds insane. How am I supposed to believe that Josh is a vampire now? Like, sure, that stuff is fun to read about and watch in movies and such, but real vampires?"

As if we were thinking the same thing, Ms. Heliotrope and I opened our mouths and popped out our fangs.

"Well . . ." Harriet sat back with a dumbfounded expression. "I guess those weren't fake fangs after all." She looked like she was about to tear up. "How is all this going to help me find my brother?"

"I've been investigating. All the children and teens are being kept by Genevieve and Danforth at their mansion." Ms. Heliotrope turned to Harriet. "Your brother is likely there. Once I determined their location, the Conclave knew they had to act quickly. We will be taking action as soon as our formalists arrive, which will be in a few hours, fortunately."

"So what do you need us to do?" I asked.

"We need blueprints of the mansion so we can figure out the best points of entry," she began. "That will be hard, as Danforth and Genevieve clearly have control of the town government. We probably won't be able to get those blueprints out of city records without showing our hands."

Des and I exchanged a glance. "You might not need blueprints," he said.

Ms. Heliotrope raised an eyebrow. "Why not?"

"Just about everyone our age explored that place before the vampires moved in. Most of us know it like the backs of our hands." Des pulled a piece of paper off a legal pad he had been taking notes on earlier and began to sketch an outline of the mansion. "There are a few hidden passages, but everyone knows where they are. The house was vacant for a while, so we all liked to go there and have crazy parties and séances and do all kinds of other weird things bored teenagers do. If those vampires wanted to live in a place where their secrets could be kept, they made a really stupid choice."

"Excellent," Ms. Heliotrope said, her eye sparkling.

We spent some time helping Des with his sketch until he had all the floors, including the basement, fully sketched out. "This should be it." He handed four pages of sketches to Ms. Heliotrope.

"You've saved me a large chunk of time. You have also shown exactly how we can use you. Could the three of you get into the mansion, while our people serve as distraction, and get the children out?"

"Definitely," Harriet said. "If anyone can do it, we can."

"Wait a moment," I jumped in. I didn't want my friends to get hurt. "Des and Harriet are regular humans, and I'm just barely a vampire. I might be able to manage, but I'm not sure it's worth the risk to send them. How can they defend themselves if we're caught?"

"Excuse me?" Harriet snapped.

"What the hell?" Des demanded.

"What?" I asked, surprised by how angry they were.

"We're part of this town too!" Harriet insisted. "We have every right to be involved in keeping our loved ones safe!"

"Right!" Des added. "What if they took Clarissa? Wait, do they have Clarissa?" He began to fumble for his phone.

"You won't be alone. The number of people to rescue is too large for you to protect and get to safety on your own. You'll be assigned a squad," Ms. Heliotrope explained. "We will need to get more people in town involved. Managing that many children and teenagers will be difficult."

Just as Des was about to make a call, his phone rang. "It's Mom!" He immediately picked up and left the room to talk to her.

Harriet spoke up again. "What do you think they're planning to do with the kids?"

Ms. Heliotrope gave her an empathetic look. "I hate to say it, but it's an easy strategy: control the kids, control the adults. The people they've glamoured won't care anymore, and the people they haven't will be so scared for their children's safety, they'll be more likely to cooperate. In the meantime, they can raise the children like cattle and use them as blood stock."

The blood drained from Harriet's face. "Oh my god!"

Even though the vampires and their actions weren't my fault, I couldn't help but feel guilty. Could I have done something more to prevent this from happening? I hated seeing the heartbreak on Harriet's face and the fear and worry in Des's eyes. I usually looked to them for encouragement. Was it time for me to be that for them? Could I manage it when all I'd been doing over the past couple of weeks was bemoaning my inability to taste pizza?

Ms. Heliotrope gave me a penetrating look. As though she had read my mind, she said, "It's not your fault, Josh. You couldn't have prevented any of this from happening. What we need to do is pull together what we can. All of you should call your families and see if they're okay. If they seem like their normal selves, get them gathered here. We can make this place a triage unit. It will be easier for the formalists to guard, and your families can see to any wounded."

"Okay," I said.

I pulled out my phone to call my dad while Harriet pulled out hers as well. After a few minutes of conversation, we had our answers. My dad was fine. Harriet's parents were fine. Des's father, Roland, was not okay, but his mother, Rhonda, was, and Jocelyn as well. Clarissa was nowhere to be found. Rhonda had thought everything was okay because Roland had told her some story about an overnight school event. Des took longer to explain what was really going on so his mother wouldn't start searching for Clarissa herself. It took a lot of convincing from both Des and Ms. Heliotrope before she agreed to come to our place instead.

Ms. Heliotrope excused herself, explaining that the formalists were meeting at her place. Harriet, Des, and I stayed behind, making calls and waiting for everyone else to arrive. After about half an hour of anxious waiting, everyone who had escaped being glamoured began to trickle in. Rhonda and Jocelyn both brought medical supplies, as did Dr. Chen, who brought some additional bags of blood for any injured vampires. I had to flash my teeth and cat eyes for a few people who were still doubtful of the truth of the situation. Some people were rightfully scared, but Jocelyn's words seemed to do more to help calm them than I ever could.

"It's good to know we at least have an answer for what happened to you, Josh," she said as she unpacked her supplies on the dining room table.

My dad looked at me with intense concern. "Josh, I . . . I wish I could change places with you, just so you could have a normal life. You deserve better than this."

"It's not great, but at least I'm not dying anytime soon," I joked flatly. Nobody laughed. The room was too tense, and people glanced at each other as if looking for advice on how to handle all of this.

"Son." My father pulled me into a bone-crushing hug. "I don't know if we can fix this, but I want you to know that, no matter what, you're always my son. We'll figure this out together. You're not alone."

It took all I had to not fall apart then and there. I knew deep in my heart that my dad would always have my back. I needed to hear it, though. I needed to know it was all okay.

I managed to blink away a few tears as I returned the hug, being careful not to squeeze him too hard. I was relieved to find that practicing self-control with Ms. Heliotrope was making it easier.

"If anyone wants to leave, you should do so now," Des said. "Josh may not be his normal self anymore, but he's still Josh. And more importantly, we need to save our town."

I watched everyone, terrified they would all leave because of me. I was also incredibly grateful to Des for putting his trust in me, even after what had happened earlier.

"You're right. This is our town. We can't let outsiders take it from us. We can't let them take our children from us. We need to show them we're stronger than them." Rhonda got up from her seat to stand next to Des. "We'll do this for Clarissa and Neil and all the other kids. They deserve to have a future."

Nods and words of agreement were shared all around the room. I slumped in relief. Nobody had decided to leave. Every single person was determined to stay and do something to defeat our monster infestation.

I called Ms. Heliotrope once everyone was settled, putting the phone on speaker. "Everyone, this is Ms.

Heliotrope. She's in charge of our plan. She's also a vampire, and she has other vampires who are going to help take down the ones trying to steal our town."

"Hello, everyone," Ms. Heliotrope said in her no-nonsense tone. "Our plan has two parts, and there will be varying roles to play. I hear we may have at least one or two additional medics, correct?"

Jocelyn and Rhonda both spoke up. I glanced at Dad, who had a strange look on his face, but I figured he was still wrapping his head around what it meant to be father to a vampire.

"Good. We will need one in the field, one at the house, minimum. Do we have anyone who can drive large vehicles, like a van or school bus?"

Harriet's uncle, one of the local school bus drivers, spoke up. "I can."

"Excellent. Out of everyone else, we'll need a group to sneak into the mansion to break the kids out. They're likely being kept in the subbasement. Interesting, that they have a subbasement."

"That's a leftover from Prohibition," said Rebecca from the diner. "The house was owned by bootleggers. That's also why it has so many secret passages. I think I should be on the rescue team. I know a lot about the history of the house. My great-uncle used to own it, and I visited a lot when I was a kid."

"Excellent," Ms. Heliotrope replied. "If you can all organize yourselves into groups of who will be going into the house and who will be outside the property to get the children loaded on the bus we provide, it sounds like we'll be prepared. Josh, make sure Des and that young lady are involved in making sure everyone who enters the mansion knows exactly where they're going."

"Yeah, sure." This felt like it was moving incredibly fast. "We're going in tonight, right?"

"Yes. If we don't move quickly, we might lose some of the children. We can't let that happen," Ms. Heliotrope replied. "And if we wait too long, our enemy will figure out our plan and be ready for us. The time is now. I suggest everyone eat and get what rest you can. We'll need you all on high alert and ready to move out when the time is right."

"Okay. Any more questions for Ms. Heliotrope before I let her go?" I asked.

"So, we should gather at the bottom of the hill and wait for word from you?" Des asked.

"Yes. We'll bring supplies for communication. Some-times it's better to use rudimentary supplies, as modern technology can be easier to trace."

"Thank you, Ms. Heliotrope. I think we're good here." I looked around, and several people nodded. "I'll let you go."

"Thank you. We'll join you once we have our distrac-tion plan in place."

She hung up, and we got to work. Jocelyn, Dr. Chen, and Rhonda coordinated supplies and made sure they had a reasonable field bag. Harriet and her mom got to work pulling together food, while Des and Rebecca consulted with each other on points of entry and the route to take through the basement to the subbasement and back.

It wasn't until after everyone sat down to eat that it really sank in that people knew I wasn't the same anymore. At Dr. Chen's insistence, I sucked at one of his blood bags as if it were an oversized juice pouch. Some people threw me nervous glances and gave me a wide berth. It wasn't fun, but after what happened earlier with Des, I couldn't blame them.

I started to wonder what would happen when Brian

came home. We couldn't let him know what we were planning. A few people attempted to take quick naps, and as time went on, Brian's absence became more and more obvious. I had a sinking feeling he hadn't just gone to mow lawns that morning. It was not a welcome thought.

By the time midnight came around, a few formalists had arrived to give us further instructions. I found it weird that Ms. Heliotrope hadn't come herself, but I chalked it up to her being the point person. She probably had a lot of information and assignments to hand out.

I didn't feel good about any of this, but it was too late to back out. By sunrise, we would have either been defeated by the monsters or saved the town.

DAY 15, PART 1

✕ FRIDAY

Which would you rather have: a roomful of ninjas or a ship full of pirates?

It was a question I had never been sure how to answer. At least, not until I met Kotaro. He was one of the formalists Ms. Heliotrope sent over. It was clear she had chosen them for how personable or reassuring they were, because our little group of townsfolk seemed less afraid of them than they were of me. After they went over the plan again in more detail, Kotaro came over and handed me another bag of blood.

"Oh, no, I'm okay. I just had one." I was still kind of squeamish about the idea of drinking something that came from another human's body, and honestly, the last bag seemed like enough. I felt better than I had since this whole mess started two weeks ago.

"*Ototo*." He gave me a pat on the back so powerful, it would have dislocated my shoulder had I still been human. He sat next to me at the top of the stairs.

"When going into battle, you must be prepared. When

I was still a human, back in the Sengoku era, I served as a ninja. A smart ninja always remembers to be prepared. Later, when Tokugawa came to power, it was difficult to find work, so I took to the seas and became a pirate. A smart pirate always remembers to be prepared. Now, we are going into battle. Extra blood will keep you alert. It's the smart thing to do. A smart vampire always remembers to be prepared."

"Wait, you were a ninja and a pirate?" Stunned, I took the bag he shoved into my hands and tentatively took a sip.

He laughed, his canines glinting in the light. "When one way of life stops working out, you have to find a new way to live. That's something all of us eventually learn to do. Not just vampires. Humans as well."

He stood and made a gravity-defying leap down the stairs. He may have been a cocky show-off, but now I knew the answer to the ultimate question. You didn't need to choose between a roomful of ninjas and a ship full of pirates. All you needed was a single ninja-pirate vampire.

I would never be that cool. I sullenly sipped at the blood bag and watched him shepherd stragglers toward the front door. If he hadn't been so damned awesome, I might have hated him.

"Hey, Josh." Harriet leaned over the railing and gave me a weak smile. "Can we have a quick talk before we leave?"

She was looking a little strangely at the blood bag. I lost my grip, attempted to catch the bag at human speed, and finally switched to vampire speed to prevent it from falling. A couple drops of blood escaped, landing on the step below me, but otherwise, the damage wasn't too bad. Des wouldn't be happy about the mess, though.

Harriet sat down next to me. "I guess this explains a lot."

"Yeah, I guess it does." I couldn't figure out whether I should continue drinking the blood. On the one hand, it would start clotting soon if I didn't; on the other, drinking blood in front of Harriet seemed weird.

"You should finish that," she said as though she had read my mind.

I nodded and gulped down the rest of the bag as quickly as I could. Then I realized in my rush, I might have made a mess of myself. I hastily wiped my mouth with the back of my hand, hoping my face wasn't smeared with blood.

"Josh, I think it's important we have a quick talk about something just in case anything bad does happen. This may not be the best time, but with what's going on, I'm not sure when would be." Her brow was furrowed, and I could tell this was serious.

"Okay," I replied, giving her my full attention.

"I . . . I've never been sure how to bring this up, but I guess we don't have time for flowery words right now." Harriet paused a moment to gather her thoughts. "Josh, I know your feelings for me are more than just friendship. I've known for a long time."

I froze for a moment. Then I remembered how obvious my feelings seemed to be to everyone else and groaned. "They were right. Everyone likes to say you already knew, but I couldn't tell if they were teasing me or being honest. Why didn't you say anything?"

"Well, I could ask you the same question. Why didn't you say anything? I waited for you to say something because I had a feeling you didn't want to confess until you felt ready. I guess you weren't ready." Harriet pulled off her glasses and busied herself polishing them on the edge of her tee shirt.

"I guess it never felt like the right time. And now it feels like it's too late," I explained.

"Did you ever stop to think that maybe I had some thoughts on all this? I mean, you've had a lot of time—a few years or so? I've had some thoughts too—"

"Wait, you've known that long?" I blurted out. Now I was really embarrassed.

She nodded solemnly. "Yeah. It was pretty obvious to me. I might have figured it out before everyone else did, to be honest. I almost stopped sharing my lunch and sitting with you guys in the cafeteria at school to try to figure out how I felt about it. Then I went away to cooking school. I dated a couple of guys and got a little perspective on the whole thing."

It stung a little to think she'd dated other guys, but it wasn't like I was in any position to judge. I had never told her how I felt, so she didn't owe me anything.

She turned and offered me her hands. I gulped, putting my hands in hers.

"Josh, you're my friend. You'll always be my friend, no matter what. If you had confessed to me before all these things started, I probably would have told you yes. I probably would have agreed to go on a date. But I think now isn't the time for you to be in a relationship. Now is the time for you to figure out who you are and how to live in the world now that everything's gone crazy." She gave my hands a squeeze. "Also, I'm not sure how this vampire thing works, and I'm not sure if I can have the kind of relationship I want under these circumstances."

Those few sentences sent me on an emotional roller coaster. I hit the high when she said she would have said yes, yet when the *but* came in, everything went downhill, fast, and I couldn't get off the ride. She was right, though. This wasn't a normal situation at all.

"I understand, and I hate to admit it, but I don't think

it would be fair to you to date someone who . . . well . . . I'm kind of a train wreck right now."

Harriet reached out and hugged me. I was startled by it and still afraid I might lose control and bite her, but all the blood I'd been drinking seemed to have staved off the hunger.

"I don't know if I'll change my mind in the future. What's going on with you is so new and everything. But, Josh, I want you to remember something, and I want you to understand that I mean this wholeheartedly. No matter what, I'm your friend. That will never change, okay?"

"Okay." I wanted to hold her longer, just to cling to the fantasy that we could be together, but I knew this moment had to end, and end fast.

"Ahem."

Harriet and I pulled apart and turned to the person standing at the bottom of the stairs.

"Dad?"

"Time to go," he said. He looked at us with sympathy in his eyes, so he'd probably at least heard the tail end of our discussion. Under normal circumstances, he probably would have wanted to give me a pep talk.

"Okay, let's go," I said. Harriet and I stood and walked down the stairs.

My heart was heavy. I felt like I had nothing now except the task ahead of us. After that? The future looked like a huge dark tunnel ready to consume me.

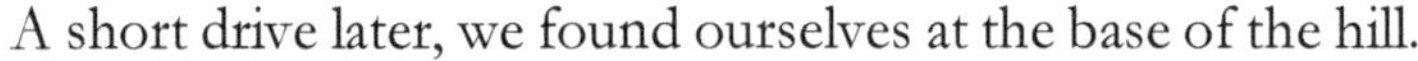

A short drive later, we found ourselves at the base of the hill.

People were still trying to give me a wide berth. The fear and tension were so thick, I could have cut it with a knife.

"You have your walkies ready?" Kotaro asked, as Ms. Heliotrope gave last-minute instructions to her team of vampires. Even Feral Doug was there, looking pumped up and ready to go. I wished she'd had a moment to give me a quick word of motivation, just to pick me up a little.

Several yeahs answered him. Kotaro used his walkie-talkie to ask the same thing of those who weren't nearby. My dad and Harriet's uncle had parked the bus and van strategically near the mansion, ready to transport hostages away from the scene. Des's family lived nearby, so his mom and sister had set up the house as a triage unit after it was determined to be a better base of operations than our place. Once Kotaro got confirmation from them, our group huddled together. Des, Harriet, Rebecca, and a couple of other familiar faces who used to sneak into the mansion for fun made up our ragtag team.

"Our team of formalists will go in first to create the distraction." The more playful, encouraging tone Kotaro had used earlier was gone. Instead, his slightly accented voice was all business. "I'll send you the signal as soon as it's time to raid. Understood?"

We all nodded.

"If anything goes wrong, those of you with little to no fighting skill are to leave immediately. Harriet and Des will act as defense since they have martial arts training. Josh, just do what you can with your vampire powers to move things along as quickly as possible and protect your friends." He stopped and gave us an approving nod. "You're all doing a very brave thing. Now wait here for the signal. We don't know how much they're monitoring the street, so don't jump the gun, got it?"

Our group offered another whispered chorus of yeahs. Kotaro gave us a deep bow of respect, then returned to the group of vampires. They quickly dispersed, and Ms. Heliotrope gave me a quick nod before she melted into the shadows.

I sat on the hood of my car, and our group waited. The tension became more and more palpable as the seconds passed. I started to wish I had some of Kotaro's charisma because it seemed like a motivating speech would have helped. Unfortunately, I wasn't good at public speaking.

Des seemed to have the same idea, but unlike me, he opened his mouth and began to speak.

"Hey, everyone. I know we're all pretty nervous right now, but I think we're going to manage just fine. We've all snuck into that mansion. We know every inch of it, so I know we can do this. It will be just like back in high school. We'll sneak in, sneak out, and nobody will know the difference."

Harriet stood and joined him. "Exactly. Just pretend we're sneaking in for a late-night party. Remember how fun those were? Who can forget the time Josh got locked in a closet because the key fell out of the keyhole?"

A couple members of the group laughed nervously, while a couple others still looked wide-eyed with fear. I didn't really mind taking the hit, though, if it meant easing tensions. Before Des and Harriet could continue the pep talk, however, the walkie-talkie squawked and emitted a series of beeps.

"That's the signal," Des said, and the group's tension ramped up again.

"Let's go," I said.

We walked tentatively up the hill, trying to stick to the shadows as much as possible in case there was any monitoring equipment the formalists had not managed to destroy. The closer we got to the mansion, the more we heard of the fighting. When we passed our first dead body on the street, the entire group froze.

I don't think any of us had seen a dead body before. The body had had its heart torn out, and the head sat a few feet away. We could clearly see vampire fangs shining in the light of a streetlamp.

"I'm not sure I can do this," said one of our team members. We were all probably thinking the same thing. Seeing the dead body made this real in a way none of our preparations had managed.

I was scared some of our team would decide to leave. Rebecca offered some calming words to the guy who'd spoken up. Then we looked each other in the eye and traded nods. We couldn't turn back now. It was time.

One by one, we began to move again as a team. Nobody left.

We continued to walk up the street and passed more bodies. Most were dismembered, and the number of arms, legs, torsos, and heads never quite added up, which meant some of the vampires were probably still alive and fighting with missing limbs. I was grateful we hadn't been properly introduced to most of the formalists; we didn't have to know which bodies and body parts came from our side.

At least one person vomited, which made me grateful my stomach wasn't as full since all I had to drink was blood. We slowed down to take care of him, then continued to move forward.

It felt like we were taking too long. None of us were soldiers. Most of us were fresh out of high school, hardly older than some of the kids we'd find in the subbasement. Even though it was absolutely necessary to do this, I was terrified that the heads of my friends might also end up littering the street.

As we inched along, I noticed a foul, iron-tinged stench that I decided must be vampire blood. It smelled entirely different from Des's blood, which was good. If vampire blood smelled different from human blood, I'd at least be able to tell which corpses were human. None of the corpses we'd passed so far smelled human. It was a small relief, but a relief nonetheless.

We finally made it to the edge of the mansion's grounds. I spotted the bus and van, which were hidden in shadows, away from the streetlights, where nobody would spot them unless they were looking for them. Since my night vision was better, I silently gestured to everyone to make sure they were aware of exactly where the vehicles were.

Then Des took point, walking through the gate and putting his back to the brick wall surrounding the estate. Everyone followed suit, with me taking the rear, and we crept along between the wall and the shrubbery. The screams and yells of vampires fighting were nerve-racking, especially when they sounded so close.

I almost yelled when an arm landed near my feet, but my throat was too tight with fear, thankfully. Somehow, that was the only sign of how easily we could have been caught by the nearby vampires if we weren't careful.

We held ourselves together until we spotted our point of entry: a window that led into the basement.

Des went ahead first. He sneaked swiftly to the window and used a screwdriver to pry it open. It responded quickly. Apparently, with all the remodeling, they had cut a few corners. Danforth and Genevieve were probably not expecting the locals to be a threat.

Des took a quick glance inside. No alarms kicked in to

alert anyone to our presence, which meant the formalists had done their job to make sure we could get in and out safely. He waved the rest of us over. Everyone sneaked across the short open space in single file and descended through the window.

The basement wasn't a wide-open space. Rather, it consisted of several rooms, and as we entered the smallest outer room, we pulled out our flashlights.

Once again, Des took point and checked the door. It was locked. He gestured to Rebecca, who had a lockpick kit with her. We all held our breaths as we listened for the tell-tale click of the lock. It came faster than I expected, and I wondered what hobbies Rebecca had and if one of them included burglary. She didn't seem the type, but considering what she'd shared about the history of the mansion and some of her extended family living there in the past, maybe some of the skills needed to hide their criminal activities were passed down through the family.

It was eerily quiet as we made our way down the hall, checking each door. While it seemed most likely they'd keep the kids in the subbasement, we didn't want to miss anyone. Unsurprisingly, though, they had chosen not to lock the kids up in rooms with windows through which they might es-cape. We had to take the stairs down to the subbasement before we started to hear signs of life.

"This way," Harriet whispered, pointing toward a door that led to a large wine cellar. It made sense that the vampires had chosen it, as it was the largest room in the subbasement and could probably hold the most people. There was also only one door and no windows to escape through. We could hear voices on the other side, and I heard the sound of the tumblers in the lock moving. Someone was clearly trying to get the door open. Unfortunately, as Des had done when he locked me into his studio, the vampires had added several padlocks on the outside of the door and even put a heavy bar in place to prevent anyone from getting out. Even the door was made of thick steel.

Rebecca began to work on the padlocks. I think we all wanted to talk through the door to reassure everyone on the other side, but anything more than the briefest of whispers was bound to be heard if one of the vampires was nearby. Every second seemed like an hour as we waited for each padlock to open.

Once they were finally off, Des tried to lift the heavy bar, but it wouldn't budge. Harriet joined him, but again, it was stuck. Then I realized I had the advantage here. What vampire would have set up a door a human could easily open if they meant to keep their victims inside?

I gestured for them to back away. They moved, and I stepped forward. It was time to do the exact opposite of what Ms. Heliotrope had been teaching me about gentling my touch. I took a deep breath and lifted the bar from its spot. It was still heavy, probably weighing as much as Des did, but I managed to slowly lift it and set it on the floor.

Des gave me an appraising look in the low light. We usually worked out together, but he had always outdone me when it came to lifting weights. It seemed I had the advantage now. Were circumstances different, I would have celebrated my victory. Now, though, it was yet another reminder that I was different.

Rebecca stepped forward to tackle the final lock on the door, but she ended up having trouble. "Hey, whoever's on the other side, stop messing with the lock," she whispered through the keyhole. "We're here to get you out."

"What?" came a voice from the other side. The sounds from within the room began to dim. "Who's there?"

"We're here to rescue you."

A few gasps of excitement met the announcement. Apparently, whoever had been messing with the lock from the inside backed away because Rebecca returned to working on the lock. Once we heard the final click, she put her lockpick kit away, twisted the latch, and pushed the door in.

We were met with a few fearful yelps and a less than pleasant smell. It seemed nobody had thought to tend to the hygiene of all the kids and teenagers in the room. I was repulsed that the kids had been treated like that, but somehow, I wasn't surprised.

"Shh, we're here to get you out," Harriet said reassuringly.

"Harriet? Josh?" Renato's familiar voice came from the crowd.

"Shh . . . we need everyone to stay as quiet as possible," Des began. "It's still dangerous out there. Renato, quick. Help us get everyone out. Do you know how many of you guys there are?"

"Yeah," Renato said. "I'll keep count."

Harriet scanned the crowd. "Neil!"

Neil ran over and gave his sister a bear hug. "Harriet! What's going on? Are we going home?"

"Shh. Yeah, we're getting you home." Harriet's voice was thick with unshed tears.

We started moving them out after another quick warning to stay absolutely silent. We made sure to pair the younger kids with older kids and teens who were responsible enough to keep them quiet while moving quickly. I stayed with everyone in the subbasement while the others got the first groups out to the bus and van.

As we continued to move everyone out, I started to worry. There were a lot of kids, and we were shoving as many of them onto the bus and van as possible, but it was still going to require a few trips to get everyone. By the third trip, Harriet reported that one child had yelped while they were outside. A vampire had been thrown, landing near the shrubbery they were creeping behind. That one yelp had almost gotten the entire group caught.

We finally got down to the last handful of kids, and I started to feel a weird sense of elation. This could work! This could actually work!

"This is great, Renato! We're going to save everyone." I grinned at him, but he returned it with a pensive look. "Uh, what's wrong?"

"There's a kid missing. I think it was that toddler? He likes to hide. What was his name? Timmy?" Renato stepped over to a cabinet and started opening doors.

I felt the blood drain from my face. "Was it Tommy?"

"Yeah, that's it! Tommy. That kid always seemed a little extra scared, like he'd seen some shit, you know?" Renato started to call out. "Tommy? Where are you, kid?"

"Renato, we need you to come with us," Des said. "If we don't move quickly, we'll get caught."

"But the kid," Renato began. "We have to—"

I pulled Renato back from where he had crouched to look inside a cabinet door. "I'll look for Tommy. You go with everyone else. It will be fine."

Des gave us a pointed look. "That makes sense. If anyone can get that kid and get him out of here quickly, it's you."

He must have been remembering the time I grabbed Tommy and got him to safety last week when he wandered into the street. "Yeah, don't worry, Renato. I can do this."

He nodded. "Okay, see you on the other side."

Everyone else left, and I started looking around, trying to take advantage of my vampire vision in the dim light.

"Tommy? It's okay. It's safe to come out. I'll help you get home to your mom, okay? There's nothing to be scared of." I walked around the room, scanning for movement as I looked around cabinets and boxes.

After a few tense minutes, I heard a small shuffling sound I probably wouldn't have noticed if I hadn't had enhanced vampire senses. I turned and walked toward the back of the room, where a large insulated blanket draped over some boxes. I carefully moved the blanket.

"Hey, Tommy, you there?" I asked as gently as I could manage.

I found Tommy wedged in a large box, tears streaming down his face. He saw me and yelped. "No! Scared!" He waved his hands out at me, trying to slap me away.

I realized then that what I had done last week had come back to bite me. He wasn't scared because of the situation. He was scared of me. An intense wave of shame came over me. He had seen me grab his dad and act like a vampire— probably just like the vampires who had put him and all the other kids in the subbasement.

I sat back on my heels. I had to convince him I wouldn't harm him. All I could think of was to say comforting things in the hopes something would stick.

"Tommy, I promise I won't hurt you. I'm here to help, okay? I want to get you home to your mommy. Remember how I helped you when you ran in the street? Kind of like a superhero, right? I was so, so fast. Can you run that fast?"

Tommy continued to cry, but he stopped trying to slap me away. "I run fast."

He seemed a little calmer, so I tried again. "I'm your friend, remember? I just want to get you somewhere safe, away from the bad guys. Will you let me carry you while I run really fast again so we can get you back to your mommy?"

He sniffled and seemed to run the idea through his head, then nodded. "Uh-huh."

"I need you to hold really tight, okay?" I opened my arms to him.

He looked at me for a moment, still a little unsure. Then he climbed out of the box and jumped into my arms. He wrapped himself tightly enough around my neck to be uncomfortable.

"Not that tight, kiddo," I gasped.

"Uh-oh." He loosened his grip a bit.

"That's better. Now, I'm going to run really fast once we get out of here, okay?"

"Okay."

We sneaked out of the room and up the subbasement stairs as quietly as possible. Thankfully, my vampire abilities gave me extra strength, because the kid was so solid, I probably would have gotten too tired to keep carrying him after a while.

I wasn't sure how this would go, since me staying behind hadn't been part of the plan. I hoped everyone had gone ahead to safety. I looked down at Tommy and wondered if I could still have kids now that I was a vampire. I had no idea, but the way Tommy was innocently holding me like a lifeline was kind of endearing. I wondered if either of my parents had ever felt that way. It was kind of nice.

Then I remembered what Harriet had said earlier and deflated. I wasn't sure having a family was in the cards for me anymore.

I managed to continue holding Tommy while climbing out the window. I had to go through backward, though, with

Tommy still in my arms, and scoot out on my ass. Just as I tried to get myself up, a hand appeared in my field of vision. Someone must have stayed behind to make sure we made it out.

"Oh, thanks." I took the hand and stood, only to realize too late that the hand held mine tighter than a human's would have.

"You're welcome, Mr. Buckmilter," came a strangely familiar voice. I turned and saw the hand belonged to someone I didn't want to see.

The butler, Mr. Wellington, stood before me.

My heart began to beat wildly. I jerked my hand back and put Tommy down. "Run, Tommy! Run to the bushes!" I yelled as loud as I could, hoping one of the others heard and would come get Tommy to safety.

Luckily, Tommy must have picked up on my fear; he immediately ran to the shrubs along the brick wall.

"Now, now, Mr. Buckmilter, I'm afraid you've caused some problems for Madam Genevieve and Mr. Danforth. It's quite rude to steal food."

Something about the comment set me off. I looked at Tommy and saw a sweet kid who deserved a life. This vampire looked at Tommy and saw a midnight snack. I might have drunk all that blood in preparation for the evening so I wouldn't go feral, but I felt the tingling in my mouth again. Pure rage replaced the fear that had been plaguing me all night. All I knew was that if I wanted Tommy to survive, I needed to fight.

What happened next was a blur. I jumped on the butler and clawed at his face like an angry cat. Wellington's hands grabbed at my throat, but I was somehow able to grab one of them and twist it hard enough to break. I wildly punched and kicked with a severe lack of skill, having never taken a single martial arts class in my life. I may not have been capable of much, but at least I could buy some time for Tommy to flee.

Soon, Wellington and I were on the ground, and I heard a sickening crunch. A sharp jolt of pain hit me, and I realized he'd repaid the broken wrist with a broken arm. Suddenly, the berserker rage started to wane, and I felt incredibly weak. A bone stuck out of my arm, and the odious smell of vampire blood came from my own body as blood dripped from the open wound.

The adrenaline rush was gone, and Wellington, who was clearly stronger than I was, carried me over his shoulder, holding me there with his good arm. He used his vampire speed to bring us straight through the front door and stopped in the entry, where a disheveled Genevieve and Danforth stood off against Ms. Heliotrope and Feral Doug.

"We have a guest." Mr. Wellington unceremoniously dumped me on the floor. I fell hard on my back and howled in pain as my arm flopped strangely.

I was quickly grabbed by the hair and forced to my feet by Danforth, who smirked at me and held me in front of him. It was clear he was using me as a shield.

"Well, well, look who we have here. If you don't back off,"—Genevieve put a knife to my throat—"we'll bleed little Joshykins until he's weak, and then we'll torture him . . . unless the Conclave agrees to back off and let us take over the town. We still have most of the town under our control, after all."

I gasped as the sharp tip of the blade pricked my skin. A couple of drops squeezed out of the puncture wound and trickled down my neck. My eyes went blurry with tears, through which I could just make out Kotaro and a couple of other formalists running up behind Ms. Heliotrope.

Out of the corner of my eye, I saw my dad at the open door, Tommy in his arms. At the same time, Ms. Heliotrope screamed four completely unexpected words.

"Don't hurt my son!"

My jaw dropped. "W-what?"

Dad's gaze turned from me to Ms. Heliotrope. "Carolyn? Is that you?"

Ms. Heliotrope looked regretfully at Dad. "Carl, I—"

Genevieve interrupted. "Ah, look, if it isn't a family reunion . . . how touching. Don't you think, darling?"

Danforth laughed. "Ah, yes. There's something about a family reunion that just warms my ice-cold heart."

He tightened his hold on me with one arm, freeing his other. My brain was racing, trying to make sense of the whole thing, and the pain I felt only made it more difficult to sort out the pieces. Ms. Heliotrope knew Dad. Dad knew Ms. Heliotrope. He had called her Carolyn, like Genevieve had . . . and Ms. Heliotrope had yelled for them to not hurt her son. Could she be . . . ?

I looked straight at her. "Mom?"

A fist hit the side of my head at superhuman speed. As I tried to retain consciousness, I saw Kotaro grab my dad and Tommy, while Ms. Heliotrope and the others ran toward us, blood-covered swords ready to slice. It was too late, though. The combination of my adrenaline rush running out and the intense pain in my head made my vision blur to black, and all was nothingness.

DAY 15, PART 2

FRIDAY

My head felt strangely fuzzy as I blinked my eyes open. My distance vision was blurrier than normal, even from before having enhanced vampire vision. All I could tell was that I was in a brightly lit room and there were white bars around me on all sides. I tried to sit up, but my body wouldn't cooperate. I was starting to panic when I heard a soothing voice.

"Awake, my sweet one?" said a feminine voice.

My brain was so jumbled, I couldn't really tell who it was. It sounded like something Genevieve would say, but the tone seemed more genuine.

I blinked again and saw a shadow hovering over the bars. I couldn't quite make it out, but it looked vaguely human shaped. It reached out and touched my cheek gently.

"Don't worry, baby. Mama's here."

What? The last thing I remembered was rescuing children from the vampire mansion, and what I was experiencing now was almost the polar opposite. I decided the best thing to do was speak.

What I didn't expect was what came out of my mouth. "Ma-ma?"

I knew I had moved my mouth, but that wasn't what I had intended to say. And why the hell did I sound like a baby?

The shape reached down and picked me up. Closer now, I could make out the face. It was Ms. Heliotrope, but her face was free of the eyepatch and scar it covered. Two whole eyes looked at me with intense sadness.

A tear trickled down her cheek. "Goodbye, my little Joshua."

No! I thought. *No, this can't be happening!* I wiggled as much as I could, trying to do anything I could . . .

Well, what could I do if I was a baby?

I started to cry as loudly as I could . . .

And I sat straight up, awake.

It took me a couple of moments to realize it had been a dream. I took a few deep breaths, then looked down at my body to make sure I was still me. My arm was expertly set in a splint. I tested it gently to see how it felt. I had broken my leg once as a kid, and the pain had been horrible, but this didn't feel like a freshly broken bone. It actually felt nearly healed. Was I healing faster, the same way Des had after I licked the blood off his knee?

I was lying on the couch in Ms. Heliotrope's house. Dr. Chen sat next to me, and I heard the muted sounds of Ms. Heliotrope and my father's voices. No, not Ms. Heliotrope. Carolyn Buckmilter. My mother. Or . . . had I imagined that?

My head pounded with the worst headache I'd ever had, and I had to take a few more deep breaths to keep from vomiting. Part of my face felt swollen and a little heavy.

"Take it easy, Josh. You'll heal faster because of what you are now. But the more you panic, the longer it will take.

It's better if you lie back down so the blood can more easily go to your head to heal you." Dr. Chen guided me down gently until I was flat on my back and handed me a blood bag to sip on.

I took a few sips, then gently turned to look at Dr. Chen. "What happened?"

Dr. Chen smiled hugely and raised his arms in triumph. "You saved the day!"

"Huh?" was all I could manage.

"The kids all got out, and the formalists overwhelmed the enemy. You did it!" he explained enthusiastically. "Well, we all did it, really. You just need to take it easy."

I blinked. His answer wasn't satisfying at all. My exasperation must have shown in my face because his triumphant expression faded. He adjusted his glasses, cleared his throat, and explained.

"Once you went unconscious, the remaining formalists managed to take on Danforth, Genevieve, and Wellington. While the three of them had guards, of course, they hadn't expected any local townspeople to be part of the rescue. We were able to send in a bigger force of formalists than they were prepared for, and all their people were called to the front of the mansion, where the formalists took the upper hand. We lost a few of our vampires, unfortunately, but while the guards were formidable, our forces were better trained. All that was left was Danforth, Genevieve, and Wellington. Ms. Heliotrope—I mean, your mom—completely destroyed Danforth after what he did to you. The formalists could barely keep her off Wellington. After what your mom did to Danforth, Wellington and Genevieve surrendered. They'll be executed by the Conclave, agents will be sent in to wipe any memories that need to be wiped through glamour, and everything can go back to normal."

Back to normal? Who was he kidding? Maybe back to normal for everyone else, but for me? Clearly, nothing was normal for me. I was still drinking blood. I had survived a neck-breaking punch in the face from a disturbingly strong vampire who probably would have killed me if I were still human.

And wiping memories? Whose memories? Would my friends be allowed to remember what I was? Would I just be alone again, trying to figure out how to live in the world now that I was changed? Would I have to distance myself from my friends because of what I was? What would my future be?

And most importantly, Ms. Heliotrope was really my mother? As the pain in my arm and face subsided with every sip of blood, my thoughts became increasingly more organized. Dad had gotten rid of all his photos of my mom after she'd left. It had been too hard for him to look at them. That had left me to only guess at what she might look like. Thinking about it, though, Ms. Heliotrope did have the same hair and eye color as I did. Not just brown hair and brown eyes, but the shades were the same. Her hair sparkled with red highlights in the sun, just like mine. The flecks of gold in the earthy brown of the iris of her one good eye were the same ones I saw in the mirror every time I looked at myself. I didn't get any of that from Dad. Whenever I asked people what Mom looked like, they'd always said I favored her in coloring and features rather than Dad.

"It's great, right, Josh?" Dr. Chen continued brightly as I processed everything. The huge smile he wore slowly faded. If I weren't feeling the weight of the world crashing in around me, it might have been comical.

"Uh, yeah. Um . . . is Ms. Heliotrope . . . I mean . . . my mom?" I was having trouble putting words together into something coherent. I may not have been the baby I had been in my dream, but that didn't change how helpless I felt.

I'd always wondered what I would do if my mother came back into my life. The emotions I'd experienced growing up without her had been all over the board. I had been angry at her for leaving. Furious. My father had been so lifeless for most of my childhood. Other kids' dads were either enthusiastically involved in their lives in some way or present but more focused on their careers than their kids. It always seemed like my dad wanted to try, but he couldn't. People would talk to me about how boisterous he had been when he was younger. Popular, handsome, loved—he had been a natural leader, according to them. The Carl Buckmilter I knew was just broken. He might have been alive, but his heart had stopped somewhere along the line. He still loved me, I knew that, but he had never quite pulled his heart back together after Mom left.

I still wanted her in my life, though. I yearned for the mom I had dreamed of. Maybe she would have helped me learn to ride a bike or taught me how to dance so I wasn't the awkward guy hanging out against the wall at parties. She could have made me help her cook dinner and not let me go out to play until I had finished washing the dishes. She would have given me a kiss on the cheek in front of all my classmates when she dropped me off at school, and I would have cringed in embarrassment but secretly been glad for the reminder I was loved. All those things my friends had complained about were things I longed for. Things I wanted but had never had the chance to have. At the very least, seeing my dad loved and happy would have changed so many things. The man I knew who had so little hope left inside would have been brimming with warmth and happiness.

I wanted a mom so badly, I could taste it.

"Yeah, you should talk to them about that," Dr. Chen replied nervously, waving his arm in the general direction of their voices. My dad's voice rose briefly, and Ms. Heliotrope's voice in response sounded like she was about to break into tears. Then Dad's voice became softer and more tender. I couldn't make out the words, but it sounded like Ms. Heliotrope either said "I love you" or "I'm sorry."

I gave Dr. Chen a burning look. "Is. She. My. Mother?" I said it in such a slow, fierce whisper that Dr. Chen gulped.

He nodded.

"Thank you."

I gulped down the rest of my blood bag and started to stand but fell back even before Dr. Chen could force me onto the couch again.

"Crap," I said.

Dr. Chen patted me on the shoulder. "Don't worry. There's time for that."

I felt the pinprick of tears at the corners of my eyes. They didn't fall, and I didn't really feel comfortable crying in front of Dr. Chen. But "there's time for that"? I'd been waiting for almost my entire life, for as long as I could remember. I was done with time. Time could fuck off.

"It hurts too much," I whispered. It all hurt too much. I had been broken before I knew what it was like to be whole. And now? The mother I had been too young to remember was real, and she'd been in my life for the past several days, teaching me about what I was . . . just like I wished she had been there to do when I was a kid, except without the whole being-a-vampire thing.

"I'll give you some room," Dr. Chen said. "Just . . . if you decide to get up, do it slowly. Don't stand if you start to feel dizzy. You gulped that blood down pretty fast and it's enough to heal you, but it will take several minutes at minimum to do its job. At least give yourself half an hour before you stand. Okay?"

I didn't respond, but the look he gave me said I didn't need to. He took the empty blood bag with him and walked toward the hallway in the direction of my parents' voices.

I finally let a few tears flow freely. I was filled with so much doubt and grief. I had thought I'd magically be so happy my mom was in my life again whenever I had imagined meeting her. This was nothing like that. Of course, I'd thought she'd be human. I'd thought I'd be human.

I heard a pair of feet walking down the hall. I turned my head to look, but it wasn't anyone I expected.

Feral Doug was walking perfectly upright. It was like I was getting a glimpse of the man he had been before he found himself in the same situation I was in. He sat down on the edge of the couch and took my hand. With slow, painful words, he spoke.

"She . . . love . . . you . . ."

If I hadn't been listening carefully, I wouldn't have caught the words. I hadn't even known he could speak.

I wiped my face with my hands and took in a rattling breath. "Does she?"

He nodded. "She . . . proud . . . you."

I stared at him in shock. Me? What was there to be proud of?

He put the hand that wasn't holding mine over my heart. "Stronger . . . than . . . you . . . know."

That put me over the edge. I began to sob out all my feelings. Heartbreak, relief, fear, hope, disappointment—all those feelings were there and more. Feral Doug handed me a blanket and smiled, then curled up in his dog bed in the corner of the room.

By the time I stopped crying, I felt a little better. My

emotions were still a jumble, but I didn't feel as over-whelmed as before. I worked on sitting up in small incre-ments. As I did, I realized how much I took the simple act of getting up from lying down for granted. I took deep breaths anytime I felt on the verge of dizziness, then conti-nued on.

Once I'd finally gotten into a sitting position, I stopped to breathe and check how I was feeling. I wasn't sure I could stand up, but at least I wasn't on my back. It was an improve-ment. Not a huge improvement when what I wanted more than anything was to run down the hall and find my parents. I didn't know what I'd do once I found them, but that didn't really matter.

I held back when I realized that maybe they needed some time too. There was no way they didn't have years of baggage to unpack between them. Now that I could see how complicated everything must have been, I was grateful Har-riet already knew what I was, knew how I felt, and had told me her feelings. Everything was out on the table. Nothing was hidden anymore. But Ms. Helio—Mom? She'd been hiding this for about eighteen years.

Feral Doug sat up in his dog bed, alert to something I hadn't noticed because I was too deep in thought. Then I heard it too: several feet walking along the hallway toward us.

I looked at the doorway between the hallway and the living room in anticipation of seeing the familiar faces I craved. I held my breath without realizing it until a Victo-rian-style shoe entered my vision, followed by the leg the shoe belonged to and then the rest of the woman who had once held me in her arms. She was followed by my dad, whose eyes looked more vital than I'd ever seen them.

The three of us stared at each other until I realized just

how long I had been holding my breath. I sucked in a huge lungful of air and coughed.

Before I knew it, arms were wrapping around me. The desperation in those limbs made her grip that much tighter.

"My son," she sobbed, all iron and steel completely gone from her voice. "I'm so sorry. I wanted to tell you. I was so scared that the Conclave would harm you if I did." The words came so fast, it was hard for my confused mind to follow.

I started to cry again, and I felt the familiar arms of my dad wrap around us both.

"M-mom?" I stuttered out, not waiting for the tears to stop. I had needed to call someone that for so long. The word felt both completely alien and utterly right at the same time.

Ms. Heliotrope pulled back and wiped my face with her handkerchief, even though she probably needed to use it on her own face. "Yes," she choked out. "Yes."

I cleared my throat. "I have so many questions."

"I don't blame you."

Dad gave a tear-thickened chuckle. "She may be tired of questions after all the ones I threw at her."

"No," Ms. Heliotrope said—no, my mother said. "I will never be tired of questions. I owe so many answers, and I've waited so long for this."

They settled down on either side of me. One larger, slightly calloused hand held my right, gently avoiding putting pressure on my healing arm. One slender hand with an inhuman grip held my left. It felt so alien but so right to just sit there with both my parents.

"So, when you were at the café the other day, had you been watching Dad?" It wasn't the biggest question I wanted to ask, but it was the first out of my mouth.

"That's where you want to start?" Dad asked, surprised. "Wait, Carolyn, you were watching me?"

Mom nodded. "Yes, I was assigned to come here because the Conclave knew Genevieve and Danforth were up to something. I was reluctant at first, and I didn't want to risk my position by letting on that I was a little . . . distracted by your dad, for lack of a better word. But I had to know. I had to see he was okay." She looked at me, her eye full of pain. "When I realized they'd done to you what they'd done to me, I was devastated, Josh. I watched both of you like a hawk. You found Doug and me outside your restaurant for a reason. I wasn't going to reveal myself to you, but you . . . you needed to know what you were dealing with."

"Wait, they did the same thing to you?" I asked.

"Yes. And I was a lot more alone than you were. They took me when I was in the city to see a specialist after giving birth to you. I didn't realize what had happened until I was holding you one night, exhausted and trying to get you to sleep, and I almost bit you and drained you dry. I was shocked by what I had nearly done, and I couldn't risk harming you or your father. I couldn't live with myself if . . ." She squeezed my hand a little harder. If I hadn't been a vampire like her, it probably would have broken a bone or two.

"So you left to protect us from yourself." I let that roll around in my head for a bit. Would I have ended up making that choice too? The same thought had gone through my head a couple of times over the past few days.

"I know all too well the horrors of what they've done to you. However, if they hadn't turned you or if they had turned someone else, I would have come, done my job, and left without saying a word. I've worked so hard to get the position I'm in with the formalists that I've earned the Conclave's trust. I knew I could never go back to the life I used to have, and I didn't want to bring you and your father pain by showing up in your lives again, only to leave a few days later. But then you—part of my job isn't just to bring justice to those who don't follow our rules. It's to help those turned against their will."

"So, what does this all mean now?" I asked. "Are we a family again?"

Mom and Dad looked at each other. I could see regret in both their expressions.

"I'm not allowed to change anyone, Josh." Mom let go of my hand. "We'd be on the run for the rest of our existence. The formalists would hunt us down and destroy us without mercy."

"But Dad—"

"Nobody should have to live this life, Josh. I'd never wish it on anyone. We may not be as obviously monstrous as the folklore says. We may be closer to human than the tales tell. But we still can't live among humans like we're as ordinary as they are. We still have to drink their blood, and the Conclave has strict rules to limit our population. That way, the human population will continue on, and we'll always have our source of blood. Otherwise . . ." She made a hopeless gesture.

I looked at Dad's face, lined with visible wrinkles and framed by hair that was a little less full than in his photos from high school. I looked at Mom's face; her skin was still as supple as it likely had been when she was in her early twenties. They were different now. They couldn't grow old together the way they had intended when they were young and happy. Even if Dad were changed into what we were, he wasn't the same person he had been when they were together. It wasn't like they could just pick up their relationship where it had left off. And if Dad were changed, he'd have to go through what we'd struggled with, and there was always the chance he could become like Feral Doug instead.

"Can we still look after him?"

"I think so," Mom said. "From a distance. The glamour didn't take with him. His feelings for both of us are far too strong for him to be manipulated into forgetting either of us. Plus, it's easier if people think you went off to college than to try to make them forget you altogether."

"Wait, what?"

"You need to continue learning what you are, and some of that can't happen here. You'll have to come with me and learn how to be a vampire according to our laws."

"Will my friends have to forget me too?" It hurt too much to think that Harriet, Des and his family, and even Brian wouldn't know me in the same way.

Mom smoothed back my hair. "You have some very determined friends. That odd boy, Brian? He was easy to glamour, but some of the others are too strong-willed to forget. Your boss at the pizza place and his family won't remember. However, Des and Harriet were resistant. So was Des's sister Jocelyn. She'll be working more closely with Dr. Chen from now on. Des and Harriet will be monitored closely to see that they maintain the secret.

"But everyone else? They'll believe you got a special scholarship to go to school as you had intended. That wouldn't be incorrect, either. The Conclave owes you for the burden you bear now. You'll have to move away from here, and they'll get you into a good school, tuition paid, in a place where nobody knows you. We'll be right there, helping you navigate your way through everything."

I was relieved to hear that some friends would still know. But I was also strangely disappointed. This whole mess had started because I was working to pay my own way through school, and now it didn't matter anymore. It was hard work, but I loved delivering pizza. I knew the town of Willow Springs in a way few did. I'd seen through the front doors of almost every house in town. So many people knew me by name who wouldn't have otherwise. I'd miss the tired parents who ordered pizza for their kids so they wouldn't have to cook after a long day of work. I'd miss the wild parties thrown by teenagers whose parents were out of town. I'd miss the kids who prank called us.

"It looks like I'll have some goodbyes to make."

"I'll miss you, son," Dad said. "Promise me you'll visit. Even if only to let me know you're okay. You can call me—" He paused and looked at Mom. "He can call me, can't he, Carolyn?"

"I don't think the Conclave could stop it even if they wanted to," she said. "They try to keep up with modern technology, but they're not very good at it. I doubt they could prevent a phone call or text from happening every once in a while."

"Good." Dad ruffled my hair.

Dad went to my place and packed a few things so I could stay with Mom while I was recuperating. Des returned with him to make sure I had my laptop. While my parents went off to have some personal time together, Des came upstairs with me to my makeshift bedroom, and we booted up our computers to play a round of *Midnight Murder Mansion.*

Des scooted his chair closer to the card table we were seated at. "So that Kotaro guy . . . do you think I could get him to train me?"

"He was so badass, wasn't he?" I exclaimed, remembering his smooth jump from the stairs.

Des nodded enthusiastically. "Yeah, it wasn't until our last round of rescues that I looked up and realized he had been shadowing us the whole time with his ninja skills. I know I wasn't supposed to, but I stuck around and watched him . . ." He paused. "At least, I wanted to wait for you to make sure you got out okay, but . . . damn. It was like that video game I was really into that one time. You know, the one with the samurai and his ninja sidekick? I'd always make you play the samurai because I thought the ninja was way cooler?"

I couldn't help but laugh. We used to get into so many arguments because I wanted to play as the ninja every once in a while, but I always eventually gave in because playing the game with Des was always more important than which character I played.

"Should I ask Ms.—I mean, my mom if he'll do it?" I teased.

Des wore a happy little smile. "That would be so cool!" He returned his attention to his laptop. "Hey, what's the modem password?"

"The modem password?" I looked around the room, trying to remember if I had seen a router downstairs. "I don't know. I never asked."

Des gave me a look. "You . . . you don't think your mom didn't get a modem set up when she moved in here, do you?"

"Well, she's been talking with the Conclave, so . . ." Then it hit me. They were vampires. Ancient vampires. And Mom had said something about how vampires weren't very good with technology. She probably hadn't been talking with them through video calls. "Uh-oh."

"Uh-oh?" Des demanded. I wasn't sure Des knew how to survive without wireless internet.

"She might not have been using the latest tech to communicate with the Conclave."

"Yeah, but if she was just using email or some messaging app, she'd still need a modem," Des said a little desperately.

"I don't think she was using email or a messaging app, Des."

"Text? Did she use text?" Des's voice went up almost an octave.

"I bet she called them on her phone." I cringed. "Some of these vampires are really old, I think. Some of them may be older than the phone. What if she had to use a messenger pigeon?"

We immediately checked to see if there were any wireless accounts we could access. All the accounts available gave off weak signals and were password protected.

"Where's my phone? I can set up a hotspot so we can get online." Des patted his pockets to find his phone, then gave me a look of sheer terror. "Where's your phone?"

I stared at him, wide-eyed. "I have no idea!" I yelled toward the door, "DAD! WHERE'S MY PHONE?"

My shout was met with silence. Then a strange thumping sounded on the stairs. Maybe it was leftover nerves from last night combined with our terror at the lack of the most basic necessity for any modern internet user, but we immediately scrambled from our chairs and backed against the wall as the sound came closer and closer. The house was creepy, after all, with its sparse furniture and old, peeling wallpaper. We craned our necks to look out the door toward the stairs and watched in anticipation as the sound continued.

A pale hand came to rest on the top step.

We screamed as a head popped up. Then we saw who it was. Feral Doug peeked up at us, my phone in his mouth.

Des collapsed to the floor. "Okay, I'm going to go to church every Sunday for the rest of my life. I don't care which church. I'm going to all of them. Keep my bases covered."

Feral Doug crawled over to me, took the phone out of his mouth, and handed it to me. One side looked a little drooly, and I wiped it off on the hem of my shirt. "Uh, thanks, but please don't scare us like that again?"

He gave me a salute, then left the room, crawling back down the stairs.

"Were we just rescued by some weird dude dressed in leather and crawling on all fours?" Des asked.

"Yup. I had a pretty similar reaction when I first saw him."

Des picked himself up off the floor and sat down at the table again. "Life's never going to be normal again, is it?"

I tapped my phone screen, got everything set up, and got my computer online. "Nope. Definitely not."

EPILOGUE

One week later

Since the school year had started a couple of months ago at colleges and universities all over the United States, we told everyone that I had been accepted to start school in the spring semester after doing an internship for a few months. We kept the details of which school I was going to attend and the nature of the internship intentionally vague, but with enough details to keep everyone satisfied. I didn't know how to glamour people yet to manipulate their thoughts, but after the whole town had been glamoured to forget events of the past couple of weeks, they were a bit more suggestible for the time being.

I sat in my room contemplating how easily my life had been packed away into a suitcase and large duffel bag. I had been so careful to save every last penny that I had ended up with very little to pack and nothing to be put away into storage. I was leaving a few things with Dad—a sort of unspoken promise that if I left them with him, I'd have an excuse to come back.

I heard a knock on my door. "Yup," I said in response.

"Hey, you ready?" Des asked.

"Yeah. It all just seems so weird. Things just happened so fast, you know? I thought this day was going to be so much further in the future—going to school, I mean. Now, it's just here. Time seems to move so much faster the older I get."

Des sat next to me on my bed. "Yeah. Imagine what it will be like when we're forty. I'll still look like my gorgeous self because Black don't crack, and you'll probably still look like yourself because, you know . . . vampires. Everyone else will probably look like trash, though."

"Maybe Brian will go bald like his dad?"

"Shut up," Brian griped as he came into the room and sat down on the desk chair.

It was weird seeing Brian back to how he used to be. He was still a complete mess of a person. However, some of the tension that had built up due to me being changed and the vampires being taken down was gone. For him, it was like it had never happened. He vaguely remembered me being sick and his annoyance that it had detracted attention away from him. He didn't remember anything from the convention other than having fun and buying his figurine, which now had a place of honor on a shelf in his room.

For me, though, I couldn't trust him the way I used to. I could only hope he made better choices this time around. I was doubtful, but I hoped he'd get the right help and learn to be a better person.

"Why were you talking about my dad being bald?" Brian asked.

Des and I exchanged a look. It seemed like he hadn't heard Des's comment about vampires, but it was a good reminder we had to be a little more careful.

"Just joking about getting old," Des said, putting on his natural charm.

"When are you leaving, Josh?" Brian asked.

"Soon. Dad's going to pick me up. You guys are going to take care of my car, right?"

"The way you talk, you'd think it was some classic instead of being held together with bubble gum and prayers." Des put me in a headlock and gave me a playful noogie.

I knew he did it for show—because who in their right mind would do that to a vampire—but still, it was annoying. "Dude, cut it out!"

Brian jumped off the chair, about to join in the male-bonding free-for-all, when someone cleared their throat gently from the doorway. We paused mid-action to see Harriet standing there. She had arrived earlier and offered to help me, but I hadn't really been ready to talk to her in depth. We both had to move on, at least for a time, until I could better grasp what I'd become. She had never actually told me her rejection was a solid no, just a no for right now, which gave me a sliver of hope. She had ended up waiting downstairs with Des for a while to give me the space I needed.

"Hey." I carefully disentangled myself from the arms and legs holding me down so I didn't hurt Des with my vampiric strength.

"Just wanted to say goodbye one last time," Harriet said.

I nodded. "Are Gino and Graziella okay, by the way? I haven't talked to them in a few days. I know things have been hard with Renato."

Harriet glanced at Brian. She couldn't answer completely truthfully in front of him. Though Danforth and Genevieve had been defeated and the Conclave's agents had glamoured everyone who could be glamoured, some of the children and teens whose parents had willingly handed them over to the vampires showed signs of feeling betrayed. They couldn't remember why, but glamour wasn't strong enough to wipe away those residual feelings. Ms. Heliotrope had explained that, due to the way human brains developed, children and teenagers could be harder to glamour effectively. It seemed to be least effective on those who had had really strong bonds with their parents, like Renato.

"I'm going to look out for him, Josh. They're trying, and Renato is still willing to deliver pizzas, but with you leaving and his change of attitude, Gino's isn't quite as cheerful as it used to be. But don't worry. It will take a little work and some patience, but things will improve."

She sighed, and I almost sighed with her. The town might be safe, but it would never quite be the same place. It was a little less shiny, like tarnished silver that needed a good polish.

"We're all really going to miss you," Harriet added. "I mean it. I hope, at some point, you can come back and let us know how you're doing. Don't be one of those guys who forgets to call home for months, okay?"

"How can I? You're the most important people in my life. I'm always going to want to know how everyone is doing. Always." I swallowed down a sob that lingered at the back of my throat.

I stood up, and Harriet gave me one of her back-breaking hugs. When we pulled back, we both laughed.

"Nobody could forget that hug," I joked. I still loved her. Nothing would change that. It was a relief that we knew where we stood, in a way. I understood why they were called crushes now. Not having to carry the secret of how I felt anymore made me feel just a little lighter.

"That's why it's the hug I gave you, silly," Harriet said.

She flopped down on the bed next to Des and leaned

her head on his shoulder. I was a little nervous seeing them that close after what Des had said about being interested in her. I never had answered his question. The truth was, I couldn't. It would hurt. I knew it would hurt if he dated her. But it was up to her to make that decision, not me. I couldn't expect her to wait for me to get my vampire shit together, and we both needed time to figure out if my being a vampire would get in the way of us being more than just friends.

I couldn't lie. It still hurt to think that my being a vampire made our paths diverge, but maybe it was time to grow up. A crush wasn't quite the same as love, and if all this hadn't happened, I might still be the same, pining away and never having the courage to tell her how I felt. Instead, I could move forward, knowing that Harriet was loved. Whatever she did about it was up to her.

A horn honked outside, and I looked out the window to see my dad's car in the driveway. "I guess it's time for me to go."

We all exchanged glances. Des, Harriet, and Brian got up from the bed, and we had a group hug. Then we separated. The room was so silent, I could hear the dry autumn leaves rustling in a sudden gust of wind.

"Bye," I said.

Harriet gave me a little wave as Des and Brian smiled. I grabbed my duffel and my suitcase, pretending they were heavier than they felt to hide my vampire strength as I had been taught, and I made my way down the stairs and out the door.

ACKNOWLEDGMENTS

It's hard to know where to start, especially because I never intended *The Pizza-Pyre* to be my first published novel beyond being posted on my Patreon account. It was simply an exercise in taking a strange little story idea based on a news article I read many years ago and seeing where it took me. I suppose I should thank that article author first (whose name I cannot for the life of me remember). The article discussed how food delivery was one of the more dangerous jobs a person could have. There's just no telling what's on the other side of the door when a pizza boy rings the doorbell. So I thought, what if there was something supernatural on the other side? And what if they took a person showing up on their doorstep with a pizza as an opportunity to create some mischief?

I have to thank Ynes Freeman and Tod Tinker, two incredible friends who have embraced this project with open arms. This book would definitely not be in your hands right now without their help. Tod and Amanda Mills Woodlee both provided valuable insight during the editing and proofreading processes. Also, special thanks to Emily Zelasko, who created the perfect cover art, and Cait Marie, who did the amazing finishing touches, as well as Andrew Alexander and Sarah V. Hines (who also has a book coming out soon with Balance of Seven) for beta reading. All these people are creators in their own right, and you should check out their work. And of course, I have to thank my patrons on Patreon, who gave my creative whims their support. Finally, I have to thank my mom, who is known affectionately as Reviewer Mom, for the initial edits on *The Pizza-Pyre*, back when it was on Patreon.

This book is, on the surface, a story of an absolutely ordinary small-town guy in extraordinary, terrifying, life-changing circumstances. Beneath the humor and suspense, however, it's a story about family, whether the family you're born with, the family you work with, or the family you create with your friends. It's about trying to figure out what happens when your life changes suddenly, disrupting your relationships with the people around you. It's about feeling isolated and alone while trying not to lose the people who keep you going. It's about finding new relationships or uncovering old ones that deserve a second chance. It's about how no matter the difficult circumstances we're in, it's always important to remember the people in our lives who help make us who we are and keep us on the path to becoming more than we thought we could be.

ABOUT THE AUTHOR

Charleigh Brennan lives across the street from a cemetery. She's grateful to have such quiet neighbors, as they give her plenty of time to be creative. Well, except when they get a little out of hand and knock items off her desk. But for the most part, it's maybe not so kind of, sort of scary or something . . . maybe.

Charleigh has lived an unexpected life, veering off into odd and unexpected paths on more than one continent. She misses the temperate weather of her Northern California upbringing yet loves seeing actual seasons in her present home in New England. If only it didn't snow for quite as long as it does. However, that does give her a good excuse to participate in some of her favorite pastimes, like reading, playing video games, trying new and interesting teas, and of course, writing.

You can find Charleigh on her Patreon account at www .patreon.com/fairygodmotherindisguise or on her Facebook page at www.facebook.com/charleighbrennanauthor.